DA NANG BOUND

A legacy of war

Frank W. Skilbeck

This work is registered with the UK Copyright Service UK©CS Registration
No:284682150

Frank W Skilbeck has asserted his right under the
Copyright, Designs and Patents Act, 1988 to be identified
as the author of this work. This novel is a work of fiction.
Names, characters, businesses, places, events and
incidents are either the products of the author's imagination
or used in a fictitious manner. Any resemblance to actual
persons, living or dead, or actual events is purely
coincidental.

Cover graphics Phannavit Samphanprat

1

They are called bui-doi | the dust of life | conceived in hell | and born in strife

Miss Saigon musical 1989

Thursday, May 5, 1988: Ho Chi Minh City, Vietnam

"If you struggle you will only get hurt," the big man cautioned Mai as he encircled her petite frame with his muscular arms from behind. Shocked at first, the attractive nineteen-year-old Amerasian girl went from terrified to hysterical as she wriggled and squirmed in an attempt to face her attacker. She struggled in vain. He had a firm grip on her hands which he quickly bound with duct tape. Overpowered, she soon tired.

Abducted in broad daylight in downtown Ho Chi Minh City, and in fear of her life, Mai screamed for help. But if anyone heard her cries they did not come to her aid. She was gagged and a hood pulled over her head but not before she caught a brief glimpse of her attacker's tattooed forearms as he bundled her into a waiting van.

"Got another one," the big man called to the driver, "and a beautiful *bui-doi*[1] at that!

"You bet your goddamned life Madame will be very pleased," he yelled in response to the driver's question. Laughing out loud he slammed shut the rear doors of the white van. Later, Mai would find little solace in discovering she was the second girl to be abducted in as many weeks.

[1] *Offensive remark of Vietnamese origin meaning "less than dust" describing mixed-race children with American fathers and Vietnamese mothers.*

Fingers pressed into the baize on the snooker table, John Mackenzie lined up on the black ball for frame and match. About to pull the trigger, his concentration was disturbed by the piercing ring of a telephone. It came from the adjoining snooker room bar. Startled, several barflies, mostly *gweilo*, looked up from their drinks. Chester Wong, long-time barman at The Royal Hong Kong Club, scuttled across the floor to field the offending call afraid of being held accountable for the disturbance. All phones should have been muted beforehand and he knew it. John Mackenzie knew it and so did his opponent.

The club had two inviolable rules: no women in any part of the premises apart from the dining room, and no telephone calls during snooker tournaments except in emergencies. Instinctively, Mac felt it was the latter and, somehow, he knew it was for him.

"Shit...is that for me Chester?" he turned and looked up from the table without breaking his stance. Turning around to look across at him, the barflies saw nothing of interest and returned to their drinks.

"Yes sir, Miss Cindy Chan; she says it's urgent," Wong answered, gently placing the phone on the bar top. He got back to polishing glasses fairly certain he was in for a dressing down when the senior steward got back from his break.

Expecting the unfinished frame to be his last for the day Mac took extra care potting the black before turning to shake hands with a bemused opponent whose chances of

4

winning died the moment the phone rang. In a spirit of sportsmanship, a much-touted hallmark of one of Hong Kong's most prestigious clubs, they promised to discuss the intrusive incident with the senior bar steward. It was a promise neither man would keep. Unseen, Mac slipped a Hong Kong hundred dollar bill into the white-gloved hand of the match referee. Tipping was frowned upon at the club. Hell, it was only a rule.

He grabbed for the phone: "Hi Cindy darling", he drooled, "just say the word and I'll be right over." It was a one-sided game he often played with the colonel's secretary, believing it boosted his chances of getting closer to her one day. Years of fruitless attempts to win over Cindy Chan had not deterred him from trying to bed the lady. She was a potential "toy" for his collection, so long as it didn't affect the business interests he had with Uncle Sam. And that wasn't just a rule; it was a red line...his own red line that he vowed never to cross. She knew that. And he knew she knew. She also knew how to play the game by Mac's rules.

A slim, long-legged, dark-haired, brown-eyed Cantonese beauty, Cindy had immersed herself in Buddhism just days after her husband had acquired a secondary wife or *er nai*. That was in 1980, eight years earlier. At the time it was common practice for Chinese men to acquire *er nai* and most Chinese women accepted that. But Cindy wasn't "most Chinese women". She took exception when she found out about her husband's philandering and ditched him without a second thought. Her actions only served to heighten Mac's interest in the lady. As for Cindy's husband, Mac thought he should be grateful his wife had not cut off his favourite appendage and thrown it to the ducks, another common practice among Chinese women whose husbands cheated on them.

Always business-like and exceptionally polite during conversations with Mackenzie, she studiously avoided being alone with him. Skilfully, she kept up her guard. Cindy would never do anything to jeopardise her job at the consulate; she loved it and she had bills to pay. In any case, Mac's reputation as a womaniser was legendary in Hong Kong.

It was generally accepted that most Chinese women were self-effacing and openly modest, but the redoubtable John Nathan Mackenzie ("call me Mac"), who often cited his vast experience of Asian ladies in general, considered this to be nothing more than a myth. And for him, myths had to be explored and, where appropriate, discredited.

A Canadian expat in his mid-fifties, Mac loved everything about Hong Kong, from its imperious skyline to the incessant noise and clatter of people and traffic and its vibrant, nonstop night life. The sometimes pungent smells that seeped out of the territory's backstreet restaurants never seemed to bother him much. His feelings about Hong Kong had changed little since arriving from Canada in the early Sixties.

He wanted to do something more exciting than selling used cars on slim margins. When he heard there was a vacancy for a general manager to oversee Orient China Airways' Kai Tak airport operations he jumped at the opportunity. He badgered the CEO to see him and was later recommended for an interview with the board. Mac knew all about aircraft ground handling, he told the board, relating his vast experience in the Canadian Arctic in the Fifties turning-around Lancaster bombers in temperatures way below zero. The board listened patiently as he related his work experience but what impressed them most was his status: "unattached", mobile and, most importantly, Caucasian. The company's ground handling contract with the U.S. government to handle government and military aircraft was not difficult to administer because the Americans did most of the physical work; but keeping in step with some of the strange ground rules set by the Hong Kong Civil Aviation Department demanded a great deal of diplomacy. And Britain's "control" of Kai Tak was becoming more tenuous as more and more airlines from the People's Republic of China began operating to and from Hong Kong after pressure from Beijing to relax the rules. This resulted in procedures being modified to a great extent; changes that played in Mac's favour. After a while, and to his supreme satisfaction, he acquired sole ownership of Orient China Airways.

For him the future held great promise. Hong Kong gave him the opportunity to be a civilian and remain close to military activities -- something important to him. He enlisted with the Royal Hong Kong Auxiliary Police and, after several years of service, including practical training in such things as crowd management, he was promoted to chief inspector. He even surprised himself by excelling in a leadership and command course.

But Mac's great love in the auxiliary police service was the police pipe band. It had links with Scotland through former Commissioner of Police Duncan William Macintosh. The band had adopted the Macintosh tartan and this provided a constant reminder of his Scottish father who hailed from the seaport and market town of Montrose.

Looking back on his life in Canada, getting married in his early twenties had not helped much. No one could credit him with contributing much to the union other than his part in fathering a boy and a girl. John Mackenzie made no secret of his attraction to the Orient. He itched to give it a try and he did. He walked out on daughter Mattie and son Mike when they were very young, leaving them to be raised by his long-suffering wife and her male partner. When he quit the marital home nobody sought to characterise the split as acrimonious in any way. In Canada in those days divorce was not an easy option. In any case, as a devout Catholic, his wife would never entertain the "D" word in her presence. Mac's claim to Catholicism was based solely on his birth right. Years later, he would question the legitimacy of such a claim -- by anybody.

Turning his back on his domestic responsibilities he left Canada and flew into Hong Kong low on cash but high on expectations. His sudden absence from the marital home did not immediately register with the children he left behind -- they were too busy growing up as children tend to do. Married now, older and wiser, they had long since forgiven their father for what they considered poor judgement on his part. They never saw it as a deliberate act of desertion. It was never discussed, at least not in front of dad. Yet there was no question on anyone's part that he loved them dearly.

To Mac's credit he never dodged questions about his marital status. "Of course my wife and I are still married..." he would say with a twinkle in his eye "...it's just that we sleep in separate beds; hers is in Ottawa and mine's in Hong Kong!"

Years before, he convinced himself that the orderly life of the quintessential married man was not for him. So it came as no great surprise to those who knew him well that

Mac's frequent affairs of the heart rarely lasted more than a couple of days. To him, lusting after a new conquest was an irresistible challenge. It was, he said, harmless fun. Nobody got hurt; at least that's how he saw it. To Mac, a woman was a plaything first and last; a toy to enjoy and later return to the toy box for another day. Yet the "toys" found him the most caring and generous beau when the box was opened and the fun began.

The man oozed charisma and self-assurance, traits neatly encapsulated in a cartoon portrait of him hanging on a wall in Jimmy's Kitchen, a popular restaurant in Kowloon. Immaculate in a safari suit he is portrayed leaning against the bar, obviously at peace with the world. Cigarette in one hand and a glass of Chivas-water nonchalantly raised in the "cheers" position in the other, the caricature depicts a man of consummate style.

Life in the fast lane earned him the dubious distinction of being one of Hong Kong's most celebrated night owls. A normal day for him started around noon with an ice-cold beer in a smoke-filled Jimmy's Kitchen and finished around sunrise. It was not unusual for him to leave Bottoms Up, a Kowloon nightspot, at five in the morning after drinking all night, take a quick, refreshing shower and be on the 1st tee-box at the Royal Hong Kong Golf Club bright-eyed and bushy-tailed for a 7 a.m. tee-off. Those who tagged along with him signed on for a hard day's night. Yes, the man had style -- and long-range tanks!

To anyone meeting him for the first time, he came across as something of an extrovert; particularly in the company of men. The truth was he preferred not to be the focus of attention.

In many ways he was living in the past: old fashioned in his dress and in his outlook on life. He did not readily accept change and often fought against it.

But among friends, Mac took centre stage. He had an enormous capacity for storytelling, mostly risqué jokes offered as a substitute for his inability to be impartial in any conversational exchange. He was, as the saying goes, quite set in his ways.

Yet he was one of the most organised people one could ever meet; never forgetting appointments and never late; always remembering somebody's birthday anniversary. His generous nature could be infuriating at times, always insisting on picking up the bills for drinks or a meal. In many restaurants he had a habit of dropping his credit card into the hand of a maître d' on the way to his table. And in full view of the waiters he would tap the right side of his nose once to indicate "it's my check tonight".

He was generous with his money and time. One of his more charitable activities was Macao's Sisters of Mercy. Every year, on Christmas Day, he would make a trip from Hong Kong to make a personal cash donation to the Sisters to help children under their care.

"Colonel Nathan is in a locked-door meeting," Cindy explained, "but would like to meet with you this evening Mr Mackenzie sir." She was aware of the club's rules and tried to keep it brief. "My boss has a late evening meeting on Kowloon-side and suggests you meet before that somewhere in Tsimshatsui if possible."

Mac grimaced, his audaciousness deflated like a popped balloon. He figured that something must have gone wrong at the airport. "Maybe we screwed up with that ill-mannered, overweight undersecretary of state", he

10

thought. It was just an educated guess on his part but he couldn't think of any other, good reason for a clandestine meeting with America's senior liaison officer (read spook). Of course, it could be something else; a matter of greater import. There was only one way to find out.

"OK Cindy," he bounced back as cheerfully as he could, "if the colonel is coming to Kowloon side let's make it 1900 hours in the Chin Chin Bar. Thank you darlin'...over and out!"

———

Living and working in Asia for fifteen years, Colonel Richard Leonard Nathan USAF was enjoying his seventh year as senior liaison officer at the U.S. Consulate in Hong Kong's Garden Road.   In the late Eighties everyone in Hong Kong and mainland China was aware that consulate staff acting as "liaison officers" were in fact spying on China and the Chinese. They functioned under the pseudonym "China-watchers", and in the late 1980s there was plenty of "watching" to do as the Peoples' Republic of China opened up to international commerce. Drawn to the region by new business opportunities in mainland China, foreigner companies poured into the region using Hong Kong as an entrepôt.

Whilst it held strategic, regional importance, Hong Kong at that time attracted a disproportionate amount of international attention because there were only ten years left before the colony's lease expired and Britain ceded sovereignty to China. The countdown had started and many Chinese mainlanders residing illegally in Hong Kong were plotting exit strategies ahead of the July 1, 1997 handover. Having escaped the grip of communism once, many residents would do anything to avoid an action replay. To the hundreds of thousands of ex-mainlanders residing in Hong Kong, it would be akin to jumping from one fiery wok into another. For many people it brought to mind an old, Chinese proverb...*Of all the thirty-six alternatives, running away is best.* And Canada's multiracial cities of Vancouver and Toronto were the most favoured destinations to run to. In preparation for the handover, many Hong Kong Chinese women were already ensuring their babies were born in Canadian cities, a move which secured a future for the whole family.

A distinguished career officer, Nathan had impressed his superiors during the early days of the "Vietnam War" or "American War", depending on which side you were on. The conflict was an undeniably gruesome encounter that sparked an unprecedented bout of soul-searching destined to go on for years in an antithetical America polarised by an unpopular war.

The colonel had taken his Vietnam tour of duty seriously. Like many of his comrades-in-arms, he was eager and ambitious to engage the foe, at least during the first three months. His approach to the conflict was to pace himself and avoid being judgemental. Do what was expected of him, and get the hell out. By the end of his three-year stint, he had picked up a bit of the language and learnt, in the main, to regard the Vietnamese people as innocent bystanders. If questioned about his time in Southeast Asia he professed his ambition was to survive the war without losing his mind or any other vital parts of his anatomy. Thousands of service personnel felt the same way, yet so many signed up for a second tour. Colonel Nathan found that incredibly odd at the time and even more so when he thought about it years later.

The long, drawn-out conflict impacted different players in different ways. For many folk it remains a timeless legacy of an unpopular and untenable struggle to bring about a change in ideology. Nathan understood this point of view but did not subscribe to it. During his tour, he saw the conflict through the eyes of a warrior. He believed the Vietnam experience could and should re-shape America's future foreign policy but remained sceptical.

As for his own future, and the future of mankind, Colonel Nathan was open-minded. Now a widower in his fifties, he was content to finish his military service in Hong Kong. He was accustomed to the pace of the place and enjoyed his job. If asked, he would probably say his preferred exit strategy was a timely hike in rank to help boost his retirement pension. In that respect, the colonel was aware of diplomatic, low-key reconciliation talks taking place between the United States and Vietnam, in which he had a crucial role to play. The talks could yet provide a grandstand finish to a distinguished career in the service of his country. Time would tell.

―――

On his way to the Chin Chin Bar at the Hyatt Regency Hotel, John Mackenzie dropped by his Tsimshatsui apartment and grabbed an outsized golf umbrella. It was a precautionary measure in case the typhoon currently barrelling in a north-easterly direction in the South China Sea suddenly changed course and headed back towards Hong Kong. It wouldn't be the first time. And light rain had begun to fall indicating the outer rain bands of the typhoon were already affecting parts of the territory.

Battling his way through throngs of shoppers in Peking Road, Mac got to the hotel a few minutes before seven. Hit by a sudden gust of wind he struggled for a moment to lower his umbrella to navigate the revolving door. Inside, he headed straight for the Chin Chin Bar.

Bar staff were busy preparing tables for the evening, lighting candles and passing out song request sheets to a largely empty house. He slipped into a booth facing the door, combed his hair and waited for Colonel Nathan to show up.

As usual, Mac was immaculately turned-out. He wore a tailored, green-and-white striped shirt, monogrammed with his Chinese initials on the left cuff, complete with gold cufflinks, freshly-laundered Tommy Hilfiger denims and brown loafers. It had long been fashionable for expatriates and tourists in the Orient to have their names monogrammed in Chinese characters on shirt cuffs or pockets and Chinese tailors were only too happy to oblige.

Not a hair of Mac's tightly-cropped crew-cut was out of place. Though middle-aged, he still placed great emphasis on being well groomed. And he could be scathingly critical of anyone he considered slovenly or unkempt - particularly members of the fairer sex. That was Mac and he would never change.

In truth, he had a heart of gold and was oft-times too willing to assist some folk he mistakenly thought to be "good friends". On one occasion, he willingly loaned over two hundred thousand US dollars to a friend of a friend. Patiently he waited for it to be returned, but never once pressed his friend. People who were genuinely good friends, and had experienced his generosity, would swear Mac had a heart as big as a football.

Tugging his leather-bound cigar case from his top pocket Mac pulled off the top to expose a triple-pack of hand-rolled Cuban cigars – his favourite smokes. He called for a cold beer from the young cocktail waitress who had watched his arrival. Resplendent in a figure-hugging red cheongsam with hip-high side vents, the waitress had immediately commanded Mac's full attention. And it was not for the first time.

"Take your time going sweetheart and hurry back," he called after her, eyes transfixed on her trim derrière. According to close friends, John Mackenzie's thoughts ought to carry a government health warning.

As a regular visitor to the Chin Chin Bar, the affable Canadian was a firm favourite with staff. But it wasn't his good looks, immaculate appearance, or sparkling wit that endeared them to him. It was the size of his gratuities. Years spent waiting on tables as a youth in Canada taught him the importance of tipping in a restaurant or bar. When the hours were long and the pay lousy, tips could be life-savers. Yep, the man was all heart.

His ice-cold beer arrived just as Colonel Nathan entered the bar squinting to get accustomed to the dim interior. In contrast to Mackenzie's casual attire, the colonel was dressed more like a Wall Street banker in his dark blue suit, light blue shirt, discreet tie and shiny, shiny shoes. His next meeting must be really important, Mac thought as the colonel sat across from him his right arm ready to grip a good friend's outstretched hand.

Greetings out of the way, Colonel Nathan got right down to business: "First off Mac," he said with a broad smile on his face, "I want to thank China Orient for taking good care of the undersecretary the other day. It was a great job on everyone's part. Henderson is a pretty demanding sort of a guy. So thank everyone for their efforts please."

It was China Orient Airways' responsibility to take care of all U.S. military aircraft including the presidential fleet whenever one of its aircraft landed at Kai Tak. The undersecretary had visited Hong Kong on important business arriving at Kai Tak aboard a military aircraft from Clark Air Base in the Philippines.

Much relieved to hear the colonel's welcome remarks, Mac took a deep breath and exhaled slowly. He signalled to the red cheongsam: "More of the same sweetheart; take your time going and hurry back!" She turned and smiled sure of a big tip when the time came.

So if we didn't screw up at the airport...what the hell is on the colonel's mind? Obviously something important enough for him to come over to Kowloon side with a typhoon closing in on the territory.

"And it's good to see you too colonel." Mac offered a cigar as the colonel settled into the booth.

Feeling better about life, Mac relaxed and concentrated on his cigar. Everyone liked to be told from time to time that they were doing a good job.

The folk at the U.S. consulate in Garden Road and the guys in the U.S. Navy Contracting Department in Wanchai openly supported China Orient Airways and were very much at ease with Mac and his team. But keeping it that way, and avoiding screw-ups, demanded constant supervision.

Though Mac had never sought or claimed to have any great intellectual advantage over anybody, he was worldly and more streetwise than most. And not just from being a used-car salesman In Ottawa. He served time as an airframe mechanic with the Royal Canadian Air Force, sometimes working in temperatures of 40 below in the Arctic servicing Canadian-built Lancaster bombers. The biggest challenge, he told anyone who showed interest in his earlier life, was to finish a job without leaving his fingers sticking to the fuselage. His frostbite story underwent plunging temperature changes over the years.

Five feet eight inches in height, Mac was of slim build but proudly sported a beer-gut he had worked on over the years. Although he had no facial hair (and was suspicious of those who did) he had a fairly prominent nose accentuated by deep set eyes. His ears appeared to stick out a little but only because he insisted on wearing his hair close-cropped with a military-style back and sides. But one look at his finely manicured hands told anyone that he was meticulous about his appearance. Yes, he was old fashioned but he got the job done and that's what he was paid for.

The U.S. government viewed him as a down-to-earth Canadian cousin with an uncanny knowledge of how Washington worked. And that counted for a lot both inside and outside the beltway as anyone knows who has dealings there. It was Harry S. Truman who once said *Washington is a very easy city for you to forget where you came from, and why you got there in the first place.* Mac kept the quote hanging on a wall in his Kowloon office, lest he forget.

It was true other aircraft handling outfits at Kai Tak airport could do an equally good job looking after U.S.

17

government and military aircraft. But, from Uncle Sam's point of view, those companies were Hong Kong-Chinese owned with vested interests in mainland China. Some had strong links to the communist party. To the Americans, a secure operating environment was essential. That consideration, along with China Orient's operational independence, was the main reason for renewing Mac's contract each year. Consequently, a great deal of mutual trust and respect had built up between the colonel and Mac over the years. All in all, China Orient was guilty of doing a good job for Uncle Sam. More importantly to Mac, it was his livelihood.

"Mac, I have always felt we have much in common," Colonel Nathan announced taking time selecting one of the two remaining cigars. "Sometimes I think the only difference between us is your goddamned strange accent!"

"For chrissakes Dick, Canadians don't have an accent?" Mackenzie fired back as part of a rehearsed response to an overworked, private joke between two good friends.

"I know you're a busy man so I'll get to the point. Thanks for turning out in such terrible weather," he smiled. "Mac, I asked to see you because we need your help with a matter of national importance."

The colonel drew on his cigar allowing the smoke to drift around his mouth and nostrils. He did not want to rush things but he did have another appointment. The two men had not met for a while and the colonel wanted to make sure this visit maintained an appropriate tone, remained cordial and was not too brief.

Mackenzie's curiosity was roused. Should he be suspicious? Did he detect a change in the colonel's

18

demeanour? "Colonel Nathan, if this is some sort of friggin' recruitment drive for the U.S. army I am not volunteering. I already did my bit in the RCAF, remember?"

"Sure Mac. How could I forget; you remind me often enough," he shot back, amused at the Canadian's recruitment crack.

Colonel Nathan was aware of Mac's service with the RCAF both in the Canadian Arctic and prior to that when he attended a heavy weapons training course, learning to fire heavy duty machine guns under supervision. Everything was on file; there were no secrets between Mackenzie and the U.S. Consulate in Garden Road.

"No, we don't want you to join our army. But we do want you to go to Vietnam -- again. This time not for business reasons but to check on intelligence reports that a couple of American ex-servicemen are up to no good over there...pushing drugs, trafficking women -- maybe both.

"This morning, at the consulate, the undersecretary of state for political affairs – the guy your people looked after at the airport -- made it very clear to all assembled that the U.S. Department of State would never allow anything or anyone to obstruct efforts aimed at improving relationships between the U.S. and Vietnam. I can't stress too much the seriousness of this matter as conveyed to me by the undersecretary"

Later, Mac would be able to add his own interpretation to the urgency being placed on this trip by the U.S. Department of State. But it was no secret to anyone dealing with Vietnam in the late Eighties that the impending collapse of communism in Eastern Europe would have a far-reaching effect on the country's economy.

Hanoi was acutely aware that a dismantled Soviet Empire was bound to impact Vietnam's position in the world as the country's main trading partners included many Soviet Bloc countries and the U.S.S.R. Worse still, in 1988 Vietnam was suffering from a famine that was inflicting hardship on millions of people.

It was only a year earlier that President Ronald Reagan had implored Mikhail Gorbachev, General Secretary of the Communist Party of the Soviet Union, to "tear down this wall" (the Berlin Wall) to increase freedom in the Eastern Bloc through *glasnost* (transparency) and *perestroika* (restructuring). Though there was no great appetite among many Americans to "engage" with Vietnam, the U.S. Department of State, on President Reagan's watch, had judged it appropriate to work towards rapprochement talks set to take place in the early part of 1989. Later, this was escalated into a priority task.

Nathan glanced over his shoulder to make sure no one was taking any interest in their conversation. It was force of habit. They had the Chin Chin Bar to themselves, which was one of the reasons Mac had chosen it in the first place.

Mac knew he was only getting part of the total story. It wouldn't be the first time he had been pressed to help. His business with Uncle Sam was of prime importance and he needed Nathan's support to keep it going. The thought of returning to live and work in Canada was unacceptable. He would take this and any assignment and Nathan knew it. But from what little had been said Mac couldn't go it alone. He would need help. And that meant getting together with his good friend Yu Lee.

After giving Mac a couple of minutes to think about it, the colonel continued with his proposal: "About now you are probably wondering where your good friend Professor Yu Lee is at this time, am I right?" Nathan had known Mackenzie for a long time: long enough to know he would not take on a job to Vietnam without Yu Lee. "Right now I'd say he's on his way to Ho Chi Minh City."

Mac screwed up his eyes surprised he hadn't heard about that. He and Yu Lee were two halves of the same coin. Tackling difficult business assignments in China and Indochina was something they always performed in tandem each trusting in one another's particular strengths. If Uncle Sam wanted Mackenzie to go to Vietnam, Mackenzie would want Professor Yu Lee with him. But they hadn't seen one another for six months.

"I don't suppose you have the vaguest idea what he's doing there."

"As a matter of fact I do: He's looking for a sixteen-year-old girl...daughter of a former USAF pilot called David Gervasoni who served in Vietnam. Gervasoni flew over from California to see me...to ask for some advice on how to find the daughter he left behind. I put him in touch with Yu Lee and left them to talk it over."

"Jesus, Dick...never a dull moment at the consulate eh? So Vietnam and my little buddy Yu Lee are back in the frame...and searching for a *bui-doi*...some lowlife's long lost Amerasian daughter; is that right?"

"Talk to Yu Lee. He's got all the details."

In front of Colonel Nathan, John Mackenzie was an open book. Over the years, he never tried to hide his thoughts from the colonel and their relationship had grown because they were open and as honest as they could be with one another.

Nathan could sense from Mac's screwed up eyes and contorted facial expressions that something was troubling him. The Canadian's history, warts and all, was well-documented and stored in a secure file in a safe at the consulate. Uncle Sam knew all about John Mackenzie. It was for his protection, Nathan told him at regular intervals and whenever the U.S. ground handling contract came up for renewal. The colonel was always right.

As Mac thought about Gervasoni and his abandoned daughter, he mulled over his own past lapses and indiscretions. Memories of Ottawa crept back into his mind. It was a long time ago but guilt has a habit of hanging around. Lacking the courage to be a hands-on father, he recalled how he had walked out on his own kids when they were young. Flashes of remorse and anger began boiling up inside him: remorse for this own shortcomings so many years ago, and anger at the news that this asshole David Gervasoni had abandoned his daughter. How could anyone do such a thing?

For a couple of minutes the colonel let Mac battle with his conscience; it would help get him into the right frame of mind, he thought.

"When you get to see Yu Lee," Nathan said breaking Mackenzie's train of thought, "tell him it will weigh heavily in his favour if he works with you on this assignment. His passport request, remember?"

"Jesus, that sure sounds like blackmail to me Dick," Mackenzie bit back, full concentration back on line. "And if I know Yu Lee then as sure as a horse craps in a barn it will sound like blackmail to him too."

22

"Not blackmail Mac...just a bit of friendly arm-wrestling among good friends."

Mackenzie decided to drop the smart talk: "Suppose we find these two American retards colonel, and they turn out to be up to the yin-yang in contraband and/or prostitution or whatever... what then? Neither of us is spoiling for a fight. I hope you're not thinking that way."

The Canadian's dramatic depiction of the assignment was more for effect and the colonel knew it. He also knew there was no way Mac could refuse to track down these American miscreants – not if he wanted to keep his special relationship with the consulate. Yes, it was blackmail but that's how Uncle Sam operated. If there was some way the CIA could be involved they would have done so. Relationships with Vietnam had not progressed sufficiently for that to be an option. Anyone found or suspected of conducting covert operations in Vietnam would set back rapprochement talks for months, even years.

"And my good buddy Yu Lee – unless he's changed and forgotten to tell me -- is a devout pacifist. He won't even fight over a piece of tail," Mac added. Again, it was for good effect.

From what he'd heard at the department of state briefing Colonel Nathan was fairly certain the assignment involved drugs and trafficking. "There is even the prospect of these two guys enjoying protection from someone in the Vietnam government or one of the country's many state enterprises -- which amounts to the same thing right Mac?

"Having considered that, I only see this as a locate-and-report exercise at the present time. Old buddy, you and I have sat through enough UNHCR meetings in Hong

23

Kong to know what terrible things are happening in Vietnam with drugs and human trafficking. Not to mention the present famine. Reports that cross my desk, and those brought back by refugees taking to boats, strike a similar tone. It is only natural for persecuted people to try and shake themselves loose from persecution by running away." Mac tried to bring to mind the Chinese proverb about running away often quoted by Yu Lee.

The colonel's chilling assessment was accurate. And it was not difficult to reach such a conclusion given the boatloads of economic refugees washing up on Hong Kong's beaches on a daily basis.

"But just think where this could lead to Dick. These two troublemakers may turn out to be part of a government-sponsored cartel that goes right to the top. You know how it works in that part of the world, right?"

Both men had been in Asia long enough to know that many governments in the region – communist-run and those headed up by dictators and despots -- were adept at keeping their citizens cowed. And if it resulted in some semblance of order in the world, the U.S. tended to turn a blind eye; at least until such events interfered with their own plans for a better world.

Nathan had to put an end marker on the meeting and called for the check. "Mac, we can't stop a lot of things from happening in Vietnam and we don't have to. But we must act responsibly...you know, do the right thing. I can tell you this much in confidence: Low-level rapprochement talks are going on at the moment between us and the Vietnamese. The state department does not want anything to disrupt or interfere with this process. I am sure you can fill in the blanks pal."

Colonel Nathan chose not to inform Mackenzie that Washington planned to enter into initial bilateral discussions with Vietnam in the early part of 1989. For the time being such information was considered too sensitive and on a need-to-know basis only.

After a quick glance at his watch, Nathan handed Mac the check and smiled apologetically. "Got to go...I have another appointment. Find these guys Mac and earn your keep."

"I was hoping you'd bring that up Dick. I was beginning to think you wanted this done on a pro-bono basis."

"Well, you know the U.S. can't fund clandestine ops, particularly with personnel from a foreign country...and that includes our Canadian cousins." Nathan would have loved to make an exception but rules were rules.

"The good news is the undersecretary of state authorised ten thousand dollars a month for this assignment plus expenses – for an initial six months. It's up to you how you share with Yu Lee.   Talk it over with him because I guess he's under contract with David Gervasoni to find his daughter. Come to some arrangement to work together on both cases. Searching for a missing Amerasian girl seems like good cover to me." The colonel drained his glass and stood up to leave.

"Thanks a million Colonel Nathan. Sounds like another fun-filled mission impossible," Mac said sarcastically. "I can't wait to get started!" He didn't mean it and the colonel knew as much.

"I know it's not great Mac but you guys will get more in the long run. Yu Lee will get U.S. passports for his family and you get to keep your special relationship with Uncle Sam. What more could you ask for?"

Mac smiled at the thought: "Colonel, I was planning to take you to Hugo's for dinner; ply you with another Cuban cigar, a Hennessy XO followed by a *bon surprise* at Club Volvo. But I guess she'll have to wait."

"Maybe some other time buddy. Give my regards to the professor when you catch up with him. One more thing: Britain's ambassador in Hanoi is in the loop. I will also brief him about Yu Lee's search for the Amerasian girl. If you need to get in touch with me call this secure number," he said passing over a scribbled note.

"You are asking us to locate-and-report right colonel?" Mac wanted to be absolutely clear.

"Locate-and-report...that's the general idea Mac," Nathan confirmed, leaving a perplexed Mackenzie holding the check in one hand and the note in the other.

———

At the time the diminutive, five-feet-five-inch tall Yu Lee met with David Gervasoni at the U.S. consulate he was lukewarm about searching Vietnam for the man's daughter. Here was just another missing Amerasian. But, like John Mackenzie, when Colonel Nathan wanted something doing he did it. Getting U.S. passports for himself and his family was extremely important and would become critical nearer to the handover of Hong Kong. In Yu Lee's case it was a time bomb. He needed the passports because he had no desire to return to a life under communism.

After years of living and working in Hong Kong, but still lacking what the Brits called "right of abode", Yu Lee was desperate to remove any incongruities affecting his status. Failure could mean all of them leaving Hong Kong when the territory reunited with its true masters. And they wouldn't get far without internationally-recognised passports.

Over lunch at the Hong Kong Hilton's popular Cantonese restaurant in Queen's Road, Yu Lee changed his mind and agreed to assist Gervasoni. His reasoning: Any sensitive, non-judgemental human being could readily empathise with Gervasoni's dilemma. That was his conclusion after weighing up Gervasoni's story against what he knew of the war years.

Pilots in the USAF lived from day to day. It became a mind-set among crews tasked to fly sorties over North Vietnam from bases in the South. Each mission was fraught with danger; crews not knowing if the next sortie would be their last. The prospect of being shot down over northern Vietnam filled the heart of every young aviator with the fear of being captured. Horrific stories of torture techniques used on POW's in Hoa Lo prison – the "Hanoi Hilton" -- kept them awake when they were in their bunks and wide-eyed alert when they were strapped inside their cockpits.

During off-duty hours, this was a subject flight crews were reluctant to discuss. After each sortie they headed for the officers' mess and got drunk. At the time, David Gervasoni was no different to any other young airman far from home.

But Yu Lee wanted to know more about the man and what made him tick. Particularly the time he spent in Vietnam and why he had left behind a daughter.

"It was twenty years ago but I remember my time there as if it were yesterday. I just did what I was ordered to do," Gervasoni recalled unemotionally.

"Exactly what did you do Mr David?"

"I flew F4 Phantom's out of Tan Son Nhut Air Base, mission after mission. And every time I got back safely I hit the bars around the air base. Everyone did it...well, those that got back."

During the war, air and ground crews had a post-sortie routine. The only way to take their mind off the last mission and prepare for the next was in the company of booze and girls, normally in that order.

"A short while after I started my tour I met and fell in love with a very beautiful girl called Thien. I thought it was love at the time but, looking back, I was very young and impressionable I guess," Gervasoni said apologetically.

Over the years and on a hundred different occasions Gervasoni had questioned himself on the true status of his feelings. "Anyway, she became pregnant and had a baby in the following June – a girl."

Reaching out with both hands and bowing his head politely, Yu Lee accepted from Gervasoni a postcard-size photograph of him in uniform with Thien and daughter Linh. The baby had light brown hair and light blue eyes like her father. She was definitely *bui-doi.*

"Keep it, I have other copies. I guess there isn't much more to add other than I was shipped out of Vietnam at the end of my tour of duty in '73. I didn't think I'd see either of them again. At the time I thought that was probably a good thing. But that's not how I think today. I made a mistake and it's time I put things right."

"I understand…and thank you for sharing that with me.

"At the consulate, Mr David, you asked about my background," Yu Lee pulled out a fan from the top pocket of his safari suite and began swishing it back and forth. It was more for emphasis than to keep cool.

"At first I was not sure I wanted to help you. I thought over your story and changed my mind. Now, I am ready to tell you a little about my background and how I came to be here.

"I was born in Cholon, Saigon's Chinatown, which, if you don't know, is on the west bank of the River Saigon. At the age of nineteen, I went to China and studied Mandarin and political science at Beijing University. There was only enough money to support one son at university so my younger brother, Yu Ming, had to remain in Vietnam."

Yu Ming never forgave his father for failing to support his education, and Yu Lee had to learn to live with Yu Ming's disappointment. This became the main reason for Yu Lee developing a close relationship with his brother; a bond that became stronger over the years.

It was at Beijing University that Yu Lee met his future wife, Gabrielle, also from Cholon.

"It never occurred to me that I would marry someone so beautiful – I would describe her as a Eurasian beauty…her father was French, mother Vietnamese. We

29

married in 1950. Our first child, a boy, was born a year later."

After university, Yu Lee landed a job as a facilitator in China's ministry of foreign relations. Adding Mandarin to his French, English and Vietnam language skills, he was much in demand as an interpreter at business meetings. He was so accomplished in his work he was assigned as interpreter at the 1954 peace conference in Geneva.

"I remember everything about the Geneva Accords meetings as if they were yesterday. This was probably the highlight of my life. I was the sole interpreter for Zhou Enlai and Ho Chi Minh when they met on the side-lines of the conference during a recess on May 8, 1954. It was a great privilege Mr David. I can recall every detail.

"But that is not the reason for telling you this. Before returning to China, comrade Zhou thanked me for my efforts graciously addressing me as 'Professor Yu Lee'. That name has stuck with me over the years and it is why I have it stitched on my safari suits and shirts in Chinese and English. When I am not travelling I teach Mandarin at the U.S. consulate so everyone there calls me 'professor' though I do not have the academic qualifications to warrant such a title. I want you to know that."

It was the outbreak of hostilities between North and South Vietnam in 1958 that dramatically affected Yu Lee and his family after they moved from Beijing to Shanghai. By then their second son had joined the family. Through hard work after arriving in Shanghai Yu Lee had judiciously managed to scrape together enough money to buy a small, two-storey house in Nanking Road not far from the racecourse.

"We were doing well and were quite comfortable for several years. Then, in 1966 everything in China went crazy and we found ourselves trapped by the Cultural Revolution. Our lives changed."

Yu Lee held a South Vietnamese passport and as South Vietnam's main ally was the United States the young, fanatical guards considered it proof of espionage. The young Red Guards were jubilant at catching a spy!

"I pleaded with them, Mr David. I tried very hard to get them to understand that I was in China to help the country. I told them about the work I did as an interpreter for comrade Zhou Enlai. I do not think they were listening. If they were, they did not believe me. As I was from South Vietnam I had to be a spy for my country and the Americans. That was their reasoning. I will never forget the hate in their eyes or how they taunted me by waving their little red books in my face."

Along with the children, Yu Lee and Gabrielle found themselves under house arrest for a year. Every morning, young Red Guards, boys and girls in their early teens, dragged Yu Lee from his bed and hustled him downstairs to the kitchen. Holding him face-down on the kitchen table they would beat the soles of his feet with a bamboo cane. Although his feet would swell up the skin was never broken.

"My wife and my young sons were forced to stand and watch everything, Mr David. Can you imagine my shame? After each humiliating beating they made me write in a tiny book 'I am a Vietnamese spy...I am a Vietnamese spy...' one hundred times before they left us for the day.

"After almost a year of these beatings my spirit began to weaken. I was hurt and humiliated mostly by the distress felt by Gabrielle and our sons. I could not take much more. It was not just the physical beatings I felt I was losing my mind."

He spent a month thinking how to handle a difficult and deteriorating situation. What came to his rescue was something mentioned years before by his father.

Meditation!

"First, to reduce stress, I meditated to shut out all negative thoughts. I found it difficult to begin with but I continued with what became a daily routine. Before the guards made their daily rounds, I meditated to calm my mind. Every time they entered our house I smiled and greeted each boy and girl in turn. I ran around like a houseboy offering sweet tea and steamed buns of mung bean that Gabrielle had prepared so expertly.

"But the beatings continued so I had to find a way to live with the pain. You may find this hard to believe Mr David, but after a few weeks I trained my mind not to accept pain until I succeeded in totally suppressing it. I followed my father's wise counsel that body and mind must work together; the more I practised the more I appreciated the wisdom of his advice. Meditation saved my life."

One beautiful summer's day in 1967 there was a dramatic change in the family's fortune. Yu Lee was not dragged downstairs for his ritual beating. Tiptoeing silently from the bedroom to the top of the stairs he listened for signs of Red Guards moving around below. For the first time for almost a year it was eerily quiet throughout the house.

"Somebody had called at the house earlier that morning because the front door was wide open. That was my first surprise."

Brilliant sunshine streamed into the passageway. Yu Lee went downstairs, wandered into the living room and looked around. On the table was a large, buff-coloured envelope. It was marked in Chinese "For the attention of Professor Yu Lee". He called the family together and opened it in front of them.

"This was my second surprise Mr David. Inside were four, open-dated air tickets from Shanghai to Hong Kong," Yu Lee smiled recalling the wonderful moment that changed their lives. "There was also a letter of safe passage signed by Chinese Premier Zhou Enlai. You can imagine how relieved we were."

One door closed and another one opened. Business opportunities in Hong Kong beckoned and Yu Lee responded accordingly: "When South Vietnam fell to the communists, I found out what it was like not to have a country. I regarded myself as an 'Asian Jew': no country, no passport and nobody wanted me or my family. At least today we all have Certificates of Identity thanks to Zhou Enlai."

David Gervasoni was warming to Yu Lee. He was grateful the little man had opened up to him and was beginning to understand what Colonel Nathan had meant when he said he would be hard-pressed to find someone better qualified to help him find Linh. In return, he would try to help Yu Lee. Colonel Nathan had urged him to use whatever influence he had to support the family's application for U.S. passports and he would get his California office working on it.

33

As a defence lawyer with a big firm in Los Angeles, Gervasoni had done well for himself and his wife Mary largely because the company's clientele included a few, big-name Hollywood movie stars whose dysfunctional lifestyles provided a steady supply of courtroom business. Thank God for Hollywood he said to himself on more than one occasion.

He spoke to Yu Lee about his clientele: "They are the sort of people who need people like me. They can't think or look after themselves in the real world; someone has to do it for them.

"But this situation...my own problem...well I hardly know where to begin. I would probably handle it better if it was one of my client's problems." His sincere confession brought a smile to Yu Lee's face. Offering to help Gervasoni was the correct decision of that he was sure.

"*Ladies and gentlemen of the jury...,*" Yu Lee mouthed to himself, imagining he was in a California courtroom. *"...David Gervasoni is correct to point out the insincerity of this case. He stands before us, a very rich and important California lawyer who has no likely defence in the matter of the daughter he abandoned sixteen years ago! I rest my case..."*

"As I mentioned at the consulate, Mr David, and would like to remind you again, some American parents show disappointment after being reunited with their missing children...because some *bui-doi* do not want to be found. The children often show anger and unhappiness towards Vietnam and America in equal parts. Please keep this in mind.

"And, if you do not mind, I also wish to ask you why you waited nearly seventeen years to search for your daughter."

Gervasoni had been forewarned by Colonel Nathan that Yu Lee would ask. "I understand how this may seem strange to you. It doesn't make sense to me either. All I can say is things were different in 1970. I was only twenty-five years old when I got posted to Saigon."

Yu Lee listened politely as he explained how young aircrew lived on the edge. How, back from a mission they would get drunk and look for girls to help ease the pain.

"My pain-reliever was Thien a stunning looking eighteen-year-old. She was from Tan Thoi Hiep village outside of Saigon but seemed to spend most of her time in bars around the air base hustling for drinks...doing what had to be done to feed herself I guess, and her parents and younger siblings at home."

Yu Lee had an alternative view on Gervasoni's situation. "I think she saw things differently to you Mr David. You may not have known at the time but, in those days hundreds, perhaps thousands, of Vietnamese girls saw people like you as a passport to America. They did not hate the Americans. And that is something that has not changed thirteen years after the end of the war.

"For relief, as you put it, you turned to Thien. She was struggling to get out of poverty the only way she knew how and would do anything not to have to live under the communists. She wanted to go to America and you were her ticket out of Vietnam. I am sure she was very disappointed to be left behind with your child."

Gervasoni became concerned that Yu Lee was about to withdraw his offer of assistance: "Are you still going to help me? I mean...you haven't changed your mind have you?"

"Mr David, this morning I called my brother Yu Ming in Ho Chi Minh City. The search for your daughter has already started."

In the month of May, warm-humid weather was the norm for Ho Chi Minh City. And like any other busy city in Southeast Asia, townsfolk scuttled about attending to early-morning chores. Some folk were buying fresh produce in local markets, others carried out errands on motorcycles. Thousands of the city's residents got around town on bicycles; hundreds more boarded pedal-powered cyclos -- or pedicabs – Saigon's ubiquitous, pedal-powered tricycle with a front-loaded "bucket" seat.

Eager to get started, Yu Ming joined other pedestrians jostling for cyclos. It was a ten minute ride to Dien Bien Phu Road and the house of his good friend Phan Duc Dang. Soon, Yu Ming would know if he would be able to help Brother Yu Lee to find David Gervasoni's daughter.

Please talk to your friend in general terms, Yu Lee counselled when he briefed Yu Ming about the assignment. Do not be too concerned about names and dates for the time being; just get a list of the month and year of birth of any female *bui-doi* born in the metropolitan Saigon area.

Phan Duc Dang, director of Vietnam's national airline Hang Khong Viet Nam (HKVN), was also director of Tan Son Nhut airport the airline's main southern base. Apart from responsibilities for southern Vietnam and the airline's outstations in Thailand, Singapore and Malaysia, he had oversight of migrant flights staged by HKVN on behalf of the International Organisation for Migration (IOM). In short, he was a key employee of HKVN.

After the Indochina War ended in 1975, IOM flights became a permanent feature of the airline's daily operations out of Tan Son Nhut. At a time when only a few, privileged Vietnamese had passports to travel out of the country, IOM flights, largely sponsored by the United States, proved a lucrative business for the airline. Inbound travel to Vietnam, on the other hand, comprised a relatively small number of businesspeople from within Asia and adventurous travellers mostly from France, the country's former colonial power.

Desperate to grow the airline's business as the country struggled to cope with punitive, American-imposed embargoes, HKVN saw an opportunity to make substantial profits at the expense of its former foe. The airline routinely transported to Thailand children born of an American-Vietnam liaison. In Bangkok the children transferred to America-bound flights and a new life in the land of their fathers. It was true that in the late Eighties many Vietnamese still felt uneasy living alongside Amerasian children. Some said it kept alive painful memories of the "American War" so there were no tears whenever *bui-doi* left for the United States, except from those left behind.

Similar to other, older buildings in Vietnam, Phan Duc Dang's modest house was the worse for wear. It was hardly surprising because little restoration work had been done in Ho Chi Minh City since the end of the conflict. The only buildings that appeared capable of holding up to the rigours of the communist takeover were those built during French colonial times.

"... remember that French people built houses to last a thousand years," Yu Ming recalled Yu Lee saying on numerous occasions. "Even the communists cannot destroy them!"

Not so far, perhaps, but they hadn't quit trying Yu Ming thought as he pushed open the weather-ravaged front door of Mr Dang's house.

While his friend prepared cups of *cà phê sữa nóng*, a hot milky Vietnamese coffee, Yu Ming opened up about his visit. "I know you are a busy man Brother Dang, so I will come straight to the point. I am here to ask a favour on behalf of my brother. He is trying to locate a *bui-doi*...the daughter of an American client."

The two men had always liked one another and felt comfortable in each other's company. They often drank coffee together and sometimes played cards to pass away the time. Their friendship had blossomed over the years.

"Exactly what is it you require my friend?" Mr Dang asked sincere in his wish to be of assistance.

"I need your help to obtain a registered list of names and addresses of all Amerasian girls born in the Saigon area in June 1971. Is this something you can help me with brother?"

It was a straightforward request easily fulfilled by Mr Dang. "I assume you know it is my duty to check on the repatriation flights and give whatever support I can for IOM's Orderly Departure Programme. I am sure I can help you brother. Wait please, I wish to check my diary. I think I am due to visit Bangkok this month."

During the war the two men had found themselves on different sides of the political divide. But that was more than a decade ago and life had to go on. Neither man spoke much about the war which had divided families and communities alike. Both knew it was time to move on.

"Yes, I was right in my thinking. I will make an outstation inspection visit to Don Mueang airport in a couple of weeks...I will travel on May 19. So, please ask your brother to meet me off our flight. I will prepare a list and be happy to provide a door-to-door service for you. Was there anything else I can help you with?"

———

The next day, wasting no time in following up with Yu Ming's request, Phan Duc Dang parked his motorcycle outside the IOM office in Pham Ngoc Thach Street and entered the building. Because of his position as director of Tan Son Nhut Airport, and as a regular visitor to the IOM office, he did not require permission to inspect migrant files. But, out of politeness and to keep relationships smooth between the airline and the IOM director, he requested permission to make photocopies of a name list consistent with the specifications outlined by Yu Ming.

Throughout the war years, on the occasion of childbirths, it was common practice to include the name of at least one parent, along with a child's place of birth (hospital or village), on documents processed by the IOM. It was also commonplace for many southern Vietnamese to register their Amerasian offspring out of fear of persecution from their communist brethren when South Vietnam fell to the North. Records were generally in good condition and updated regularly by IOM staff.

Many Vietnam citizens who supported America and its allies in the war ended up in "re-education" camps to be "transformed into good communists". The only way to escape such humiliation was to go to another country, preferably the United States.

The good news for would-be migrants was that the U.S. Government readily accepted those who had supported America during the conflict. Amerasians and their immediate family, including grandparents, were eligible to migrate to the United States if they wished to do so and if approved by the IOM. In setting and meeting the established criteria, Uncle Sam did not set the bar too high.

"Always a pleasure to see you Mr Dang," IOM director Leslie Shaw said as if he was greeting a long-lost friend. "Help yourself to coffee...I will have my secretary prepare the list for you exactly as you specified."

"That is kind of you Mr Leslie."

"Not at all Mr Dang; it's my pleasure. If there is any further information you require please let me know."

As far as the IOM was concerned, Mr Dang was not just director of the national airline, he was the national airline.

At midday, Yu Lee and David Gervasoni converged on the arrivals terminal at Bangkok's Don Mueang Airport in good time to meet director Phan Duc Dang from Vietnam. Gervasoni's expectations of finding Linh had been bolstered by Yu Lee's assertion that the list would help narrow the search.

Yu Lee had already expressed thanks to Yu Ming for securing Mr Dang's valuable assistance: "If all goes well," he told him during their phone call, "we will find Gervasoni's daughter in a matter of days...weeks at the most thanks to your good work brother." To Yu Lee's way of thinking this assignment presented an opportunity for Yu Ming to make a valuable contribution working inside Vietnam. It would also strengthen the bond that had existed between the two of them since their childhood days in Saigon.

Colonel Nathan would also be pleased, Yu Lee thought, envisaging his passport application finding its way to the top of the colonel's in-tray.

Yu Lee's mild bout of euphoria was about to be brought to an abrupt end. Above the noise and chatter of the busy concourse, the airport's public address system crackled into service: *Hang Khong Viet Nam flight 072 from Ho Chi Minh City is delayed arriving. There will be another announcement later.*

The men looked at one another quizzically. The aircraft had left Ho Chi Minh on time -- the airport manager had confirmed that when they informed him they were meeting Mr Dang on arrival. So what could have delayed a non-stop flight?

"Please wait here Mr David. I will check with the airport manager."

As Yu Lee reached the fourth floor airport offices he peered out of the terminal window. A thin plume of smoke was rising from the airfield not far from the terminal building. He experienced a sinking feeling in the pit of his stomach. Looking again, for longer this time, he saw dense smoke rolling across sections of the airfield.

The airport manager had already left his office. Yu Lee re-joined Gervasoni just as a second announcement came over the PA system confirming that HKVN's aircraft from Ho Chi Minh City had crashed and burst into flames one kilometre short of the runway.

Police were already sealing off the arrivals area. Meeters and greeters were ushered out of the building. The airport authority threw a security blanket over the incident as crowds of worried people milled around, pressing airport staff for information. Galvanised into action to handle an increasingly tense situation, the Civil Aviation Department directed armed police officers to restore order outside the Customs hall as people poured out onto the streets.

Grabbing Gervasoni by the arm, Yu Lee steered him towards the bridge adjoining the airport and the airport hotel. "They may close the airport. We must get out of here," he said hustling Gervasoni towards the hotel.

At the busy hotel reception desk Yu Lee requested a call to Ho Chi Minh City. Anxiously waiting to be connected, he turned to Gervasoni: "We must get confirmation that Mr Dang was on the flight. I expect this will be difficult if not impossible so soon after the accident. I will ask my brother to check with the airline office in Ho Chi Minh City. They may refuse to discuss this over the telephone. In which case, Mr David, I may have to go to the airline's head office in Hanoi with your approval of course."

"Let's hope on this occasion that he didn't make the flight," Gervasoni responded with great concern at the same time trying to understand what had happened. "But, if he did, how can we proceed under such difficult circumstances?"

The receptionist interrupted: "Your call to Ho Chi Minh City sir."

"Brother, listen carefully please," Yu Lee said. "I have some bad news. The aircraft from Ho Chi Minh City crashed near the airport. I want you to call the airline offices at Tan Son Nhut to confirm if your good friend Mr Dang was on board or not. Let us hope he missed the flight.

"If necessary, please call the airline's director in Hanoi. He is Mr Dang's boss and will be among the first to know what happened. If you are unable to obtain information over the phone, please try to make an appointment for me to see him in Hanoi as soon as possible. For now, I suggest you do not contact Mr Dang's family; leave that to the airline.

"And brother, I am very sorry to be the one to bring you such bad news."

2

After several failed attempts to contact director Nguyen Van Trang by phone, Yu Lee left for Hanoi. From recent developments it was important in the context of seeking help from the airline to speak to Mr Trang. After all he was Mr Dang's immediate boss. He would be aware of the man's fate. Yu Lee also wanted to explain first-hand the reason Yu Ming had contacted Mr Dang in Ho Chi Minh City.

It took a week to organise the visit; top officials of the airline, including the director, were weighed down with work. Some executives were dealing with the next of kin of those who perished in the Tupolev accident; others were in discussions with the authorities in Thailand and Tupolev Aviation the TU-134's manufacturers.

Airline staff had no time for visitors, Yu Ming was told quite bluntly when he made contact. However via other airline contacts he succeeded in arranging an appointment for Yu Lee to meet with the director at Noi Bai airport.

Travelling on board a sister aircraft of the downed TU-134 caused him some concern until they were airborne. As things turned out, however, the flight proved to be uneventful; just the same he meditated for most of the journey to calm his nerves.

"Keep in mind that director Trang is a patriot and staunch communist," Yu Ming had stressed when he

45

briefed Yu Lee during their telephone conversation. Although director Trang and his subordinate Phan Duc Dang were both born in the communist north, director Dang, during his time in Ho Chi Minh City, had grown to be less dogmatic, less sensitive about his communist background. Nonetheless, he had always been careful to toe the party line at official meetings to dispel any doubts as to where his loyalties lay.

Director Trang, on the other hand, never missed an opportunity to demonstrate his loyalties to the Party and his past exploits flying MiGs with the 921 Sao Dao regiment underscored his commitment to Hanoi. No one ever questioned where his loyalties lay.

"Director Nguyen Van Trang," Yu Ming had cautioned, "is one of Vietnam's four war heroes. That's another thing you should bear in mind brother."

After a short taxi ride from the terminal building to Hang Khong Viet Nam's headquarters Yu Lee found himself outside the director's office. He was warmly greeted by two staff members – a slightly-built gentleman called Mr Hiew, who turned out to be the note taker, and an attractive young lady who took care of refreshments in the conference room.

"Director Trang is expected shortly," Mr Hiew announced. "He has been informed of your arrival."

Shown into the small conference room, Yu Lee was taken aback at the sparse furnishings. The centrepiece was a very old, light-blue, Formica-topped conference table and twelve matching plastic chairs – unattractive relics from the past. A water heater with a coffee/tea station stood in one corner of the room. Not much to see, Yu Lee thought to himself, but at least the room was clean.

"Mister Hiew, is it true that director Trang enjoyed a distinguished career in the People's Air Force?" Yu Lee posed the question as he briskly waved his fan back and forth for effect.

"You are well informed professor," the note taker responded staring admiringly at the monogrammed pocket of Yu Lee's light green safari jacket. "Our director is a national hero of the American war...decorated for shooting down two enemy aircraft over the Gulf of Tonkin," he added with great pride. It was a rehearsed response but the short exchange had the effect of promoting a relaxed atmosphere, which was Yu Lee's intention.

Even in the late 1980s, more than ten years after the war, northern folk tended to distrust strangers, particularly those who fought on the "wrong" side. They were even more suspicious of people like Yu Lee, a Vietnamese-Chinese who had no part in the conflict. With that in mind, and heeding Yu Ming's good advice, it was important to create a congenial atmosphere and get off to a good start.

Minutes later a smiling director Nguyen Van Trang entered the conference room. He walked towards Yu Lee who got up from his chair, pocketed his fan, and leant to shake the outstretched hand offered by the director.

"Sorry to be late," he said politely in a strong northern dialect. "I trust Mr Hiew has been taking care of you brother. Thank you for coming to see us today. Let me see...has your visit got anything to do with the loss of one of our aircraft in Thailand?"

"It has everything to do with that Mr Trang. I tried several times to reach you on the telephone from Thailand but was unsuccessful. I am sure you are especially busy right now...and I do not wish to add to your burden, but I am anxious to learn the fate of director Phan Duc Dang who I believe was on the flight."

The director raised his eyebrows. "Do you mind if I ask what your business was with Mr Dang?"

"I was at Don Mueang airport to meet him off the flight.   My brother Yu Ming, a close friend of Mr Dang, asked the director for a list of names of Amerasian girls in the Ho Chi Minh City area. My client, an ex-American serviceman, asked me to search for his daughter. Director Dang said to meet him on arrival and he would hand me the list. I understand he had a planned inspection visit at Don Mueang airport on the same day."

Director Trang's eyes narrowed. "I must inform you brother that I do not approve of airline staff passing such information to the general public. But I will answer your question: Everyone, including Mr Dang, perished in the accident."

He did not wait for Yu Lee to respond.

"My advice to you professor is to apply directly to the IOM office in Ho Chi Minh City to get the information you need. If you have good contacts with the Americans you should be able to get a letter from an embassy official to back up your request. After all, the Americans underwrite most of the costs for the Orderly Departure Programme. We just provide the aircraft to carry the passengers."

The director was not convinced by Yu Lee's story. That much was clear by the incredulous look on the man's face and the lopsided nature of the conversation. There had to be more to this than Yu Lee's search for a *bui-doi*.

Although it wasn't his business, it was his duty as a patriot and Party member to report anything suspicious to the secret police. At the very least, the director decided, Yu Lee's movements had to be monitored during his time in Hanoi.

"I have already approved a vehicle and driver to take you into the city," the director said as he got to his feet and put an end to the meeting. "I expect you will be staying overnight," he added. It was a safe assumption as there were no more flights leaving for Thailand until the following day.

"You are very kind brother. And thank you for seeing me at this difficult time for everyone in HKVN."

It would have been impolite of Yu Lee to refuse Mr Trang's offer of transportation. In any case he would have to hire a private taxi for the forty-five minute trip downtown to the Metropole hotel. As he was travelling alone, there would not be any opportunity for the van driver to overhear any private conversations. In any case his quest to find an Amerasian girl was hardly of national importance or even a security risk.

With nothing more from director Trang, Yu Lee was anxious to leave Noi Bai and get to his hotel in Hanoi as quickly as possible. He was keen to call on a dear friend he had known since his days as a youth.

————

Thirteen years since the end of the war and the main road linking the airport with Hanoi was still strewn with potholes. Every rainy season more of the road got washed away. Hanoi's financial woes meant road repair

49

work was a hit-and-miss affair much like the country's early attempts to integrate South Vietnam with the North.

It was heart-breaking to look out of the van window at the sight of poor Vietnamese people living in squalor, unable to do anything to alleviate their suffering. Only a few kilometres from the nation's capital, in rural backwaters, citizens were engaged in a fight for survival.

On both sides of the road paddy fields were scarred with deep craters, a legacy from years of strife and forty thousand tonnes of ordinance dropped from America's B52 bombers on and around Hanoi. Thousands of craters that peppered the landscape had long since filled with water and were now thriving duck farms. If nothing else, the Vietnamese were innovative and enterprising and determined to survive.

Kilometre after kilometre, village after village, impermeable parachute silk hung between house walls bringing families some protection from the elements. The chutes played another, important purpose trapping and channelling rainwater into waiting barrels. Yu Lee doubted that the American pilots who had parachuted into captivity to keep an unscheduled appointment with the "Hanoi Hilton" would appreciate the irony of it all.

On both sides of the road, neat stacks of red bricks, fired in local kilns, were arranged outside a few houses -- mostly homes belonging to Hanoi's communist party cadres and others who had managed to save enough money to rebuild. They were the lucky ones.

Children and old people were everywhere. Missing from the rural demographics was the better part of a whole generation. More than three million Vietnamese died in the conflict, many in the prime of their lives. Thirteen years after the war half the population of Vietnam was less than twenty years of age including many children suffering from malnutrition.

The smell of wood smoke from hundreds of charcoal fires drifted aimlessly across the landscape signalling preparations for the early evening meal.

Subconsciously, Yu Lee's thoughts drifted back to China, to the Cultural Revolution and the terrible damage inflicted by communist ideology as he had experienced it. Always, it seemed, the poor people suffered most. His year under house arrest in Shanghai was a personal humiliation as real as if it happened only yesterday. But, all things considered, it could have been much worse. And that was something he would always keep in mind.

Alighting from the van around the corner from Ngo Quyen Street, suitcase in hand, he walked the short distance to the Metropole Hotel. Looking back, Yu Lee spotted the van driver peeking from behind a wall. It was to be expected. Director Trang would soon know where Yu Lee was staying which meant officials at the Ministry of Public Security, more commonly known as the secret police, would also know before the end of the day.

———

A throwback from the French era, the once magnificent, colonial-style Metropole Hotel opened for business in 1901. The hotel's gloomy descent into its ruinous condition was another tragic example of a failed political system. Similar to other colonial-style buildings in the capital, it suffered from lack of maintenance due to scant interest on the part of the communist leadership; a frustrating state of affairs stemming from an unhealthy mix of homespun lethargy and sanctions blocking international investment.   After years of inattention, the once-magnificent wide staircase, a centrepiece of the lobby, was sparsely covered with worn-down linoleum with frayed edges turned upwards like day-old toast.   All public areas cried out for a deep clean. The whole place was in desperate need of renovation but that would never happen until America agreed to lift the embargo.

Inexplicably still functioning as a hotel, the Metropole stood as a fine example of French architectural excellence from a time when colonisers – though hated by many -- constructed buildings of great beauty destined to last for years.

Yu Lee tapped on the desk bell: "Hello. Is anybody there?"

As the nation's capital, Hanoi was faced with social problems ranging from poor housing to inadequate sanitation and drainage particularly in the Old Quarter. During the rainy season, residents endured widespread flooding in the city and surrounding areas. Unwilling and, in some cases, unable to voice their disapproval, stoic Hanoi citizens went about their business with quiet resolve.

Life throughout Vietnam was not only difficult it was tenuous; citizens were threatened by a different kind of danger than war. There was a deep uncertainty about their future and the future of their families. Millions were trapped in a slowly-changing totalitarianism system because the benefits of a series of economic reforms introduced in 1986 had not yet trickled down to the masses.

Yu Lee's ruminations were interrupted by the sudden appearance of a bright-eyed, dark-haired receptionist. Stunning in her light-green *ao dai*, she gracefully stepped forward and beamed a captivating smile that could light-up the darkest room – even the dingier parts of the hotel lobby.   What was it about young, Vietnamese girls wearing traditional *ao dai* – particularly sheer silk – that got ones adrenalin flowing Yu Lee mused. It had been a very long day.

The hotel was all but deserted. In minutes he had secured a room. Key in hand he reached for his suitcase. "Second floor sir," she said. "Take the staircase please; the elevator is out of service." It had been like that for years.

"No sir, there are no restaurant facilities within the hotel," she said in answer to his question. Shrugging his shoulders Yu Lee headed for the staircase unconcerned about the hotel's lack of restaurant facilities. The Piano Bar and Restaurant in Phung Hung Street was open every evening and he was looking forward to meeting up with Madame Ho, the restaurant's owner and a very good friend from a bygone era.

———

After unpacking, Yu Lee took a peak out of the window looking for signs of anyone trailing him.   His thoughts turned to his friend at the Piano Bar; she would most certainly welcome him, but as it was some time since he last called on his former school friend there was a chance of getting scolded for not keeping in touch. It was an occupational hazard.

Well-known and popular with artists, particularly street painters, the Piano Bar in Hanoi's Old Quarter was just a short walk from the Metropole.

In this small, picturesque city of wide boulevards and narrow streets, it was not difficult to imagine how earlier generations of French expatriates enjoyed life in the Orient. Hanoi once boasted much of the sophistication of Paris including fine dining at street-side cafés that shared space with the many art galleries. It was easy to visualise sidewalks bustling with elegant French ladies dressed in crinoline dresses, holding high their colourful parasols to ward off the strong sun as they strolled through the Old Quarter shopping for artefacts to send back to Paris. During periods of hot and humid weather they might retire to a typically French café to cool themselves under whirring ceiling fans. They would order baguettes, croissants, butter and fruit conserves accompanied by a milky-iced coffee *(cà phê sữ'a đá)*, or *cà phê sữ'a nóng* the hot version of the same drink -- all the while dreaming of being home in France.

———

After a refreshing shower, his senses thoroughly tested by the rhythmic clatter of ancient plumbing, Yu Lee dried off and laid out a freshly-laundered, dark blue safari suit. Dusk was approaching as he set off for the Piano Bar.

Always on the lookout for bargains he also kept his eyes peeled for signs of Hanoi's secret police, a difficult task in the fading light.

"But that works both ways," he thought crossing to the other side of the road, "if I can't see them, then they probably can't see me!" He reproached himself for being so suspicious, an unfortunate legacy after spending years working and living with communists.

The streets were unusually quiet; just a few cyclos, one or two motorcycles, and a handful of local folk heading home at the end of another busy day. "But what have I got to worry about," he said to himself, "I haven't done anything wrong."

Although much too early for talk of total freedom, Vietnam had made a start. The introduction of *doi moi* economic reforms was a positive beginning. Looking ahead, how ironic, he mused, that the warring factions that wrought so much dysfunction and unhappiness in Vietnam – China, France and the United States of America --- were now among those most likely to offer the best hope for the country's future. Poetic justice perhaps?

Daylight was fading as Yu Lee rounded a corner into Phung Hung Street. With much anticipation he stepped into the Piano Bar to be greeted by a lively rendition of the First Movement of Mozart's Piano Concerto No. 9.

———

Flinging her arms around Yu Lee's neck, a very surprised but openly delighted Madam Ho pulled him inside. For him it was a magical moment and the next best thing to an official homecoming.

Similar to many other parts of Asia, the Vietnamese frowned upon overt displays of affection in public places. But on this special occasion Yu Lee considered a warm embrace was permissible. After all he was about to become reacquainted with an old and very dear friend.

"My dear, young sister," he whispered in her ear, "I am so happy to see you. You have not changed and neither has the Piano Bar," he added looking around at a packed restaurant.

On Friday evenings business was always brisk. Waiters rushed between tables struggling to keep up with patrons' demands. The clientele was a mix of students, local shop owners, and office workers. Yu Lee detected an air of excitement as customers prepared for their weekend break. Excellent food was accompanied by piano recitals performed by students from the Hanoi National Academy of Music who ate there for free.

"Whenever we meet," Yu Lee said reassuringly, "I always think back to our schooldays in Saigon." Both had attended school in Cholon, Saigon, one of Southeast Asia's oldest Chinatowns.

"But that was when we were much younger dear brother and ready to take on the world. Today it is different and we live in a different world than before."

It was a little under two years since they last met in Hanoi, but their embrace carried the weight of an enduring friendship.

A great beauty in her prime and still attractive at sixty, Madam Ho pushed Yu Lee away from her so she could smooth away imaginary creases from her *ao dai.* Conscious of being the centre of attraction she smiled politely at several patrons before turning back to confront her friend. With faked annoyance, hands on hips, she glared at him as he braced for what she considered a well-deserved scolding.

"It is always a pleasure to see you my dear professor," she said teasingly as she brushed the right shoulder of his safari suit. During their embrace the six-inch-taller Madame Ho had involuntarily deposited some of her face powder on his safari jacket.

"You did not come to my restaurant during your last visit. Why was that?" she demanded. Nearby, a few students found the impromptu exchange amusing. They watched with interest as Yu Lee received a dressing down from their host as the piano played on.

But how did Madame Ho know he had been in Hanoi two years ago and not visited her? Later, he would pose the question.

Like a ten-year-old schoolboy caught smoking cigarettes in his bedroom Yu Lee absorbed the barrage, his face a picture of feigned embarrassment. Diners judged it part of the evening's entertainment losing interest only when Madame Ho guided him to a table. Undaunted by everything going on around her, the young girl playing the piano turned the page and launched into a spirited rendition of Bach's Piano Concerto No 1 in D minor with great approval from the music students to her left and right.

Admired by many, Madame Ho was the embodiment of Oriental grace and sophistication from a golden era. Looking radiant in flower-patterned, green and white *ao dai,* she cut a fine figure. Her elegant dress sense was complemented by long, black, waist-length hair and a warm and generous smile willingly shared with everyone in the restaurant. She was a handsome woman who, for unknown reasons, had never married. It was hard to accept that she was sixty years old. Her only concession to age was a hint of sadness betrayed by her brown eyes whenever she allowed her thoughts to drift back to those halcyon days in South Vietnam. But, as she had already made clear, that was a world ago and the world had changed.

It was time to get down to business and the reason for Yu Lee's sudden appearance at the Piano Bar.

Although he was conscious of Madame Ho's influential connections among government officials, many of whom dined at the restaurant, he had to make sure he could count on her support.   Not in terms of her direct involvement in locating Linh but advice and guidance to successfully navigate any bureaucratic roadblocks if and when the time came to take her out of Vietnam -- though he didn't anticipate any.   Assurances solicited by Madame Ho from a deputy prime minister, for example, could be the difference between success and failure in the event of a glitch in proceedings.

Since the end of the war, the restaurant had developed into a popular haunt for many of Hanoi's government and state enterprise officials, but only at lunchtimes. Evenings saw a different clientele mostly younger people working or studying in the city. The restaurant was situated close to many ministries and its unique ambience shaped its popularity. Madame Ho was on first-name terms with many government representatives and Yu Lee had experience of this. If not for her contacts in the ministry of foreign affairs, he would not have been able to establish trading and business links in Vietnam – particularly in the North. She was important to his business and his affection for her had not diminished over the years.

It was time to apologise: "I am sorry I did not see you during my last visit dear sister.   In truth, I did not have much spare time to myself," he said squeezing her hand.

"As you know only too well, foreigners are always in a big hurry to do business in Vietnam. The people from the Dutch company I was helping did not even stay overnight during our visit from Saigon. One of them fell ill; he kept losing his stomach and did not want to stay in Hanoi for treatment."

It was true. The company had received approval to dredge heavily silted stretches of the Red River that runs through the city. However, when one member of the group went down with chronic diarrhoea the port authorities curtailed a planned tour of its facilities.

Clasping Yu Lee's hand and holding it to her cheek she said: "I was just teasing brother...friends never have to apologise to friends."

A passing waiter set down the menu: "You must be hungry. Since your last visit I have added a few new dishes. Take a look," she suggested, opening the menu before him.

They were seated at a table across from the door, and close to the piano to avoid being overheard. Yu Lee studied the menu while Madame Ho updated him on political developments in Hanoi.

"The secret police still watch me closely. It is a sad fact of life that the communists are still suspicious of me." But she wasn't being singled out; they were suspicious of anyone of Chinese ethnicity particularly citizens born in Cholon who had moved to the nation's capital after the war. After all, Cholon was one of the biggest Chinatowns in the world and, until the fall of Saigon in 1975, functioned almost as a city within a city, its residents able to pursue Chinese cultural traditions without interference as they had for generations.

It was only after Saigon fell to the communists in 1975 that everything changed. Thousands of southerners were rounded up and transported to re-education centres to be transformed into "good communists". It was a worrying development that prompted Madame Ho to forge closer links with officials in the ministry of foreign affairs; something she managed to achieve and maintain for over ten years. But she knew she could never let down her guard. Being ethnic Chinese and from the South, her allegiance to the Hanoi government would always be kept "under review". And she would have to keep on proving herself a worthy citizen.

After placing his order Yu Lee discussed his search for Linh including the earlier setback when the Tupolev crashed in Bangkok. In less than ten minutes, and before his course of *cua farci* had arrived, Madam Ho was up to speed.

"Where do you go from here?" she asked after he related his conversation with HKVN's director Trang.

"I have other alternatives. You see, I believe if we are to find the American's daughter it will be in Ho Chi Minh City. I plan to go there tomorrow and consult with my brother."

"What are your options?"

"You remember my good friend John Mackenzie. He does great work for the UNHCR supporting refugee repatriation programmes. This means he has contacts in the IOM. We can get back to my original plan to obtain a list of Amerasians from the IOM office. Kim, my secretary, is familiar with the metropolitan area of Saigon and I plan to ask her to make some house calls for me."

The outcome of the meeting with director Trang called for a review of tactics.

"I feel I should be able to do more to help you," Madame Ho said signalling for a waiter to clean-up a nearby table. "But when you find Linh I may be able to help get her out of Vietnam – assuming she wishes to go of course."

"I was hoping you would say that my dear friend and..." Yu Lee wasn't able to finish his sentence. Suddenly, with a loud crack, the restaurant door burst open, attacked from outside with such force it was left hanging on its hinges. Seconds later, three plainclothes men, recognised by Madame Ho as secret police, stormed into the restaurant. Everyone was ordered to stand with hands on head, including the student playing the piano.

Two men approached Yu Lee. They ignored everyone else. A third man remained by the door. Madame Ho looked on helplessly as Yu Lee had his arms gripped. In seconds he was bundled out of the door and into the street. Not a word was spoken. He glanced back at his friend. Her eyes relayed the message: "...stay calm, my friend I will find a way to help you". Visibly shocked, she restrained herself, knowing it would be a waste of time to remonstrate with the secret police during a raid. For now, patience was the order of the day.

Cautiously, diners slunk back into their chairs. Many of them were shaken by the surprise raid but no one left the restaurant. If anyone departed too soon after Yu Lee's arrest it could look suspicious.

Outside, Yu Lee was pushed into a waiting police van, hands cuffed behind him. In silence he absorbed the pain of the cuffs pinching his skin. There had been some dreadful mistake and he was confident he could set things straight at the police station.

But the van didn't go to a police station. A hurried glance at the dateline of 1886 above the prison gate immediately told him he had arrived at Hoa Lo, the "Hanoi Hilton".

Built by the French when Vietnam was still part of French Indochina, Hoa Lo was Hanoi's *maison centrale*, copying the euphemism used all over France to describe prisons. It was left to American POW inmates to dub Hoa Lo "The Hanoi Hilton".

Thoughts of his year under house arrest in Shanghai came to mind.

Inside the prison, he was relieved of his possessions, including his fan, and pushed into a small, single-bunk cell with one chair, a bucket and a washbasin that leaked water onto the cold, stone floor. He was not questioned, and was told not to ask any more questions after asking and being refused permission to make a phone call.

In less than an hour claustrophobia began to set in; visions of the past came back to haunt him. He broke into a sweat fighting fleeting thoughts that Red Guards were outside his cell. Were they waiting to beat the soles of his feet? Subconsciously, another voice questioned the purpose of that line of thought. After all, he hadn't done anything wrong. He had to stay calm and remain awake.

Lying flat on his bunk and staring at the ceiling he went over the events of the day. He knew Madame Ho would do everything she could to get him released. With luck he would be released by morning.

But that did not happen. Good luck was not on his side. Friday night would be the first of three nights he would spend in the "Hanoi Hilton".

———

Concerned for the safety of her good friend, Madame Ho knew she had to act -- but how? The work he was engaged in, as explained by Yu Lee, seemed harmless enough. Was there more to it? She had to be careful not to get dragged into something that could prejudice her special relationship with government officials.

At the first opportunity she would seek help from the British Embassy in Hanoi. The ambassador and his wife were regular diners at her restaurant and, in matters of foreign policy, she was aware that Britain looked after Hong Kong's interests in Vietnam. Surely they would help her friend.

———

Alighting from her cyclo right outside the British Embassy, Madame Ho asked the driver to wait for her. Being forced to hang around all weekend had weighed heavily on her conscience. She had discounted thoughts of making a direct approach to Vietnam government officials for fear of worsening the situation. All in all, it had made for a long and worrying weekend.

Inside the embassy, His Excellency Anthony J. Braithwaite, her Britannic Majesty's long-serving Ambassador to the Socialist Republic of Vietnam, listened patiently and carefully to Madame Ho's account of Friday's incident at the Piano Bar.

"That is exactly how it happened, Mr Ambassador and the last I saw of Yu Lee he was being pushed into a van."

"Dear lady, I am very much aware of the existence of Yu Lee and know something of his consulting work in Vietnam. I also know he has excellent connections with the American consulate in Hong Kong.

"I will put a call through to them right away and inform them of Yu Lee's detention and my intention to have him released at the earliest opportunity. Clearly, someone has overstepped the mark and we'll get to the bottom of it."

"Thank you Mr Ambassador. I was very concerned and didn't know who I could turn to for help."

In Madame Ho's presence Braithwaite spent a few minutes on the phone.

"There now...you heard what I said to Colonel Nathan...that I will personally intervene to have him released right away. You did the right thing by contacting me. Thank you so much for bringing this incident to my attention. May I wish you goodnight and see you to your cyclo. Meanwhile, please try not to worry I am sure Yu Lee will be alright."

In truth, the ambassador suspected Yu Lee's spirits would be flagging after three nights in Hoa Lo in the insalubrious company of political outcasts, dissidents and thieves. Time was of the essence. He was already working on a plan as his driver opened the car door. "Take me to the ministry of foreign affairs if you please."

———

Trang Dinh Te, Vietnam's deputy minister for foreign affairs, was an important member of the Vietnam team engaging in regular meetings with British trade delegations. Ambassador Braithwaite's arrival at the ministry was unexpected but he was always welcome nevertheless.

The deputy minister was as keen as Braithwaite to help grow trade between both countries. For some strange reason he had not been briefed, but he anticipated the meeting was in connection with trade. So it came as a complete surprise when the ambassador opened by saying he had come to see him about Professor Yu Lee from Hong Kong.

Sitting comfortably, with a cup of warm oolong tea at hand, Ambassador Braithwaite settled back in his chair. He knew how the deputy minister worked and had planned his approach accordingly. He got straight to the point.

"Yu Lee's business in Vietnam Mr Te," the ambassador stated, "is to locate an Amerasian girl abandoned by her American father sixteen years ago just before the end of the war.

"This rather minor matter," Braithwaite said in a serious but beguiling manner, "hardly seems to warrant our joint intervention. Indeed, if it were not for Madame Ho – the delightful proprietor of the Piano Bar -- bringing certain matters to my attention, I would not be troubling you today."

At the mention of the "delightful Madame Ho", Mr Te stiffened. Clearly feeling a modicum of discomfort he looked anxiously at his telephone as if expecting it to ring at any moment. Madame Ho was not only well known to him but was someone for whom he held great respect as did his boss, the minister. There was need for caution.

But what could have happened to warrant this urgent visit on the part of Britain's ambassador?

"You are always welcome at the ministry Mr Ambassador and I thank you for visiting us today. Yes I am aware of Professor Yu Lee's valuable assistance to my country. But just how can I be of help to you this morning?"

"Mister Te, you can do me a great service by having Yu Lee released immediately from the Hoa Lo dungeon," Braithwaite countered in an unwavering tone. He had decided to portray an air of aloofness. It wasn't difficult for him.

If Mr Te thought the ambassador's description of Hoa Lo was a bit melodramatic he chose not to let on. He knew Braithwaite had visited the famous jail on several occasions, and refuting the ambassador's description of the facility would be imprudent and may even evoke a challenge.

"Hoa Lo!" Mr Te repeated. "Are you quite certain?"

"Am I to believe that you are unaware of the distasteful episode that took place in the Piano Bar last Friday evening?"

Under normal circumstances Braithwaite would not expect the deputy minister of foreign affairs to know everything that was going on in Hanoi's restaurants or prisons. But this was different; he had a point to make and he was quite enjoying watching the man squirm.

"Moreover," Braithwaite said, maintaining his air of aloofness, "I don't believe any formal charges have been levelled against the unfortunate man. So he has now suffered three nights of unwarranted detention and associated discomfort. You do see my concern Mr Te do you not?"

These were assumptions on the part of Braithwaite but it ratcheted up the level of discomfort being experienced by the minister. Had they been playing chess, Mr Te's king would now be surrounded with no chance of escape.

In a way it was a game of political chess though neither Britain nor Vietnam would permit such an incident to sour bilateral relationships. The minister was well aware that Yu Lee returned to Vietnam after the war to help the country. This was evident from his excellent reputation in business circles and not just in Vietnam.

In the early days following *doi moi* only a handful of foreigners and *Viet Kieu* had answered the call to help the country. Understandably many people were not sure of what sort of reception they would receive as former supporters of the South. In Yu Lee's case, he returned by express invitation of the government of the newly constituted Socialist Republic of Vietnam. And like many other Vietnamese who spent the war years abroad, Yu Lee was not entirely trusted by the ruling communist cadres. People of his ilk were considered by some to be deserters during a time their country needed them most. But try telling that to a man who had fallen foul of totalitarianism twenty years earlier earning him a year of forced detention. So far, Yu Lee had steered clear of any controversy in Vietnam. But things could change and Mr Te knew that. It was nothing more than diplomatic chess and, for now, both players had to be careful with their next moves.

"I will take immediate steps to have him released," Mr Te said anxious to make amends on the spot. "I am sure it was a dreadful mistake on somebody's part for which I extend my country's sincere apologies Mr Ambassador."

"That is most courteous of you Mr Te and a prudent decision if I may say so. Thank you, I will make sure Yu Lee learns of your gracious response.

"I dare say that neither of us would want such an unfortunate misunderstanding to muddle relationships between our two countries. Or indeed to interrupt rapprochement talks that could affect Vietnam's standing in the international community." The deputy minister had to be aware of the improving political situation between Vietnam and the United States.   The importance of reconciliation between the two countries was of paramount important in both Washington and Hanoi.

The point had been made and enough had been said. The meeting was at an end; it was time for Braithwaite to take his leave.

————

Indebted to Britain's ambassador for his timely intervention, the first order of the day for Yu Lee was to get back to the Metropole for a welcome shower and to wash-away feelings of exasperation and indignation after spending a wasteful and unproductive weekend in Hoa Lo. A change of clothes would definitely help. Then he would respond to the ambassador's request to meet with him. Before doing so, he had to get rid of the smell and taste of the Hanoi Hilton.

Being offered a lift to the Metropole in a Hanoi police car and on to the British Embassy underscored Mr Te's efforts to keep things sweet with Britain's resolute ambassador. It also underscored Ambassador Braithwaite's statesmanship when it came to dealing with ministries in Vietnam.

For Yu Lee his hot shower was sheer bliss. He even found himself singing in synch to the beat of the dancing pipes. Although there was no evidence that his room had been searched during his absence he assumed the secret police had been around. He had nothing to hide so he had nothing to fear.

After being under house arrest in Shanghai, Yu Lee figured he could take anything thrown at him though the thought of spending four or five years in Hoa Lo, recalling the fate of some American POW's, chilled him to the bone. During the short time he was there, the cries and screams from some of his fellow inmates had kept him awake for three nights. The old man in the cell to his left, who benefited from Yu Lee's untouched food, had open wounds on his arms and legs consistent with being beaten. From his accent, Yu Lee knew he was from the South and probably not considered to be a "good communist".

Being deprived of simple everyday things normally taken for granted was, in itself, a form of torture. In just a couple of days Yu Lee had shed around four pounds in weight through a combination of inedible food and needless stress. But he was free again and able to redouble his efforts to find Linh. If anything Hoa Lo had strengthened his resolve.

———

"Would I be correct in assuming you are somewhat relieved to be out of that dreadful place?" Expressions of understatement, so typical of British people, was something Yu Lee had never really got used to. Braithwaite, a product of England's public school system, typified the breed.

"Quite correct, Mr Ambassador, and I thank you very much for securing my release. Given a choice, I would much prefer the Metropole to Hoa Lo. I could only recommend a stay at that prison to someone who was finding it difficult to lose weight."

"That's quite understandable. I see you have not lost your sense of humour. And one must not forget the role that Madame Ho played in bringing this sordid affair to our attention. She was extremely concerned for your wellbeing."

"I will be sure to thank her."

"But that's not all I wanted to say. Colonel Nathan asked me to inform you that he would be most obliged if you could link up with John Mackenzie. I understand he is due in Ho Chi Minh City in the next day or so."

"Meet with Mr John you say? What could that be about; do you know Mr Ambassador?"

"Well, I am at liberty to give you an outline briefing," he said, shepherding Yu Lee towards his private office although they already had complete privacy in the drawing room.

"I do not possess all the details but I do know that Colonel Nathan has asked your friend John Mackenzie to try to locate two ex-servicemen...Americans who served in Vietnam during the war," he said consulting a notebook plucked from his desk drawer.

"Why does he want to find them?" Yu Lee was curious but his thoughts were elsewhere – very much

70

focused on finding Linh. He was concerned that David Gervasoni would be impatiently pacing up and down anxious to receive a progress report.

"The Americans believe these men may be up to no good...drugs, trafficking young women, that sort of thing."

"Do you have any names?"

"Yes, Robert Johnson and William Petroni both of whom were reportedly sighted in Ho Chi Minh City some months ago." The ambassador handed Yu Lee photographs of the pair.

"Colonel Nathan also asked me to inform you that your application for passports was still under review. I trust that means something to you.

"Our American friends seem to be extremely anxious to find these two gentlemen. I should tell you this was a pressing reason for intervening to expedite your release from Hoa Lo...plus Madame Ho's insistence of course."

Smiling at Braithwaite's reference to passports, Yu Lee followed the ambassador to the outer gate unaware that deputy minister Te had issued orders for the secret police to follow him.

Back in his room at the Metropole he drew the curtains, bolted the door and fell into a deep sleep the moment his head touched the pillow.

Waiting in line at the United Airlines' check-in counter, Lily Crenshaw focused on returning to Vietnam to be reunited with her parents and other members of the family. It had been a long time.

In her check-in line and adjacent check-in lines she observed a good number of Asian-looking travellers of similar age clutching what looked to her like brand new U.S. passports. Were they also overseas Vietnamese *(Viet Kieu)*, she wondered, making their first trip back to Vietnam after immigrating to America after the war? Everybody knew that Vietnam was opening up and *Viet Kieu* with business expertise were actively encouraged by the Vietnam government to return to help kick-start the country's moribund economy. Lily had similar thoughts: *doi-moi* (market economy) promised a new start for the war-ravaged country she left as a child.

But first she had to find out why the regular stream of letters from her family had dried up. There was no other way to get in touch with them and that gave her cause for concern.

Secreted close to her chest – literally -- Lily had five thousand dollars as a homecoming gift just in case her parents had fallen on hard times. That, she presumed, was the main reason for not hearing from them.

Another good reason for taking a break with her family was provided by her ne'er-do-well husband Harold. Of course he objected to her decision to go to Vietnam. Lily had anticipated as much knowing that his main fear would be running the restaurant without her. He wasn't up to it. Serve him right, she thought smiling to herself. She pictured her inept husband stumbling around the kitchen and restaurant upsetting staff and patrons alike.

For now her thoughts were on finding someone to help her get five thousand dollars into Ho Chi Min City. She wasn't concerned about the first stop in Taipei where she would be required to wait in the transit lounge, or Bangkok where she would overnight at the airport hotel. What preyed on her mind was being singled out by the sticky-fingered Customs officers at Tan Son Nhut airport when she arrived in Ho Chi Minh City. Stories were rife in the U.S. about how some *Viet Kieu* were victimised.

That is something I must work on, she thought, as she stepped aboard the Boeing 747 on the first leg of her journey into the past.

Around the time Yu Lee was released from Hoa Lo, his good friend and colleague, John Mackenzie, was in line at Thai Airways' check-in desk at Don Mueang, Bangkok's international airport. Boarding pass safe in hand, he was able to kick back and relax until his flight was called. Though never fearful of flying he was feeling slightly apprehensive following the news of the Tupolev accident just days ago.

Mac wasn't in the best of spirits because early morning rises had a detrimental effect on his disposition unless he was heading for an early tee-off time at the Royal Hong Kong Golf Club. In truth, he also felt cheated after leaving behind a warm bed in Hong Kong and an even warmer bodyguard. *Colonel Nathan could never understand and appreciate the many sacrifices he'd made for Uncle Sam he muttered as he dragged himself into the bathroom.*

In his rush to leave he had barely enough time to shower and grab his pre-packed crew bag. Half-dressed he'd bolted out of his apartment block looking for his housekeeper. She had been running up and down Peking Road for half an hour trying to fulfil her boss's instructions. *I know it's the morning rush hour but you must find a bloody taxi driver willing to take me to Kai Tak airport. Offer more dollars: I don't have time to screw around.*

In Thailand it was a little after midday and the area around Thai Airways' check-in desks was awash with passengers. Dozens of would-be travellers jostled for

74

boarding passes some anxiously waving a ticket and passport overhead to attract the attention of airline staff.

The absence of direct services from northern Asia to Vietnam in the late Eighties meant passengers had to route via Bangkok.   As a result, flights to Hanoi and Ho Chi Minh City were invariably overbooked. Transit passengers from Japan, Korea, Taiwan and Hong Kong were funnelled through Bangkok's Don Mueang airport resulting in Thai Airways and Hang Kong Viet Nam services being invariably oversubscribed on a daily basis.

Overbooked flights offered a golden opportunity for astute airline staff to make money on the side by "auctioning" seats to the highest bidder.   Airline agents kept a wary eye open for passengers holding up tickets with partly-concealed dollar bills. There was no such thing as a "firm booking" out of Thailand to Vietnam. Travelling to Hanoi or Ho Chi Minh City, in a sellers' market, meant you played by local rules or got left behind.

Surveying the crowded forecourt, Mac suspected *Viet Kieu* were at the heart of the mêlée. From a safe distance he watched as security officials moved in to control the crowd.

Economic reforms, or *doi moi,* a centrally-planned socialist-oriented market economy, were only introduced into Vietnam in 1986. Relaxation of the rules had encouraged many *Viet Kieu* to return to Vietnam. They came to pursue business opportunities or reconnect with loved ones left behind during a bloody conflict that had torn apart thousands of families.

Checking to make sure his boarding pass was safe Mac reflected on the sound advice often suggested by his friend Yu Lee: *Be easy Mr John; relax and enjoy the good life.*

"I hear you my friend," he said aloud. He couldn't wait to get on-board and down a glass or two of Champagne and smoke a choice Cuban cigar.

It seemed an age ago, but it was only a year earlier that Mac had made his first peacetime trip to Vietnam. Navigating a way through Vietnam's bureaucratic minefield, with Yu Lee's assistance, he managed to put together a string of cargo flights between Sydney and Ho Chi Minh City carrying much needed medicines, clothing and food for hundreds of thousands of sick and half-starved Vietnamese. The airlift established a crucially important lifeline for thousands of citizens displaced by years of ground fighting and incessant bombing raids. And the vital, organisational role played by Mackenzie and Yu Lee had not escaped the gaze of government officials in Australia and Vietnam.

The Indochina wars cost the lives of over three million Vietnamese. No family was left unscathed in the north or south of the country. Now, some thirteen years on, the country's young people yearned for stability. Quite simply, they sought a better life than their parents and grandparents; something other than unrelenting conflict. For many years peace remained an illusion, a dream. Could new, economic reforms bring forth change? Importantly, these much needed reforms required the support of the international community – the United Sates in particular – and little progress had been made thus far.

It was true that Vietnam's expansion of diplomatic relations in the West, and with countries in East Asia, foretold of better days ahead. But real progress would not come about until the United States played a more active role in the process. The outline briefing Mac had received from Colonel Nathan offered some hope in this respect.

If only for humanitarian reasons, something urgent had to be done to staunch the flow of illegal immigrants arriving in neighbouring counties in their rush to get out of communist Vietnam. Even now, as *Viet Kieu* competed to board flights to visit relatives and friends in Vietnam, dozens of Vietnamese refugees were washing up on the shores of Hong Kong in small, leaky boats. Their objective was to gain political asylum in any foreign country that would take them.

By 1988 over thirty thousand "boat people" were incarcerated in Hong Kong as economic refugees. China insisted all must be repatriated to Vietnam before China re-established sovereignty over Hong Kong in 1997.   Helping to airlift these people had become part of Mackenzie's responsibilities working with Hong Kong government departments under a UNHCR mandate. There were only ten years to go. The clock was ticking.

But that was not today's challenge and would have to wait. Colonel Nathan had a sensitive and highly important, job of work to be undertaken.

Firing up a Marlboro Lite, Mac pondered the task ahead. Finding two wayward Yanks in Nam could be difficult, even dangerous, especially if the colonel's description of their backgrounds was half accurate. As soon as he could, he would sit down with Yu Lee and hammer out an action plan. It was top priority.

———

Mac was still deep in thought when he felt a light tap on his right shoulder. Turning on his heels, he found himself staring down at the smiling face of an exceedingly attractive Asian lady. For one moment she took his breath away: "Jesus, Joseph and Mackenzie...aren't you a sight for sore eyes?" he blurted out almost choking on his cigarette. Although slight of stature, the lady was incredibly well-endowed. "Sweetheart," he said, "with that cleavage you could hide...let me think..."

"Five thousand American dollars Mr John; I know because I've done it," she proclaimed nonchalantly, one hand brushing strands of long dark hair from her eyes.

"That's one helluva place to keep your Ben Franklins." Mackenzie teased at the same time battling hard to drag his eyes away from her ample chest. He lost the battle.

Eagerly eyeing her up and down, his gaze zeroed in on her mini skirt. No one could argue that it offered a formidable challenge to the international norms of decency. But that was okay by Mac. The lady's spotless white blouse fitted snugly around a trim waist. Shapely legs confirmed she was a frequent visitor to the gym. Five inch heels brought her up to five-seven. Another toy perhaps? Had they met before?

"Do I know you?" he asked stubbing out his cigarette.

"No. But I know who you are Mr John. The Thai Airways station manager told me you were a regular traveller to Vietnam and that you might be able to help me," she said fluttering her heavily-mascaraed eyelashes for effect.

78

"And just how might that be?" he responded, eyeing her even more closely and liking what he saw. She certainly looked Asian, but her mannerisms and sense of humour marked her as all-American.

"Mister John I believe we are taking the same flight to Ho Chi Minh City. This is my first trip back to Nam since I was evacuated."

"Is that so…and when was that?"

"Nineteen sixty-four. I was ten."

Was she looking for help or just looking for company? Either way, Mac had time to kill and nothing better to do. And she was easy on the eyes.

"Little lady, let's go into the Thai Airways lounge and you can tell me all about yourself before they call the flight."

"I will be happy to tell you a little about myself," she said with a smile. "My Vietnamese name is Nguyen Thi Minh Lili, but you can call me Lily. My family are from Hoi An in central Vietnam, do you know it?"

Mac lit up another cigarette. He had already grabbed a beer from the self-service counter and was making himself comfortable. "Heard of it, but haven't been there. Tell me about it."

"I will tell you about my family if that's alright," she suggested settling into her chair.

"Go ahead I'm all ears."

"During the war my father fought with the ARV, attached to an American unit. As the war dragged on with no end in sight, dad said the Americans could not win and would have to withdraw. He told me he was concerned

79

about my safety and arranged for me to be evacuated to the United States."

"How did you feel about that? Did you want to go?"

"Well, to be honest, I didn't want to leave my family behind, but they insisted. That was twenty-four years ago. Now, I'm going back to help my family because they gave me a new start in America. I owe them that much."

"Tell me about your time in the States."

"Well, after graduating from a teachers' college, I married a guy called Harold Crenshaw. Within a few years we had a Vietnamese restaurant in Venice and I managed to save some money from the business," she said, pointing to her chest. "I also made some money teaching Vietnamese at a local school. I have teaching qualifications with me," she said patting her small carry-on case.

In the beginning Lily had found it difficult to adjust to life in the United States, but she persevered with her English language skills and, over time, learnt to adapt to an American lifestyle.

"Mr John, this money," she said, pointing towards it again, "is for my family. I want to help them."

It was a familiar refrain in the late Eighties. And like any other *Viet Kieu* who decided to return home Lily could easily become disillusioned in a radically different Vietnam to the one she had left behind. Vietnam's socialist ways would be a challenge after California. But it was her choice, her business. If she wanted to try her luck in the old country then nothing John Mackenzie or anyone else could say would put her off.

But was she sure of what she was leaving behind?

80

"Tell me about Harold...does he fit into your plans?"

She frowned at the question: "My husband is a miserable son of a bitch. He took up with another woman years ago and left me to run the restaurant on my own. Harold treated me badly and I won't mind if I never see him again. This is my money, not his."

"But you are still married right?"

"Right, but all I know and care about is getting back to Hoi An to see my family. That's my priority and why I need your help. If I don't see Harold again it would be a prayer answered."

"You can tell me it's none of my business Lily, but I think you should prepare yourself for what could be a big shock when you get back to Hoi An." He lit up another cigarette: "True, Vietnam has changed for the better for a few lucky people, but most Vietnamese are living on the edge and your folks could be among them."

Irrespective of what Mackenzie told her -- and she did take on board his concern -- Lily had made up her mind. She was determined to go back to her birthplace. Mac saw that in her eyes: "I am just making sure you know your own mind Lily. You are going back to a Vietnam you won't recognise and may find strange."

That said he never could resist a damsel in distress, particularly those who carried their problems on their chests. He had decided to help from the first moment he clapped eyes on her. Lily offered a mouth-watering challenge to a man like Mac.

He had another question: "How do you plan to get your lifesavings into Saigon?"

"This is where I need your help Mr John. I want you to carry my money please. I heard that foreigners were not checked the same as *Viet Kieu*. I also heard rumours that *Viet Kieu* women were sometimes strip-searched."

"They're not rumours Lily. It is common for *Viet Kieu* to have their cash taken from them for 'safekeeping'. That's the last they see of it. In your case...with your looks...you could lose more than your money. And how do you know you can trust me not to run off with your hard-earned cash?"

It was a good question, but she had to trust somebody. Even so, she had decided not to tell him about her backup plan. If he refused to help her she would go back to the Thai Airways station manager. Earlier in the day he said he couldn't help because it could cost him his job but she would press him and offer cash if necessary.

Regular travellers to and from Vietnam in post-war years were wary of customs and excise officers at Vietnam's ports, particularly Ho Chi Minh City's Tan Son Nhut airport. It was a sensible precaution. Many uniformed officers were jealous of *Viet Kieu* whom they regarded as foreigners. They were easy to spot. Compared with local Vietnamese, *Viet Kieu* were presentable, well-dressed and looked healthy. Some officials found that intimidating so they relieved *Viet Kieu* of some of their valuables. To their convoluted way of thinking, it helped level the playing field.

As Vietnam introduced a more open market economy thousands of *Viet Kieu* heeded the call to go back and help the country recover from years of war and stagnation. For airport workers such a situation provided a golden opportunity to make a dollar or two. Everyone had to eat, and there were plenty of hungry mouths to feed in post-war Vietnam.

An absence of official fund transfer services between the United States and Vietnam meant that cash-in-hand -- or cash-in-cleavage in Lily's case -- was another way to transport valuables. Customs officers offered speedy clearance for a little "tea money" with no questions asked.

Lily had been correctly informed that foreigners were rarely body-searched. Nevertheless, Mac figured Lily to be an obvious target for such attention.

"Lily Crenshaw, in my rush to shower this morning I just knew this trip would be different. But, if I was told I would meet someone whose cleavage was a hiding place for five thousand dollars I would have said they were either sniffing something or in need of psychiatric counselling. OK, let me have it. Hand over your bundle little lady!"

"Thank you Mr John. You won't regret it, believe me," she proclaimed with a tempting smile and a flutter of her heavily-mascaraed eyelashes.

"You are so right about that."

Unseen by other travellers, Lily unbuttoned her blouse, and parted with her bundle of cash.

"Take your time Lily," he grinned, reaching forward for the cash. Expertly and unseen, he split the bundle into two halves and stuffed them into his trouser pockets.

"I have to say I think you're a very gutsy lady," he told her watching as she buttoned up her blouse.

Selecting two iced coffees from the trolley, he sat down again and opened his crew bag. As per normal practise, he was wearing a freshly laundered white, long-sleeved crew shirt with two, button-down top pockets and black trousers. He could pass as a member of the aircrew. His shirt had epaulet straps but he never wore epaulets. His uniformed appearance gave the impression he was an off-duty crew member. The standard crew bag he carried helped support the illusion. From time to time Mackenzie's strategic camouflage came in useful.

The lounge had filled up. Discreetly, Mac plucked two company envelopes from his crew bag, slipped in the cash and deposited one envelope in each top pocket of his shirt buttoning the flaps. Everything was secure.

The flight was called for boarding.

"Meet me outside the Customs Hall at Tan Son Nhut airport and have a good flight," he winked at her as he picked up his bag and headed for the gate. She had placed her trust in him and would find out soon whether or not she had chosen wisely.

———

True to character, John Mackenzie kept the cabin attendants busy running back and forth on Champagne duty. Savouring a cigar, he mulled over Lily's case. In Ho Chi Minh City he would invite her to meet Yu Lee; that much he had already decided. She could spend a few days at Yu Ming's house until she got her bearings. In any case, it would be good to have her around for a while.

The uneventful Airbus flight to Ho Chi Minh City was two-thirds full with *Viet Kieu* all excited to be returning to Vietnam. Some, like Lily, were going back after long absences abroad. Customs officials, Mac thought, are

84

going to have a great time with many of them. He prepared for a quick exit from the plane.

The aircraft slowed to a halt right outside Tan Son Nhut's sole terminal building. His objective was to be first in line so he could to take care of the senior Customs officer before Lily arrived inside the building.

Striding along with the confidence of a member of the aircraft flight crew, he passed through passport control then into the arrivals hall, pausing only to light up a cigarette. He was on plan and ahead of the game. So far so good!

With a pronounced click followed by a grinding of gears, the carousel jerked into action carrying the first few bags into view, Mac's included. His very heavy, extra-large suitcase was stuffed with a variety of giveaways from Hong Kong including fake watches and jewellery, lingerie, shoes, handbags and a personal supply of cigarettes, whisky and his favourite brand of Cuban cigars -- items not easily sourced in post-war Vietnam apart from cigars. A strategically-placed hundred dollar bill should deter Customs officials from becoming too inquisitive. It had worked before on several occasions.

Stubbing out his cigarette, he surveyed a growing crowd of excited passengers swarming around the baggage carousel. Too late he spotted Lily. She was being escorted to an office at the rear of the Customs hall. Not overly concerned, he watched until she disappeared from view. With her strength of character and other noble attributes Mac felt sure she would be able to handle the most inquisitive officials.

Wheeling his suitcase out of the Customs hall he turned to look behind just in time to see Lily emerge from a back office. Grabbing her suitcase, she whisked it past waiting Customs officials and into the warm, muggy air of Ho Chi Minh City. She had a cheeky grin on her face.

"What the hell happened in there?" Mac looked for signs of dishevelled clothing. "I saw you disappear into a room at the back of the hall."

Sheepishly, Lily adjusted her skirt. It had ridden up her backside as a result of dragging her suitcase behind her. "I did as you suggested...picked out this older guy. He asked me for 'tea money' so I gave him fifty bucks. Then he started to grope me. I told him to back off and get my suitcase out of the door. He pulled a face, waved me through but would not help with my suitcase."

"Well, it's hats off to Lily. The head honcho got a hundred from me. What the hell...we paid twice but we bucked the system and able to talk about it."

Grabbing a passing porter Mac steered her towards the exit. "Let's get the hell out of here. The smell of corruption always brings on a headache."

"Little lady, I would like you to stay at my good friend Yu Ming's house for a day or two. That's if you don't have any other plans." They were settled comfortably in a taxi. The drive into town would take forty-five minutes.

"I would like that Mr John; I don't have any other plans except organising my trip to Hoi An."

In the short time they had known one another Lily had begun to warm towards Mac. She liked his upbeat style and was confident she could handle his sexual overtures given sufficient recovery time between attacks. He had done her a great favour helping smuggle her money into Vietnam and she would not forget that in a hurry. In any case, it would take a day or two to arrange transport to Hoi An some seventeen hundred kilometres from Ho Chi Minh City.

"If all goes well my plan is to spend around two months in Vietnam taking care of my family. We have a lot of catching up to do, I'm sure you know what I mean Mr John."

"Sure I know what you mean Lily. I just hope you find the family in good shape."

Mackenzie tried to take in everything she said as Lily continued to talk about her family but his mind was on what lay ahead. Yu Lee, he knew, was not entirely trustful of his brother Yu Ming. Not a lot had been said on the matter but, intuitively, he sensed something had happened between the two of them in earlier years that had strained their relationship. Ethnic Chinese family feuds can last for years particularly where money or favours are concerned. He was also aware that Yu Lee was trying hard to involve his brother more and more in his business undertakings.

Mac was quite fond of Yu Ming, and found him a reasonable and helpful sort of guy.   And Yu Ming had excellent connections inside Vietnam which could come in useful -- with his brother's agreement of course.

Whatever transpired over the next weeks and months as the duo pursued their commitments in Vietnam, he knew he could rely on his good friend Yu Lee to come up with a back-up plan. And he was sure it would be a plan that took into account his father's wise counsel: "...always remember, my boy, a smart rabbit digs more than one hole!" Yes, the professor always had a back-up plan. And he had probably started digging already.

Surrounded by heavy traffic on Dien Bien Phu Road, and out of the driver's line of sight, Lily took hold of two bulky envelopes offered by Mac with a nod and a wink.

———

The detached, French-colonial period house in District 1 in downtown Ho Chi Minh City belonged to Yu Ming but was viewed as a family residence rather than his own personal property. He spent more time in the house than Yu Lee so Yu Ming took care of it.   And the professor used that as an excuse to send money to Yu Ming from time to time to help pay the bills.

The house's main attraction was its proximity to Saigon Central Post Office an imposing, French-built structure in the heart of the city.   It was a place where you could buy more than just stamps and envelopes or make phone calls: it was a meeting point for people living and working in and around Ho Chi Minh City and a favourite place for friends to congregate and exchange news.

A Gothic edifice constructed in the early part of the 20th century by famous architect Gustave Eiffel, the post office was one of the grandest colonial buildings in the city. Situated close to the Notre-Dame Basilica it was yet another magnificent example of the splendour and grace of 20th century French architecture.

A busy, public place, this was where businesspeople sent and received overseas faxes away from prying eyes. In Ho Chi Minh City, self-styled security personnel were implanted in every hotel in the downtown area. Their main role, Yu Lee maintained, was to report to the secret police at the Ministry of Public Security on the comings and goings of foreigners and their contacts. Listening into private telephone calls to and from the city's major hotels was another way of accomplishing the same task. Little wonder, therefore, that the post office's private booths were viewed as safe havens from where private telephone calls could be made or faxes sent and received.

Two years had passed since the introduction of economic reforms yet few motor vehicles were seen on the city's streets. Appearing affluent had its risks in communist Vietnam. Even those who could afford a vehicle opted for a motorcycle; by choice the ubiquitous Honda Dream bike was one of the most popular modes of transport. In Vietnam, as in most parts of Southeast Asia, motorcycles were regarded as "small cars". It was not unusual to see families riding four-up, with the family dog sitting on the driver's lap or in a basket hung over the handlebars.

With great courtesy, Yu Ming greeted Lily as she disembarked from the taxi.

Paying off the cab driver, Mac added a ten thousand dong tip. It did not go unnoticed by his fellow passenger. "You are very generous Mr John. Are you always like this?" she asked obviously impressed.

"Work it out Lily...at thirty thousand dong to the dollar I gave him a thirty cent tip. But you're right; it's way too much for a forty-five minute cab ride!" The taxi was already pulling away from the kerbside when he called out "...use some of it to send the kids through college!" His insensitive remark earned a frown from Lily. It wouldn't be the only time she would admonish him for being insensitive.

After making two trips between the kerbside and the house Yu Ming managed to walk his visitors' luggage indoors. He could not hide his delight at seeing John Mackenzie again. He was a firm favourite with Yu Ming: "I am always happy to see you Mr John," he said, enthusiastically hugging a reluctant Mac. "But I see you have a friend with you.

"Yu Ming...Mrs Lily Crenshaw. Lily is from California coming back to Vietnam after a long, long time away. I hope you don't mind I invited her to stay here for a while before she joins up with her folks in Hoi An."

"You and your friends are always welcome in this house Mr John. And I am sure my brother will agree. He should be here soon. Now, please excuse me. I will prepare some food and drink while you unpack and take a shower," he added panting heavily as he dumped the luggage on the upstairs landing.

Lily was visibly exhausted; a combination of jetlag, the excitement of the journey and Ho Chi Minh City's oppressive humidity in May. Having waited twenty-five years to savour the moment, when it arrived, she was overcome with emotion. Sleep would put that right. There was time to talk later.

"If you will excuse me gentlemen, I must take a rest. I have been on the move for over twenty-four hours non-stop and I am very weary." She brushed back strands of her long, black hair. "I am in desperate need of a hot shower," she said with a deliberate flutter of her eyelashes that did not escape Mac's attention.

But Yu Ming mistook her remark for a slight rebuke. "Please excuse my very poor manners Miss Lily. May I ask you to go to the far end of upper passageway and take room on right; room with pink walls and curtains? You will find towels in the dresser. I bring your luggage right away."

"Let me take care of Miss Lily's things," Mac suggested, as Lily headed upstairs, "while you do me the great favour of pouring out a very cold beer."

The front door slammed announcing Yu Lee's arrival. For a moment he just stood inside the door, shaking his head from side to side like someone with bad news. Finding his voice and remembering his manners, he went into the kitchen to greet his brother and good friend Mackenzie. "It is so very good to be back brother, and to see you of course Mr John."

Yu Lee was also worn out. Placing his small attaché case to one side he embraced both men. It was good to be back among friends. A good night's sleep would help dispel lingering thoughts of the Hanoi Hilton.

"It's been a while professor," Mac said enthusiastically, pleased to be reunited with his old friend. "I don't know what you've been up to but from the look on your face I would say you have had a tough time in recent days. Am I right about that?" He had in mind the search for the Amerasian girl, as yet unaware that Yu Lee had spent a frustrating weekend in prison.

"We need to talk Mac...about my time in Hanoi, the hunt for Linh and our new assignment. But I need to take a rest first.

"Another thing," he added, lowering his voice, "I think I was followed here by the secret police – just a feeling."

"Understood; I will see you in the morning. Get some rest prof."

Mackenzie watched as Yu Lee picked up his attaché case and headed for the stairs. "Just one thing: don't go into the bedroom with the pink walls and curtains; I will update you tomorrow," he added before downing the last of his beer.

———

Without making a sound, Mac opened Lily's bedroom door and peaked in. She was in a deep sleep. Carefully, he closed it again and tiptoed to the room next to hers.

More than anything, he wanted to take a shower which was his first priority. It did little to dispel his tiredness but he felt less tense as he dried off. Drawing back the duvet, he climbed into bed and flicked off the light. It was replaced by a faint glow in the bedroom from a streetlight.

Mac was concerned about Yu Lee. If the professor was being tailed by the secret police it could affect their plans. The work that lay before them was vitally important. Such concerns would have to wait until morning was his final thought as he drifted into a deep sleep.

After what seemed to be just a few minutes he awoke with a start, his nostrils under assault by a strong smell of perfume. He recognised the scent – Lily!

There was no telling how long she'd been there, but that was unimportant. What was important was that she was in his bed and naked.

"I guess it's show-time," he declared turning to face her. She looked refreshed, her face radiant in the dim light.

"I must protest this outrageous intrusion into my privacy," he announced with feigned indignation, at the same time surveying every inch of her as he slowly pulled down the duvet.

"Were you expecting someone else Mr John?" she asked defensively.

"Hell no Lily; but in Vietnam you never can tell." Her nakedness was accentuated by the low glow of light from the streetlight.

"Let's get something straight Mrs Crenshaw," he said admonishingly. "I don't know what your game is but you have just three hours to get your ass out of my bed."

"And if I don't," Lily asked enjoying the tease, "what then?"

"Well, you could ask for a time extension. I have been known to be lenient when faced with situations that challenge my masculinity."

———

Early next morning a rejuvenated and visibly relaxed Mrs Crenshaw tiptoed noiselessly downstairs, leaving Mac snoring competitively with hordes of tree crickets and bullfrogs revived by overnight rain. Determined to earn her keep she went directly to the kitchen to prepare breakfast for the men.

Lily smiled broadly on seeing Yu Lee in the kitchen and enthusiastically shook him by the hand as Yu Ming made the introductions. Bringing him up to date with her plans to visit her family in Hoi An she also told him about the invaluable assistance she received from Mac.

"Yes, I do understand Miss Lily. Mr John can be very helpful particularly where attractive young ladies are concerned," he offered politely.

In truth, Yu Lee was a little concerned that Lily's arrival on the scene may have some sinister overtone. His involuntary incarceration in prison, still fresh in mind, had rekindled a degree of fear and suspicion that had lain dormant for some time. There was nothing to support this concern other than his intuitive feelings and an inclination for cautiousness.

After a hearty breakfast and cosy chat with Lily and Yu Ming, Yu Lee went upstairs and tapped on Mac's bedroom door. He wanted to talk in private.

The sound of running water told him his friend was taking a shower: "John...just to let you know I have spoken with Lily...had quite a good conversation in fact. She is a very likeable lady don't you think?"

He had to shout above the noise of the shower. "She seems to know a little about me…I guess from Thai

94

Airways staff. I suppose her approach to you at Don Mueang must have something to do with that."

"That's what I figured prof; but nothing for us to be concerned about. She plans to join her family in Hoi An. I suggested she stay here a while until she gets her bearings and arranges her onward trip."

"That seems a good idea," Yu Lee replied fidgeting with the duvet so he could sit on the bed.

Mackenzie grabbed his bathrobe. "From what little I have learnt of Lily she is a strong and sensible lady quite capable of taking care of herself." He had in mind her gutsy approach to him and the way she handled the Customs officials. "It crossed my mind she could assist us in the future; assuming she's interested."

"Would that have anything to do with last night?" Yu Lee did not expect an answer. "You may consider it none of my business Mr John, but can you be sure of Lily? Why did she pick you out at the airport in Bangkok and not someone else to help her? Can we be sure she is who she says she is," he added. Had he been in Mac's shoes at the time, Yu Lee would have exercised greater caution.

"I think you are being a bit overcautious professor but I hear what you say. CIA implants aside," he said jovially and dismissively, "let's discuss something more important. Tell me about the secret police. What makes you think you're being followed?"

"After what happened in Hanoi I expect to be followed," Yu Lee said putting the question of Lily's dependability to one side. Mac was probably right. He was being overcautious. "Let me update you my friend."

Mac, more than anyone except perhaps for Yu Lee's wife Gabrielle, was aware of Yu Lee's capacity to deal with adversity and his proven ability to handle challenging situations. Physically slight of build he was in the heavyweight class when it came to mental strength. Lesser men would have been driven insane facing a year under house arrest in China watching the country descend into a state of cultural psychosis. A weekend in Hoa Lo, no matter how bad, could never compare with being a prisoner of the Red Guards during China's Cultural Revolution. But that did not prevent him from being naturally cautious and Mac understood as much.

Waiting for everyone, including Lily, to assemble in the kitchen Yu Lee recounted details of his visit to Hanoi. He would take Lily into his confidence.

"As I feared, Mr Phan Duc Dang died in the Tupolev crash near Bangkok. I had it confirmed by HKVN's head office. I want both of you to know that my brother and Brother Dang were close friends," he said putting his arm around Yu Ming's shoulders, "so please understand if he seems a little quiet for a few days."

Unaware of the search for Linh and the Tupolev accident, Lily was puzzled by Yu Lee's remarks but refrained from making any comments. Bearing in mind Yu Lee's previous observation, Mac decided to watch Lily's movements closer than before.

He turned to Yu Lee: "Don't worry professor, we will find Linh," he said reassuringly and after digesting Yu Lee's update.

Still confused, Lily sat patiently as Yu Lee related his recent experience in Hanoi.

As she was going to stay in the house for a few days -- even longer – the men would bring her into their confidence notwithstanding Yu Lee's previous concerns.

During his weekend stay in Hoa Lo, Yu Lee had pondered alternative ways to handle the search without help from the national airline. For Lily's sake, and to bring Mac up to date, he ran over details of his visit to Hanoi that had been sparked by the air accident in the search for Gervasoni's Amerasian daughter.

"I have decided to ask Kim to make enquiries and try to put together a short list of candidates in the Ho Chi Minh City metropolitan area. She knows the city as well as anyone and can ask questions without attracting too much attention."

A long-time girlfriend, Yu Lee had implicit faith in Kim. And she would do anything for him.

The alternative option of asking John Mackenzie to use his contacts in IOM was put to one side by Yu Lee after learning about the additional undertaking thrown at them by Colonel Nathan. Both men agreed the two assignments would be better tackled at the same time.

"John, we have to discuss the task given to us by Colonel Nathan. I am a little upset that everything gets linked to my request for US passports for my family." He said it with a smile but Mac knew how Yu Lee felt. To him it was a massive loss of face.

"The colonel knows I have no choice but to carry out his request. So when do we start Mr John?"

"Where do we start would be a better question my friend," Mac fired back. "First things first professor; you and I need to agree a plan to find the Americans. But before we get to that I suggest you go and see Kim and see how she feels about helping us find Linh. That will get one assignment underway. Do you agree?"

Yu Lee had already called to check that Kim was at home: "I will take a cyclo to her house and make a detour via the central post office. As you know, it is a great place to meet, get lost, or lose someone."

And it was another way of finding out if he was being followed. Everyone else would stay safely indoors until Yu Lee got back.

———

As the driver slowed down at the busy entrance to the post office Yu Lee leapt off the cyclo. Head down, he made his way through a throng of people who were shoving and pushing each other into and out of the same, main door. The cyclo disappeared from sight and circumnavigated the immediate area before returning to a prearranged pickup point.

Each day, local folk visit Saigon Central Post Office to send or receive money or make telephone calls to relatives living upcountry. Its cavernous interior, capable of housing several hundred people at a time, was a secure place for citizens to socialise with one another. Within, it was nigh impossible to track any single person, which is why Yu Lee had chosen it as a detour just in case he was being tracked by the secret police.

Walking confidently towards the bank of telephones on the left hand side of the building he joined the long line of people waiting to make a call. Twenty minutes later and without making a call he retraced his steps to the entrance.

The wind had picked up and rain was in the air. Satisfied he was not being followed he boarded the cyclo as it cruised by the busy main entrance.

———

Watching from behind drawn curtains Kim saw the cyclo parked across from her house.   With furled umbrella in one hand, she ran across the road, leapt onto the cyclo and fell into the bucket seat as the driver pushed hard on the pedals to get up to speed in the heavy traffic.

"I am so happy to see you Kim. We have much to talk about," Yu Lee held her hands tightly. He had to shout to be heard above the noise of passing motorcycles. "Please do not be angry with me but a proper reunion will have to wait until another day and another time. Right now, I need your help with an important assignment."

Had it been anyone else asking for her help under similar circumstances Kim would probably have rebuked them for being so rude.   Though it was uncharacteristic of Yu Lee she could see from his face and sense from the urgency in his voice that he had his reasons.

"I want you to help me to find a sixteen-year-old *bui-doi* girl," he said, explaining how he had been approached by David Gervasoni via the American consulate in Hong Kong.

"Mister David left his daughter in Vietnam after the war. We do not have much to go on except her name is Linh and we have this family photograph of her when she was about eighteen months old." He gave Kim the photograph and a brief account of Gervasoni's service in Vietnam.

"I am very happy to see you too my dear after such a long time," she said accepting the photograph. Still smiling, she shook head from side to side. "Have you not considered that this girl could be anywhere after sixteen years. Do you know how many Amerasian girls there are just in Saigon?"

"No I do not know, and I did not say this would be easy Kim. But we must find her. Linh's father wants to take her to the United States to take care of her...help with her education and a new life. Try to understand how he feels, even after such a long time. Can you help?"

No stranger to adversity herself, Kim's marriage had failed because her husband, just a few days back from the war, chose to gamble and drink rather than find a job to support her and their only daughter. The family suffered. It was Yu Lee who helped her put her life back on track for which she would be eternally grateful. His concern for her predicament helped her to regain her self-esteem. More than anyone, Kim knew Yu Lee's intention to find Linh was sincere.

Unable to support her eight-year-old daughter, Kim had sent her to live with her parents near the southern Vietnam city of Vung Tao. That arrangement allowed her to take up a job in a clothing factory although her greedy husband took everything she took home.

But all that had happened before she met Yu Lee. He had spotted her during one of his visits to the clothing factory when he was consultant for a Hong Kong company owned by his friend.

As described to him at the time, her situation seemed hopeless. Unless she could find work and avoid falling into poverty, she was in danger of losing her self-esteem and possibly her sanity – not uncommon among many citizens who were just barely surviving in post-war Vietnam.

Within a year Yu Lee had arranged to rent a house for her in Ho Chi Minh City. He also promised to reunite her with her daughter as soon as possible. That still had to happen.

After moving into the house Yu Lee kept her busy with small jobs acting as his private secretary. She arranged meetings, typed documents and organised visits to state enterprises and government entities in the city. An enterprising lady, with a good head for figures, Kim was totally reliable. And she was willing to do whatever he asked of her. She had complete faith in him and he had total trust in her. She got paid for her trouble and for the first time in years felt she had two feet on the bottom rung of life's ladder and, with luck, good prospects for advancement -- given Yu Lee's continued support of course.

On the far side of the street Yu Lee spotted a man paying a great deal of attention to them. It could be somebody from the secret police. It was time to make a route adjustment.

"Go down Dong Khoi Street," Yu Lee instructed the cyclo driver. Was he becoming paranoid -- again? Hoa Lo can do that to a man. Dong Khoi Street was gridlocked with traffic. It was time to end the meeting with Kim and find his way to Yu Ming's on foot.

"Please try to find Linh. Ask your family and friends. Let people know you can arrange for them to be paid up to five million dong if they can provide information that helps us find her."

"I will do my best professor. If I have any success I will contact you."

Yu Lee was sure he would get a positive response to his offer. The equivalent of one hundred and sixty-five dollars was a windfall for most people living on less than two dollars a month.

The minute she got back indoors, Kim set about calling family members and friends she trusted most. Two brothers and three sisters living in the metro area of Ho Chi Minh City were the first to get a call from her. She gave them the girl's name, date of birth -- nothing more. There was little more to offer other than the old photograph which she would keep to herself for the time being.

After a couple of days' anxious wait a call came through from one of her brothers. His information looked promising.

"A cousin of ours," he told her, "a policeman called Phan Van Nguyen had access to a name list of *bui-doi* living in the metropolitan area of Ho Chi Minh City."

It sounded encouraging.

Unknown to Kim, metropolitan police routinely maintained an updated account of movements of Amerasians. Many were under review as potential emigrants under IOM's Orderly Departure Programme. It was important to know their whereabouts so they could be contacted at all times and informed of opportunities to migrate.

"Where can I find Officer Nguyen," Kim asked her heart beginning to race.

"At the police station at the lower end of Dong Khoi Street near to the Majestic Hotel. I will call him and tell him you want to see him."

Cranking her motorcycle Kim joined the busy flow of traffic heading downtown towards the River Saigon.

Fortunately for Kim, Phan Van Nguyen was on duty when she arrived. He stopped what he was doing and stepped forward as she entered the police station. He guessed she was his cousin from the description he'd been given by Kim's brother.

Looking him over, Kim could not see any family resemblance. She was quite sure they had never met before.

Officer Nguyen greeted her as if they were old friends reunited after a long absence: "Welcome cousin Kim. Please wait in there," he requested indicating a small interview room. "I will join you in one minute." She sensed her cousin's exaggerated welcome was more for the benefit of his fellow officers than for her.

Sparsely furnished with a small table, a table lamp and two chairs, the interview room also boasted a coffee pot and several mugs on a small side table.

A minute later Officer Nguyen joined her: "You are my cousin Kim, is that correct?" He poured himself a mug of coffee but did not offer her anything to drink. Strange, she thought.

"Yes, I am Kim," she said showing him her ID card. "Thank you for agreeing to meet with me cousin. My brother says you may be able to help me locate a *bui-doi* girl called Linh. Do I understand correctly?"

Taking a seat across from Kim, Nguyen took his time lighting up a cigarette. Amazingly, to her anyway, he put his feet on the table and blew a large smoke ring in her direction. He pondered her through the cloud of smoke. "I

104

can help you but I expect to be paid for my trouble," he said in a curt and offensive tone. It was not what she expected from a family member even a distant cousin.

His sudden, aggressive behaviour so soon after they'd met took Kim by surprise. Perhaps it was a bad idea, she thought, to have reached out to her siblings with details of the reward for finding Linh. Had she opened a Pandora's Box?

Nguyen was insistent: "Listen up cousin, I have a good idea where to find the girl and I am sure you are not doing this work for nothing. So it is only fair I get paid," he told her temptingly waving a clipboard above his head.

"You can have this list of names for six million dong. That's the deal; take it or leave it, it's up to you."

"But what if the girl is not on the list and...?"

"That's your problem; it is a chance you have to take," Nguyen said cutting her off.

She was taken aback; not by the amount which was around two hundred dollars, but by her cousin's unnecessary aggressiveness and apparent greed. She felt uneasy and would rather be somewhere other than in the police station.

Sensing she was in something of a dilemma Nguyen pressed her further: "You have to understand I am taking a risk letting someone have addresses of Amerasians. It could cost me my job if anyone found out." It wasn't true, but how was she to know?

Cousin or no cousin, Kim sensed she could not trust him. She desperately wanted to get her hands on the list and the asking price would, she thought, be acceptable to Yu Lee.

In post-war Vietnam, everyone was battling to survive. In Officer Nguyen's case it was a matter of life or death. Debts he'd accumulated for being unlucky at card games, as he put it, had driven him to seek help from loan sharks. He was now out of his depth and desperate for money because loan repayments were months overdue. Within days his creditors were due to pay him a final visit.

News about Kim's search had given him an idea, a lifeline. He would extract as much money from her as possible for a list of *bui-doi* in the Ho Chi Minh City area. Once she'd delivered the money to him at the police station he would have her arrested for subversion. In the late Eighties many Vietnamese from the South refused to accept Hanoi's plans to integrate the country under communism. Nguyen's plan was to have her arrested knowing that his sergeant would have her presented before a magistrate for a ruling. In court, Kim would have to face her accuser whom Nguyen planned to be a friend of his with the secret police – someone who also owed money to loan sharks.

In all likelihood, Nguyen figured, she would be sentenced to a period of re-education at an up-county location. Confident he would be able to extract more cash from Yu Lee, Nguyen would later seek her release on the grounds of misidentification. His friend in the secret police, for a price to be agreed, would attest to Kim's arrest being a case of mistaken identity. She would be released after Nguyen received enough money to pay off his debts and pay off his friend. That was his plan; hastily-hatched perhaps, but he was warming to it nevertheless.

Right now, sitting across from Cousin Nguyen, Kim was having second thoughts. Perhaps naively, she had expected better from someone in the family. How could she trust him going forward?   She could not; would not; it was time to leave. She stood up and started for the door.

"Cousin Nguyen, I have decided I do not need your help," she stated as firmly as she dared to. "I am sorry I troubled you. I am doing a favour for a friend and I will ask someone else for help," she said reaching for the doorknob.

Instantly, Nguyen jumped to his feet and jammed one foot against the door as she tried to pull it open. "Not so fast cousin. Listen to what I have to say before you decide to leave. I have already checked this list and you will want to know what is on it."

What was she to do? As a visitor inside a police station common sense told her she should feel safe. She had to avoid making a scene at all costs. Would it be sensible to sit down again and listen to what her cousin had to say? She returned to her chair.

The information he had was compelling, including as it did details of four Amerasians living in the city area, two of them boys. Of the two girls one was called Linh.

Her interest rekindled, she began to wonder if she'd been a bit hasty in deciding to leave. Feeling rather foolish, she nervously crossed and uncrossed her legs. "Tell me more please about the girl called Linh."

"I will if I have your full attention," he said sarcastically.

"Let me see…she was born in June 1971. She lives with her grandparents in Tan Thoi Hiep," he read from his clip board. Nguyen had regained the high ground in their exchange and felt smug about it. Tan Thoi Hiep was only fourteen kilometres from the police station so it would be easy to check his information.

"There's more," Nguyen said. "Auntie Vanh – your aunt and mine I guess – lives in the same village and can take you to see the girl at her grandparents' house. So what do you have to say now Cousin Kim?"

Though nurturing a growing dislike for her smug cousin she had to accept the fact that he'd done his homework. Yes, she could recall her aunt -- vaguely, though she had not had any contact with her mother's sister since childhood.

"As you can see cousin, I have worked hard on this case and pieced together a lot of information in just two days. I will tell you something more: Auntie Vanh has lived in Tan Thoi Hiep since 1970. She moved there after her husband died in the American War. Now, listen carefully to what I have to say to you."

He stretched across the table and, in a whisper, said: "For one million dong more, I will ask Auntie Vanh to call you or give you her number." Nguyen intended to milk the situation for all he could, confident that Yu Lee would pay up. He'd made discreet enquiries and learnt that Kim was working for Yu Lee. For the first time in months he felt he had a chance to pay off some of his debts.

Though she did not feel good taking auntie's telephone number from Nguyen, she had little option. She had to trust the man -- at least for the time being. Once again, common sense stopped her from walking out of the police station. She had to see it through: "I will work with you for now cousin," she conceded with a fair degree of reluctance.

It was the only sensible option.

"Cousin Nguyen, you will get six million dong for the list and another million after I have spoken to Auntie Vanh," she said in a take-it-or-leave-it tone. It was a bold bluff assuming, on her part, that Nguyen could not be seen accepting money from anyone in the public domain let alone inside a local police station. Not that she had any cash with her. This time, Nguyen did not resist when she opened the meeting room door. Moving towards the front desk in the reception area she found herself among several police officers and one or two members of the public talking loudly among themselves while busily filling in forms.

"I will see what I can do to help," Nguyen called after her from the meeting room. "And thank you for bringing this matter to our attention," he added. Everyone in the police station knew her visit was official police business.

Three days after her intimidating experience at the police station the harsh treatment meted out by police officer Phan Van Nguyen still rankled with Kim. But it was important to move on, and give Yu Lee her full support despite her cousin's arrogance and greed.

The 'phone's shrill ring startled Kim and set her heart pounding. It was Auntie Vanh calling and her news was encouraging.

After finishing the call, Kim grabbed her handbag and cranked up her motorcycle. In dry, fine weather after overnight rain, she set out for Tan Thoi Hiep village. It took only twenty minutes to get there. Her aunt's house was easy to find. Auntie Vanh was waiting.

"I would recognise you anywhere child. You are so much like your mother." Mrs Vanh could not hide her joy and Kim, embracing her, was elated at being reunited with one of her mother's sisters, someone she barely recalled.

But the reunion had a downside: Mrs Vanh's physical appearance was a matter for some concern. Dressed simply in traditional, almost threadbare, black *ao dai,* she had fallen on hard times. Her hair, hastily twisted into a bun, was crudely held in place by several, multi-coloured elastic bands. Even her flip-flops were wafer-thin from constant use. Kim could not know these were the only shoes she possessed.

Despite her unkempt appearance, her aunt's mannerisms appeared to be similar to her mother's as far as Kim could tell. And, like her mother, her aunt was softly

110

spoken. Mrs Vanh's kind face carried the tell-tale signs of having lived and survived decades of war.

After being shown into a small living room, Kim guarded against rushing headlong into the main details for her visit. It could be construed by her aunt as impolite after being reunited for only a few minutes. She did not want to get off on the wrong foot. It was important to pick the right moment to bring up the subject of Linh. It was a wise decision as her aunt soon began reminiscing about a time when Kim, and her own daughter Thuy, used to play together.

She smiled at Kim as she recalled times gone by: "Do you remember how you both loved to hold hands sitting side by side in a cyclo when your mother took you and Thuy to school?"

Displaying appropriate respect for an elder, Kim smiled and nodded appropriately. It was not easy to go back to her childhood days memories of which were hazy. But she carried in mind a picture of Thuy.

"Life has been difficult for me Kim," she continued, emerging from a moment of deep thought. "I lost my husband...your uncle... during the war. And only last year my dear Thuy died from cholera." Painfully, she related that awful day at the local hospital enduring personal hurt and humiliation because she did not have enough money for her daughter's medication. "There was no-one I could turn to for help."

Cholera took Thuy because her mother did not have the money to save her. Perhaps ten dollars, at the time, would have made a difference.

Grief was etched in the lines of Vanh's face. "She was just thirty years old when she died and I am still trying to get used to the idea of being on my own." Her aunt forced a smile because Kim's visit was by far the best thing to happen to her since that dreadful day. A visit from her niece was a moment to savour and she was not inclined to let Kim slip away too easily.

Though deeply distressed, she had somehow managed to relocate her place of abode from Ho Chi Minh City to Tan Thoi Hiep in 1970. "Despite the difficulties I enjoy living here. My neighbours are kind and help me get by."

Her aunt's plight seemed to Kim to be quite alarming. How sad to be reunited after so many years, she thought, only to learn of cousin Thuy's untimely demise. How cruel life can be at times.

"Exactly how do you get by auntie? I mean how do you make a living for yourself?" She would find a way to help her aunt next time she spoke with Yu Lee.

"I do a bit of stitching and mending for people in the village. I make a little money from time to time."

"Aunt, I do remember my cousin Thuy." Kim took a seat by the window. "And I recall my mother talking about both of her sisters and how it distressed her not being able to keep in touch with everyone."

"And now that you and I have found each other my dear niece, we must keep in touch. It is important we do not lose each other again."

"I suppose we have to thank Cousin Nguyen for this chance reunion auntie," Kim said with scant conviction.

"But to be honest with you I really do not care for him. He is rude and very greedy."

Aunt Vanh expressed surprise. She was not familiar with that particular side of her nephew's character. She did not see much of him either, so how was she to know? For sure she would be unaware her policeman nephew was millions of dong in debt.

"It is like this aunt," Kim continued, keen now to get to the main point of her visit. "He is only interested in money. I am not sure if he told you that he would get paid for helping me…I mean the American searching for his daughter promised to pay.

"I did not feel comfortable meeting with Cousin Nguyen at the police station. I am not sure I can trust him. It was only because he mentioned your name and our family connection that I decided to accept his proposition. And, I am pleased I did because I am so happy to see you and to be able to spend this moment with you."

"About your search for this *bui-doi* girl Kim; I am fairly sure I can help you find the one you are looking for my dear. After that, you must decide how to deal with your cousin. It will be for you to judge later."

Between sips of tea, she told Kim that a sixteen-year-old Amerasian girl lived in the village with her grandparents: "Her name is Linh and she was born in June 1971. I have already spoken with Linh's grandparents. They are very nice people."

It was promising news indeed; could she be the Linh they were seeking?

"We are now in the month of June, so Linh may already be seventeen. Let us go to see her, my dear. You can decide if she is the *bui-doi* you are seeking. We can take your motorcycle. It is not far."

———

The journey to Linh's grandparents' house took a few minutes. Mrs Vanh was first to reach the front door which was ajar. "Linh's grandparents told me to knock and go right in," she said turning to Kim.

Inside the small entrance, they were greeted by the sweet smell of lemongrass combined with the acrid smell of dried orange peel slowly burning in the centre of the small living room. Traditionally, elderly folk in Vietnam burn orange peel as an easy and cheap way to confuse unwelcome mosquitoes.   Lemongrass helps temper the pungent smell of burning peel.

They looked to be in their seventies but Linh's grandparents were probably in their early sixties; a sustained period of war does that to people. Introductions over, Mrs Vanh suggested to Kim she should not discuss the purpose of her visit until grandmother got back from the kitchen.   Anxious to take care of her guests, she had toddled off to prepare tea only to reappear moments later carrying a tray of small teacups stacked alongside a very large pot of freshly brewed oolong tea.

Kim looked around the living room. It was sparsely furnished with two, small, well-worn sofas, a rattan coffee table, a chest of drawers and a few wall photographs. This was not a wealthy family.

"We know why you have come to see us," grandmother said taking the initiative. "Mrs Vanh told us you want to meet our granddaughter Linh," She poured tea for all.

It was the opening Kim was waiting for. Taking a deep breath she explained everything from the time when David Gervasoni first approached the American consulate in Hong Kong up to her meeting at the police station.

Suddenly, without prior warning, a young lady, their granddaughter, appeared from behind a bead curtain. Parting it with her hands she looked at Kim.

"Is it me you want to see?" Nervously, Linh began smoothing away imaginary creases from her freshly-ironed, sparkling white *ao dai*. Taken aback, Kim stared at the young lady before her in particular her radiant smile which seemed to light up the whole room. Was this light-skinned, blue eyed, dark-haired beauty the Amerasian girl they were looking for?

Reading Kim's thoughts, grandma put her arms around her granddaughter and hugged her tightly. "Linh was abandoned by her American father in 1971 a few months after she was born. Her mother decided to call her daughter Linh because she felt it was the start of a new life for them all." Linh is the Vietnamese word for spring.

Grandfather interjected: "We were informed at the time that Linh's father was going back to America. Our daughter Thien also told us she had managed to find a job at Tan Son Nhut Air Base." Thien parents never knew she worked the bars around the base.

"She worked hard and made enough money to keep us all alive," he added, recalling the many hardships they had endured at the height of the conflict.

Grandma picked up the story: "We were very poor…at times quite desperate." She glanced at her husband. "Over time, we found out from Thien that she

115

was particularly fond of one man…an air force pilot. He asked for her each time he returned from flying duties."

The strain from recalling past events showed on grandmother's face. Linh looked from one grandparent to the other, wanting to help but not quite understanding the significance of what was being said.

"Yes, Thien and the American pilot were very fond of one another," grandfather told Kim. "But, for some reason it did not work out." Thien never told her parents that Linh's father left for America in great haste.

Grandfather was carrying a torch for both daughter and granddaughter. He looked at Linh: "Your father went back to America after you were born Linh and we never heard from him again." She was aware of her father's sudden disappearance but, in previous discussions, it hadn't been explained in such detail.

"Are you here because you have news of my American father Sister Kim?" Naturally, Linh wondered why people were so interested in her.

Before Kim could respond, grandfather chipped in again: "When Linh was around eight years old, Thien found life quite difficult living in our community. There was a lot of ill-feeling, even hatred, towards Amerasians at the time. Linh was taunted and bullied at school as a *bui-doi* and Thien felt ashamed."

Yet again, grandmother picked up the thread: "Thien could not bear the shame of raising a *bui-doi* child who was not accepted by local people," she said reaching out to hug her granddaughter.

For the first time, Linh was beginning to feel quite emotional about her absent parents. When her grandparents had previously spoken to her about them, she had, to some extent, remained detached and dispassionate. Older now, and with her seventeenth birthday a few days away, her eyes began to fill with tears. She looked at Kim who was almost certain this was the Linh they sought.

Kim considered showing everyone the photograph of Linh as a baby with her mother and father but decided to hold back believing it could cause further distress to Linh and her grandparents.

In a very short space of time, Linh's grandparents related everything they knew about Linh's father even though it was a long time ago. Their memory recall was impressive.

Kim had been briefed by Yu Lee on a number of important facts revealed during conversations with Gervasoni in Hong Kong: He was based at Tan Son Nhut Air Base; his daughter was called Linh and her mother Thien; he flew F4 Phantoms. If Linh turned out not to be Gervasoni's daughter the day's events, as far as Kim was concerned, would amount to a chapter of incredible coincidences.

Repeated references about her parents – in particular her absentee father – unsettled Linh. Recently, she had questioned her grandparents about her father and mother; in particular why she had been abandoned first by her father and then by her mother. Now almost seventeen and entering womanhood she wanted to know more about the past. But she was reluctant to put pressure on her grandparents to reveal more.

Grandmother gazed at her granddaughter sensing her concern. "We are proud of you and love you so very much Linh. You are growing into a beautiful young woman and I know both your mother and father would be proud of you."

It was too much. Overwhelmed by events, and confused, Linh withdrew to the sanctuary of her bedroom.

"As far as we know," grandmother said addressing Kim, "Thien took up with another man around eight years ago. We have not seen anything of her but she occasionally sends us a little money. I am sorry to say we do not know how to get in touch with her."

Several minutes later a composed Linh returned and sat next to her grandparents.

Kim had decided to be direct with her: "Little sister, I want you to understand why I am here today. An American gentleman, who lives in California, is searching for his sixteen year old daughter. He wants to offer her a better life with a new start in America."

A look of apprehension returned to Linh's face. "Sister Kim, if you think this man is my father then can you tell me why he waited for sixteen years to find me? It does not make sense to me."

"I wish I could give you an honest answer Linh but I cannot. If you are this man's daughter, and I am fairly certain you are, that should be the first question you ask him."

Linh was confused but Kim persisted: "If this man is your father, and let us assume for a moment that he is, I want you to think about joining him in America, with his American wife. I understand they do not have any other children. This could be a great opportunity for you to start a new life."

Linh paused and let Kim's words sink in. It sounded like good advice and something she had to consider. After almost seventeen years waiting and wondering she could be reunited with her real father. But what would become of her grandparents if she went to America.

"Because of my American father I have never been accepted as Vietnamese," she told Kim. "I have always felt a stranger and often thought of leaving Vietnam. I would love to get a good education, but I could never bring myself to leave my grandparents." She looked at each one in turn. "I love you both so much I do not think I could ever leave you."

It was time to bring the meeting to a close. Grandfather would have the last word – at least for the time being. "Thank you both for coming to see us today; we know you are trying to help Linh," he added embracing his granddaughter.

"Everything you have told us comes as a great surprise. We will have a family discussion Kim and talk to you again soon."

Convinced she had made solid progress, Kim headed back to Ho Chi Minh City. It had been a remarkable day of events. Could the village of Tan Thoi Hiep be where the search for Linh resulted in a happy ending? Time would tell.

———

Everyone welcomed Kim's news. Yu Lee considered it was enough to make a report to David Gervasoni – a report that was long overdue.

Following Kim's meeting in Tan Thoi Hiep a growing impatience developed among everyone to learn of the family's decision regarding Linh.

Subsequently, Kim got a telephone call from Linh's grandfather. "I am sorry I did not call before. You must understand Linh had her summer exams which caused the delay." The long wait, he maintained, did not signify a lot of deliberation on Linh's part.

"The day after your visit to our house, Linh said she would like to meet the man you think may be her father."

Everything grandfather related to Kim was jotted down to be shared with the others. In particular the important decision to travel to Kim's house, with Auntie Vanh, during Linh's next rest day from school. It was all arranged, Kim was told. A neighbour in Tan Thoi Hiep village would drive them to Ho Chi Minh City in his van.

"It is important for everyone concerned," grandfather insisted during the 'phone call "…to meet face-to-face with Yu Lee. And we want to find out more about Linh's father and his sudden desire to find his daughter."

———

A few minutes before noon on Sunday, June 26, a black van, looking the worse-for-wear, pulled up outside of Kim's house. It was exactly one week following grandfather's call to Kim.

Auntie Vanh alighted first and turned to assist Linh's grandparents. Kim noticed Linh was carrying a small attaché case which she took to be a positive sign.

Watching anxiously through the window from behind net curtains, Yu Lee moved to the small drawing room ready to greet the family. There was an air of excitement.

Kim handled the introductions. At first pass Yu Lee felt it was impossible to be sure this beautiful young girl standing before him was Gervasoni's daughter. Certainly, her ethnic mix made a compelling argument, but that could apply to many Amerasians. Yet there was no getting away from the fact he was staring at the most beautiful seventeen-year-old girl he had ever seen. Linh's slender build, long dark hair and large, cornflower-blue eyes framing her thinly-defined nose set her aside from other darker-skinned Amerasians.

Was this the girl they were looking for? Trying very hard not to stare at her, he sat alongside her on the small sofa. "I have some questions for you Linh."

"Yes, I am ready for that professor," she responded with confidence.

Smiling politely at Yu Lee in anticipation of his first question, Linh reached into her small clutch bag to retrieve a photograph. Yu Lee looked at her face which glowed in the early afternoon sunlight that shone through the window. Holding the photograph in one hand he stared at it in disbelief. It was identical to the one handed to him in Hong Kong. Was this solid enough evidence to convince David Gervasoni? It ought to be.

"Who gave this to you Linh; do you remember?"

"My mother gave it to me when I was eight years old. It has been in my bedroom ever since."

Grandmother was unaware of the existence of the photograph. "Why did you not show it to us before child?"

121

Linh was embarrassed: "Before my mother left me with you and grandfather she gave this to me. She said it would remind me of her. I never looked at it at the time – not closely anyway."

Turning to Kim she reinforced her explanation. "After you and Mrs Vanh left our house I went to my cupboard to look at it again. It was my seventeenth birthday," she added truthfully. "And I remember what you said about my father wanting me to go to America. I started to think a lot about starting a new life," she smiled holding up the photograph for Kim to see.

It was a critical moment in the search for Linh. No one in the room had any doubt that this young lady had to be the daughter abandoned by David Gervasoni so long ago.

"If your grandparents agree," Yu Lee said taking hold of her hand, "I want you to stay here with Miss Kim until I can arrange for you to meet your father."

Though Linh was elated at the prospect of going to America she was sad at the thought of leaving behind her grandparents, even for a short while. And what if Yu Lee somehow failed to fulfil his promise?

"If I go to America, I ask you to do all you can to help my grandparents join me as soon as possible. Do you think Mr David...I mean my father...would agree to that?"

Linh could not yet be aware that under the IOM repatriation programme it was possible in such circumstances for next of kin to join their loved ones once the necessary paperwork was processed. Help would be required from the American Consulate and this was where Yu Lee and John Mackenzie could help.

"If Linh goes to the United States," Yu Lee said addressing Linh's grandparents, "I will guarantee you will all be reunited at the first possible opportunity."

He may have exceeded his authority but he knew that Mac would never let him down and Colonel Nathan had never failed him yet.

For the next few days Yu Lee agreed to lay low at Yu Ming's place. "I will check with you and Linh in two days' time," he told Kim. "I will ask Mr John to go to the central post office to fax David Gervasoni that we have found Linh."

———

Yu Lee briefed Mac as soon as he got back to Yu Ming's house. Discovering Linh's whereabouts in a relatively short space of time was a welcome break for both men. The photographic evidence was compelling but the final decision would rest with Gervasoni -- and Linh of course.

"We still have to tackle the assignment for Colonel Nathan prof," Mac announced very much alive to the fact the secret police might be tailing Yu Lee. "You haven't forgotten have you?"

"No, I have not forgotten about the assignment Mr John. And I am very concerned about the secret police going to Kim's house and causing more problems. They are capable of making a case out of nothing if they decide to."

His experience in Hanoi testified to that and with an Amerasian minor suddenly appearing at the house of Yu

Lee's lady friend, the secret police could claim to have a legitimate excuse to intervene.

The next move was to discuss the task outlined by Colonel Nathan and prepare a strategy. Yu Lee had already invited his brother and Lily to join the discussions.

————

Cautioning Linh to remain indoors, Kim hooked an airline bag over the handlebars of her motorcycle and headed for the police station to deliver a cash payment to Officer Nguyen. She did not inform Linh where she was going but assured her she'd be back within the hour.

Although Yu Lee had impressed upon Kim that he could not be absolutely certain that Linh was the Amerasian girl they were searching for, she would do as he said and pay off Officer Nguyen. Whatever happened, she was determined to minimise her contact with her "green-eyed" cousin.

Kim's disturbing account of her meeting with her police officer cousin had not resonated well with Yu Lee or Mackenzie. She should find a neutral venue, they suggested, for any future meeting. But, for now, they decided not to take the matter any further. Attracting unwelcome attention, such as from the local police, would not help their cause.

Peering out of a window, Nguyen watched his cousin park her motorcycle near the front entrance to the police station, uncouple the airline bag and struggle with its contents. It was bulky and heavy because the banknotes were in one thousand and five hundred denominations. At the time, the highest denominated note in Vietnamese dong was one thousand. In simple terms, change for one hundred American dollars amounted to almost one-square-foot of Vietnam dong. As such, it was common to see citizens lugging around airline bags stuffed with cash to pay for basic commodities.

Officer Nguyen popped outside and took the bag from Kim escorting her into a rear door and towards the office where she had her first meeting with her cousin.

Kim knew she could never again trust Nguyen after what happened at their first meeting. But what happened next took her totally by surprise.

"Cousin I am arresting you for subversion," he announced, brusquely pulling her hands behind her and cuffing them. Nguyen pushed the airline bag under the interview desk. He would collect it later. Leaving her standing, he drew up a charge sheet accusing her of being part of a southern group conspiring to subvert the government.

The desk sergeant looked at Kim as she was presented before him. He read the charge sheet and, without commenting, attached her ID to it and dropped it into his out tray. "Tomorrow you will be taken before a magistrate. Take her to the cells."

Nguyen pushed her down a staircase. Concerned she might fall she did not struggle. Directing her into a cell, he slammed the door, locked it and left.

"You will spend the night here. No phone calls. Someone will collect you in the morning and take you before a magistrate. Be good, don't make a scene and you won't get into further trouble."

Unseen, he repositioned Kim's motorcycle to the rear of the police station out of sight. Later he secured the airline bag on his bicycle, it was time to celebrate.

———

Depressed, hungry and in need of a shower after a restless night fighting depression and mosquitoes, Kim was desperate to contact anyone who could help her. Try as she may, she could not comprehend Nguyen's actions in double-crossing her. Inwardly, she knew she should have trusted her initial instincts about the man and acted on the advice given by Yu Lee and Mackenzie to meet on neutral ground. It was too late.

It was eerily quiet in the depths of the police station; none of the other cells was occupied as far as she could tell.

Loud banging on her cell door broke the silence and suspense of the moment. A policewoman opened the door and pushed forward a bowl of watery rice. "You will go before a magistrate today. Eat now. I will collect you later."

"Please allow me to make a telephone call," Kim called after her, frantic to contact Yu Lee or anybody. Her plea was ignored. Kim was alone, defenceless and trapped as a hapless victim of a wholly corrupt justice system.

So engrossed in thinking about her own plight Kim had completely forgotten about Linh who by now had to be wondering why she had failed to return home as promised. She resolved to stay calm. Sooner or later Yu Lee would come to her rescue. Of that she was absolutely sure.

———

With Kim securely locked-up at the station Officer Nguyen was free to drop by the Hotel Continental for a celebratory drink or two. Feeling good about himself, he was in the mood to let off steam and perhaps boast a little about his remarkable achievement. In his rush to leave, he didn't even change out of uniform.

The upmarket bar in the hotel, a favourite venue for businesspeople and well-healed locals, was not off-limits to Saigon's law enforcement officers. But it was not the place you would expect to find poorly-paid, off-duty policemen. Officer Nguyen was about to change that.

"Barman, give me whisky and I mean now!" Nguyen demanded dragging out a barstool and rudely pointing a finger at head barman Jimmy Yuen. "And not the local stuff...Scotch...good Scotch."

Jimmy Yuen was no stranger to distasteful scenes during his years tending bars. But being confronted by a noisy uniformed police officer in the ultra-smart Hotel Continental lobby bar was a first for him. "Coming right up sir...would that be Johnnie Walker Black or Chivas Regal?"

"Black Label...a large one...now!"

By presenting himself in a public bar, in uniform, Nguyen was courting trouble with his superiors and Jimmy Yuen knew it. However, he deigned to humour the man and engage him in dialogue. The bar would soon fill up with regulars so careful handling was required.

Within minutes of his arrival, Nguyen was shooting off his mouth, clearly very pleased with his accomplishments. After forty-five minutes of sustained drinking, he had ridiculed everything and everyone in a passionate outpouring assisted only by his good friend

Johnnie Walker.   Jimmy Yuen listened intently, refilling Nguyen's glass each time he banged it down on the bar top. After an hour of this, he figured Nguyen to be just a couple of drinks away from making an ignominious exit from his barstool. And that was fine by the senior barman.

Without looking up from polishing a glass, he said: "Looks like you had a good day today officer."

"A good day...yes...making easy money from my stupid cousin and I feel good about it." He was beginning to slur his words. "Yu Lee, her boyfriend from Hong Kong, wants everyone to believe he came back to Vietnam to help the country. Bullshit. He's here to help himself," Nguyen added gulping down more whisky. Jimmy Yuen just nodded. He knew when to listen and when to voice an opinion. It was time to listen and learn.

Nguyen laughed out loud: "I just helped myself to some of his money and...*hic*... there's nothing he can do about it. He can go screw himself for all I care."

Yuen could see that the police officer before him was totally repugnant. But he wanted to learn more. He knew who Kim was and he knew of Yu Lee. He had seen them together in the bar with other people. Yuen was an enterprising man, always on the lookout for an opportunity to make some money on the side. In truth he had his own agenda and the enterprise he was currently engaged in held great promise in his view.

"Another Scotch for our fine police officer?" he asked pointing towards Nguyen's empty glass.

"Make it a proper double this time you miserable cockroach," Nguyen fired back, his feet slipping on the bar rail as he struggled to keep seated on his barstool.

128

He got back to his story: "All I had to do was give my cousin the address of a *bui-doi* girl in return for a bag full of money. Here...take a look," he said opening it up wide enough to see inside. "Now tell me that wasn't easy money bartender!"

Jimmy Yuen's mind was working overtime. "Are you telling me that that all you had to do was give your cousin the address of an Amerasian girl in exchange for all that money?"

"Listen, I will tell you how easy it was. They are looking for this Amerasian called Linh whose father wants to take her to America. Well, I found the little bitch and took the fools for seven million dong. Is that brilliant...*hic*...or what?"

"More than brilliant sir," Jimmy Yuen readily concurred. "You certainly have style if I may say so officer," he conceded sensing the policeman was about to impart the full details of his day's work.

Four patrons entered the bar but sat far from the bar in a corner booth near a window. Excusing himself, Jimmy Yuen broke off to serve them. He returned and stood opposite Officer Nguyen who was still relating his story.

"When she arrived at my police station this morning...*hic*... the silly bitch brought this airline bag stuffed with money," he said leaning across the bar. "You should have seen the look on her stupid face when I arrested her for subversive activities," he added laughing out loud. Everyone...*hic*...in the station congratulated me.

More customers began to arrive and another waitress joined the evening shift. She was instructed by

Jimmy Yuen to find seats for guests as far away from the bar as possible.

"Is Miss Kim still at the station?" Jimmy Yuen asked.

"I expect so...*hic*... she won't be seen by a local magistrate until tomorrow morning."

"What about the Amerasian girl...where is she?"

"At Cousin Kim's house I suppose."

Officer Nguyen's interest in the exchange began to wane. He was anxious to make a visit to the toilet. "Get my check ready while I go and do something nobody can do for me," he drawled. Dragging the airline bag with him to the men's room he turned back to the bartender: "I don't trust anybody, including nosey barkeeps like you."

Yuen watched as Nguyen left the bar quite certain he had chanced upon a golden opportunity to make some easy money. And he had a plan in mind.

———

Early on Wednesday morning Yu Lee and John Mackenzie went to Kim's house to be greeted by a visibly shaken and distressed Linh.

"Uncle," she blurted out, "I have been alone here for two nights. Sister Kim did not return. I did know what to do because I could not find a way to contact you. I followed her advice and did not leave the house." Tears streamed down her face.

As neither man had heard from Kim in two days they were unable to shed any light on her sudden disappearance. They had been putting the final touches to a strategy for the task outlined by Colonel Nathan.

"You did the right thing by staying indoors Linh," Mac reassured her as Yu Lee checked the house. Both men felt dreadful, remorseful after leaving Kim to supervise Linh without offering her any assistance. It was a bad call on their part and well they knew it.

———

Wednesday was Jimmy Yuen's day off. Kim's address in hand, he boarded a cyclo ready to put his newly-hatched plan into action.

Officer Nguyen didn't mention Kim's home address when he was in the bar but it did not take the enterprising barman long to find it at the Continental. Yu Lee was acquainted with Tu Nguyen Dai the director of Saigontourism who oversees the management of the hotel. Correspondence between the hotel and Yu Lee at Kim's house was on a file in Mr Dai's office. It was that easy!

Arriving at Kim's house Jimmy Yuen was greeted by Yu Lee who recognised him immediately. Mac joined the party eyeing their visitor up and down. He was waiting for Yu Lee to offer some explanation.

"Mr Yuen works at the lobby bar in the Hotel Continental in Dong Khoi Street. Kim and I have seen him there on several occasions."

"Quite correct brother," Jimmy Yuen confirmed reaching to shake hands with Mac.

"Mr John, would you mind if I spoke to Brother Yu Lee in private? It concerns Miss Kim."

"That will not be necessary. Anything you have to say to me can be said in front of Mr John."

131

Jimmy Yuen related events in the hotel bar. The barman's account of proceedings upset Yu Lee. His own negligence in the matter began to weigh heavily on his conscience.

Mackenzie, on the other hand, was direct: "Are you telling us that Kim's own cousin, a friggin' policeman in Ho Chi Minh City, offered to help her then arrested her?"

"Where is she now?" Yu Lee asked becoming more and more anxious. Thoughts of being tailed by the secret police had gone right out of his mind. This was something that could not wait.

"I'm not sure," Yuen replied truthfully, "but Nguyen said he had locked her up and she would not be able to see anyone until after she has been before a court magistrate...that would have been yesterday I think."

Yu Lee's jaw fell. He knew Kim would be quite distressed after spending two days locked in a police cell. He blamed himself entirely.

Jimmy Yuen had carefully prepared his proposal for Yu Lee to consider. Shrewdly, he related to both men only those events that could easily be supported by others in the bar. He painted a picture compelling them to become acutely concerned about Kim's safety. But to set his entire plan in motion he had to get them out of the house. It was a dangerous game but Jimmy Yuen was up to it. Already, he could see he had Yu Lee's undivided attention. The man was already suffering mental anguish. A good sign, Yuen thought.

"You must understand that Officer Nguyen was very drunk. And the more he drank the more he talked openly about Kim. He said she offered him a lot of money that she brought to the police station in an airline bag. Nguyen said he took it and then accused her of subversive activities."

"Subversive activities," Yu Lee repeated in shocked response. "He must be out of his mind."

"Did you see the bag?" Mac asked.

"I did, he brought it into the bar and unzipped it just enough for me to see it was stuffed with notes, seven million dong altogether. And he boasted how easy it had been for him to take the money from Miss Kim."

Yu Lee's blood pressure was on the rise but he remained outwardly calm. A display of anger would be counterproductive. This situation called for cool heads.

"Jimmy, thank you for taking time to come here today," Yu Lee said determined to control his feelings. He was very upset though not entirely convinced by Jimmy Yuen's story. He had been around too long to take the barman's account at face value. The man could have a personal interest in the proceedings. But, this was not a good time to say or do anything rash.

"I was aware that Kim was your good friend brother, because I have seen you together many times in the hotel. I was sure you would want to know what had happened to her. I do not expect any sort of reward for coming here today," he lied gazing first at one man then the other.

"It is none of my business but if you want my advice," he continued feeling certain he could get both men out of the house, "I would get over to the police station as soon as you can."

If Kim has spent a day or two locked up, Yu Lee thought to himself, it meant she had been denied the opportunity to make a telephone call which was seriously worrying. It also explained why Linh was so distressed.

"I think you are right Jimmy; I will go immediately. Will you come with me Mr John?"

"Sure I'll come," Mac shot back. "But what about Linh, we can't leave her here alone can we?"

"We will take her with us," Yu Lee decided. "Wait a minute...on second thoughts...we don't want to risk complicating matters with the police."

It was the opening Jimmy Yuen wanted: "If I can help in any way I'd be happy to do so. This is my day off and I don't mind baby-sitting for a couple of hours."

"I guess you could help by keeping an eye on Linh and the house until we get back with Kim."

"I would be happy to be of assistance," Jimmy Yuen said. "Don't worry; she'll be safe with me."

Yu Lee asked Linh to join them. "Something has happened to Kim. Uncle John and I have to go to a police station. This gentleman is Mr Jimmy Yuen...he will stay with you until we return."

Instinctively she did not want to be alone with Jimmy Yuen. Yet she did not want to appear impolite or ungrateful to Yu Lee or John Mackenzie. "Uncle," she said, smiling to hide her deeply–felt concern, "perhaps I should go with you and Uncle John. I can wait in the cyclo outside the police station until you find Sister Kim."

Mac was less trusting, not having any previous experience with Yuen. He was one hundred percent against leaving Linh with Jimmy Yuen. Yu Lee might be familiar with the man but could he claim to really know him? "Professor, why can't we take Linh with us – Jimmy Yuen can come too?"

That was Jimmy Yuen's cue to put forward another idea: "The police station is close to Dong Khoi Street and only a short distance from the Hotel Continental. Linh can wait there with me. It is my day off and I can take care of her until you come to pick her up." That was an even better idea; there would be plenty of people and activity inside and outside the hotel.

―――――

The cyclo carrying Yu Lee and Mackenzie slowed down outside the police station. Disembarking, the two men looked across at the cyclo carrying Linh and Jimmy Yuen as it headed around the corner in the direction of the Hotel Continental. It was soon out of sight. So far so good, it seemed.

Neither man anticipated the devious and radical change of plan staged by Yuen. Abeam of the hotel, the cyclo driver pushed down hard on the pedals. Linh glanced at Jimmy Yuen whose eyes were fixed on the road ahead. The cyclo driver drove past the hotel as instructed.

Linh began to panic. "Please stop," she pleaded. "We should wait in the hotel as we agreed. Where are you going?"

His response was to hold Linh's hand tightly to prevent her from jumping off the cyclo. They were heading in a northerly direction towards the airport. The cyclo tracked down Dien Bien Phu Road which Linh recognised, but after forty-five minutes or so they entered unfamiliar territory. The nearby roar of aircraft engines indicated they were close to an airport or airbase. From the direction they had been travelling it could only be Tan Son Nhut Airport.

Well outside of District 1 Jimmy Yuen reassured Linh she was safe: "It is better if you come to my house for a couple of hours. You can take a rest and I will make sure you are reunited with the others later."

She did not trust Yuen but how could she refuse, how could she resist?

The cyclo turned into a side lane. Linh noticed two large buildings behind a seven-foot wall running the length of the lane -- airfreight sheds. An aircraft roared overhead just as they disembarked in front of a neat, white-painted villa one kilometre from Tan Son Nhut Airport.

Yuen paid off the cyclo driver and, still holding Linh tightly by the arm, walked her into the house. There were several security guards posted inside the compound. Her first thought was how could a barman working at a city hotel afford such a large villa and staff?

Pushed inside, she was directed into a back room on the ground floor. "Stay there and don't worry," Yuen said locking her in the room.

Frightened now and shaking with anger, Linh felt cheated and confused with no inkling of what to think or how to react to her predicament. She was hopping mad for allowing herself to be chaperoned by Jimmy Yuen in the first place. And she felt sad and troubled that neither Yu Lee nor John Mackenzie had singled out Yuen as someone not to be trusted. She had been let down twice in as many days. In just a short space of time her previously high approval rate for Yu Lee and John

Mackenzie had plunged. Her faith in both men was shattered.

Looking around the dimly-lit room Linh counted five other girls including another Amerasian girl all huddled together. Suddenly it hit her: she had been abducted.

"Complain all you want to," Sgt Hung Van Minh said with a smirk on his face, "it won't change anything." The arrogant, self-assured desk sergeant, who, upon their arrival, claimed to be the officer-in-charge of the police station, was obviously enjoying the run-around he was dishing out to Mac. What he didn't realise however was such bravura was misplaced because neither Yu Lee nor Mac were inclined to be messed around.

They pressed him again and again till he confirmed that Phan Van Nguyen was based at the station. But no, he was not on duty.

The sergeant said he was not aware of anybody called Kim being locked-up in the police station: "No you cannot take a look around the cells. They are off limits to all but station personnel and inmates." The sergeant was adamant.

The man's evasive action and delaying tactics were all too familiar to Yu Lee. In post-war Vietnam he had wrestled with scores of corrupt government officials, petty bureaucrats and "men in uniform". It made it extremely difficult to do business in the country and he could fill a book with past experiences.

Sergeant Minh leant across the table impolitely eyeballing each man in turn. "So, how else can I help you?

"Let me try something else," Mac whispered to Yu Lee reaching into his pocket and pulling out a large wad of dollars.

"No, please, not this way Mr John."

138

But Mac was determined. "We have to fight fire with fire prof. Sergeant Minh...let's go somewhere private where we can talk business."

Mackenzie was hoping the sergeant would find the sight of so much cash irresistible and secure his undivided attention. Also, he was pretty sure that, by now, the sergeant would be extremely jealous of subordinate Phan Van Nguyen's recent windfall. Mac was right.

"So just what do you wish to know, gentlemen?" the sergeant asked, shutting the door behind him. It was the same interview room that Officer Nguyen had used when he met Kim. Yu Lee found the thought disturbing. He would leave proceedings to Mackenzie.

"This time we'll keep it real simple," Mac said peeling off twenty dollar notes and placing them on the table one by one. "Listen carefully sergeant. Where is Miss Kim...is she here and can we see her?" Mac received another disapproving glance from Yu Lee.

He continued to bargain: "I know what you're thinking prof, but money talks and we don't have time to mess around."

For the first time since the men arrived at the station, Sgt Minh began to feel uncomfortable. He knew where Kim had been taken but he was troubled by the thought of having to explain his actions if the station commander ordered an enquiry at some future date.

He watched wide-eyed as Mac continued to peel off twenty dollar bills. Sure enough, greed got the better of him. The sergeant reached over and scooped up the cash. "She is on the way to Da Nang...left first thing this morning."

"Why is she going to Da Nang?" Yu Lee asked re-joining the conversation.

The sergeant shook his head. "Sorry, I cannot give you any further information."

Mac peeled off more notes, more slowly this time.

Beads of sweat began to form on the sergeant's forehead. Feeling quite nervous, he wanted to bring the meeting to a close, to get rid of his visitors. "At the magistrate's court this morning she was charged and found guilty of subversive activities and sentenced to spend time in a re-education centre in Da Nang.

"Officer Nguyen was the arresting officer. And his account was supported in court by a representative from the secret police."

"You should have got involved sergeant and asked Miss Kim to explain the reason for her visit to the station," Yu Lee asserted. "You did not give her that opportunity, did you?"

"She committed a serious offence," Sgt Minh countered, "and the court agreed. That is why she was ordered to undergo a course in corrective training."

"Listen to me sergeant. It is important you have all the facts. Kim was authorised by me to offer a personal reward for anybody who could help us find a missing Amerasian girl. The money will be paid by the girl's American father. Kim has never been involved in politics and would never take part in a move to unseat the government."

Mackenzie was puzzled as to why Kim was sent to Da Nang: "Why couldn't she stay in Saigon?"

With two hundred dollars tucked safely into his breast pocket, Sgt Minh felt he was ahead of the game but it was time to put a cap on proceedings. "Da Nang Rehabilitation and Re-education Centre," he explained, "is the only such facility left in the country. Look on the bright side," he added smiling through rotten teeth, "she may come back a good communist and quit her subversive activities."

Yu Lee bit his lip. Mac clenched and unclenched his fists until his knuckles went white. He stopped short from reaching over the desk to render gratuitous modifications to the sergeant's face. Just in time, Yu Lee grabbed his friend by the arm and marched him out of the police station.

Mac calmed down quickly. "I don't think we can learn much more here professor. There is a sickness about this police station. It's time to get the hell out of here. We need to regroup and decide how to get Kim back. Do you agree?"

"Of course; but before that we must check on Linh at the Hotel Continental. We have been away for over an hour."

———

The duo's largely disappointing morning at the police station turned into an afternoon nightmare on entering the lobby bar of the Hotel Continental. Jimmy Yuen and Linh were not there and had not been there. Though disheartened both men knew there was too much at stake to become disillusioned. They had to regroup, pull themselves together and pick up their game for the sake of Linh and Kim.

141

Linh was alarmed and outraged to see Jimmy Yuen openly counting a large wad of money. "Job done," he seemed to be mouthing, a wide grin on his face.

For Yuen, it was easy money. Sourcing Vietnamese girls earned him the equivalent of one hundred dollars per girl and two hundred apiece for *bui-doi*. He put the money into a rucksack and called to Linh from outside the room: "Someone will come to see you. Be a good girl, do as you are told and you will be alright."

Disconsolate at being on the receiving end of such bad luck she yearned for the security, warmth and comfort of her grandparents' house. Jimmy Yuen had caused her pain and distress. For the rest of her life she would carry in her mind the smug grin on his face as he counted his money? Being sold for cash was a degrading and humiliating experience.

Linh felt lonely, but she was not alone. Her five companions, all around twenty years of age, looked similarly crestfallen.

Mai, the only Amerasian among the five, informed Linh that all the girls had been in the house around two weeks apart from Mai. Two months had passed since she was bundled into a white van in broad daylight in downtown Ho Chi Minh City.

"Linh, like you, we feel scared and have no idea what is going to happen to us." She placed a comforting arm around Linh's shoulders. Previously a part-time bar staff at the Hotel Continental, Mai was a pretty, green-eyed girl just nineteen years old. Similar to Linh, Mai's father left

Vietnam for the United States a few years before the end of the war. Mai's mother had tried her best to raise her children (two young boys plus Mai) but found it impossible to make ends meet. Mai's mother earned a little money waiting on tables in a Chinese restaurant, enough to pay the rent but not nearly enough to feed the family.

"Mother did the best she could but there wasn't enough money to go around," Mai explained. "For me, there was little chance of getting an education unless I found a way to earn some extra money," she added tearfully as she related how difficult life was for her and her family in post-war Vietnam.

Discounting any ideas of plying the beer bars in Ho Chi Minh City's red light district, Mai had jumped at the opportunity to work as a cocktail waitress in the lobby bar of the classy Hotel Continental.

"Jimmy Yuen seemed so kind at first. He said he wanted to help me and I believed him. I was introduced to his friend who owned a restaurant where I earned some extra money for a short while."

Listening to Mai's story Linh had almost forgotten about the four other Vietnamese girls who were huddled together on one of the bunks.

Looking around her new accommodation it seemed purpose-built as a detention centre of some sort. There were no windows and just one door. Six, wooden, double-bunks were racked along one side of the room. Some had letters carved on them – initials of previous detainees Linh guessed. Behind the bunks, in a corner, were two, curtained-off cubicles each with a shower, washbasin and squat toilet. A very large, wooden table able to accommodate twenty people stood opposite the bunks.

Beyond was a dressing room and Linh spotted some of the girls' clothing on hooks – a reminder that she only had the clothes she was wearing. There was no doubt that the room was a holding area and it had been in use for some time. Linh and her roommates were not the first to be held there and probably wouldn't be the last. Two very old ceiling fans, both whirring noisily overhead, recycled stale air making the room feel stuffy and warm. She longed to be outside in the fresh air.

"Have you any idea what is going to happen to us?" Linh asked Mai.

Though just nineteen, Mai was quite mature in a street-wise sort of way and seemed to accept the role of senior girl – at least of the Amerasian duo. "One of the girls over there," she said pointing towards the bunk, "was told by Jimmy Yuen that everyone would be going upcountry in a few days. That is all we know at the moment, but we have to accept it because it gives us hope we can at least get out of this place and stay together."

A sudden crashing and banging of door bolts startled them all. A big man stepped into the room. He was alone. Standing just inside the door, the tall, stocky foreigner looked to be around forty years old. Slightly balding and in need of a shave he sported a large, fresh bruise on his right temple. He was wearing dark blue denims and a long-sleeved blue shirt turned up at the cuffs above his wrists. A good wash wouldn't go amiss thought Linh who was trying hard not to stare.

"You can call me Mr Bill," he announced motioning all six to sit at the large table. He didn't sit but looked down at each girl in turn, thumbs hooked into his belt, obviously pleased with what he saw before him.

Once again Jimmy Yuen had excelled himself, he thought. Madame Ha would be pleased.

His excellent command of the Vietnamese language underscored Mr Bill's long-standing presence in the country. From his muscular build he could have been a prize-fighter or a career serviceman. But what really commanded the attention of the girls was the large Bowie knife strapped to the right side of his belt. Sensing the girls' interest, he adjusted the sheath for maximum effect as he'd done on numerous occasions.

Linh glanced at Mai. She was trying to make herself as small and insignificant as possible to avoid being noticed by the big man as he walked around the table.

"None of you will come to any harm if you do as you're told. We are going upcountry to a school where you will be able to improve your education and earn your keep," he explained. None of the girls felt inclined to ask him how they were to earn their keep. But each one had her own thoughts on the matter.

The good news, thought Linh, was they would be together at least for a few hours more. If they were split up she would be much more afraid of what lay ahead.

Just as quickly as he had arrived on the scene, the man left, bolting the door behind him.

An uneasy quiet descended upon the room. The situation could be worse, someone said. They could have been separated. For the time being it looked like they would remain together and that had to be a good thing.

Gathered around the table the girls took it in turns to explain how they had been duped by Jimmy Yuen. Apart from Linh, the girls' stories struck a similar note; all had been given the opportunity to earn more money and all had been taken in by his persuasive promises.

Mai added a little more to what she had disclosed to Linh earlier. "I was working in a restaurant just off Dong Khoi Street," she said, her hands clasped in front of her. "Jimmy Yuen used to come to the restaurant for a break from his work at the Hotel Continental. Everyone knew him. He seemed nice enough and, after several visits, he persuaded me to work in the lobby bar of the Continental.

"I did earn more money but I had to work long hours and still couldn't make enough to pay for my education."

Mai explained how Jimmy Yuen had offered her another opportunity to earn extra money working at his friend's Chinese restaurant not far from the hotel.

"One day, just outside the hotel I was attacked from behind. All I can tell you is that my attacker was a very big and powerful man. I couldn't break free and was bundled into a van and brought here.

"Whatever happens," Mai offered, "we must try to stay together as long as possible. We are safer as a group." None of them disagreed and joined hands in an act of unity.

———

Yu Lee and Mac got back to Yu Ming's house frustrated with the lack of progress and angry with themselves. They had failed Kim and managed to lose Linh. Not much to be proud of by anyone's estimations!

"Kim is my responsibility and I will go to Da Nang to have her released," Yu Lee announced. "I will get started immediately," he added, gratefully accepting a cup of coffee from Lily.

Lily was also depressed and still having difficulty coming to grips with recent setbacks. The two men had handled things badly but could they have done anything differently under the circumstances? In any case, recriminations would not help their overall cause.

Cigarette in one hand, beer in the other, Mac spun round in his chair ready to challenge Yu Lee.

"Professor, I agree someone has to go to Da Nang but not you my friend. I say this because you could easily get picked up by the secret police and that's a risk we can't afford to take. I don't want to sound heartless, but we have other objectives to achieve such as the assignment for Colonel Nathan."

Yu Ming and Lily glanced at one another but remained silent.

Mac's remarks made sense but Yu Lee considered it his personal responsibility to find Kim and bring her back to Ho Chi Minh City.

Yu Lee's reaction was emotionally driven and Mac knew it. He also knew the professor's capacity to think logically would come to his rescue.

"Prof I want you to listen to me for a cotton-pickin' minute. Here's what we have on our plate: We have to get Kim back from Da Nang; we must solve the case of the found-but-now-missing Linh, and we are duty-bound to get moving on the other assignment for Colonel Nathan. I would say that it's high time we got our act together and started to make some progress, wouldn't you?"

But, in Yu Lee's view, it was inappropriate to ask someone else to go to Da Nang in his place. Kim was his responsibility; he got her into this mess and it was his duty to get her out of it.

Becoming increasingly concerned and quite perplexed, Lily watched as the two men wrestled back and forth. She felt compelled to intervene. After all the help she had received from both men, she felt it was the least she could do. Da Nang was just a few kilometres north of Hoi An. She could re-establish contact with her family and use her parents' house as a base and make enquiries from there. To her, it all made good sense at a time when it seemed that common-sense had left the room.

Her mind made up, she confronted the men: "We can sit here debating this for hours," she said pointedly, looking at each man in turn. "While you are arguing, Kim will be hoping that at least one of us is making a move to get her out of the detention centre," she added willing herself to get started.

"This is something I can help you with. Look, I can get my things together in a few minutes. So why don't you tell me exactly what I should do?"

Yu Lee looked into Lily's eyes and also caught Mac's steely-eyed gaze. He could see he had lost the battle.

"Lily, if you are determined to do this the least I can to is to give you some advice. First of all I think Yu Ming should go with you." He looked at his brother who nodded enthusiastically at the suggestion. Lily was a good choice but not on her own. There was no telling what she might encounter.

"Secondly, you should take a copy of Kim's ID card with you. Wait, I will get one from the file." He headed upstairs at the double.

"Lily, I also have a suggestion," Mac interjected. "Present yourself to the rehab folk as a family member...you know older sister or cousin. Otherwise they may question your motives for being there." Lily did not possess a Vietnam ID so she figured she would pose as a relation of Kim's recently returned from the United States. It was half true.

Mackenzie hadn't forgotten Yu Lee's earlier remark that he may have been too trusting of Lily from the time she tapped him on the shoulder at Bangkok airport. If she was working for some party unknown to them her offer to help get Kim released did not fit the profile. Who could tell? But he agreed with Yu Lee's idea to have Yu Ming tag along with Lily.

Yu Ming, who had already brought downstairs his backpack, grabbed Lily's suitcase and called for a cab.

"I will say I am Kim's cousin from the United States; I can't see anyone accepting us as sisters," Lily said looking at Kim's copy ID which she pocketed along with sufficient dong from Mac to buy a one-way air ticket to Da Nang. "I will do all I can to get her released – whatever it takes."

"I cannot thank you enough Lily. We will await your call, hopefully with good news," Yu Lee said handing her the telephone number of Yu Ming's house. "Now, let's get you to the airport."

Stubbing out another cigarette, Mac said he would go to Hanoi and inform Ambassador Braithwaite that they had linked up and were getting on with the job of tracking down the American ex-servicemen.

"I will tell him we are making progress. No point worrying people until we are sure what is going on.

"The ambassador is sure to put a call through to Colonel Nathan and that could buy us some breathing space. I will also call on Madame Ho, if you want me to, and let her know you are safe and sound in Saigon."

———

Lily's long-held hopes of being reunited with family in Hoi An was an exciting prospect. But it did not work out the way she'd envisaged.

After just twenty-four hours in the family home her hopes and dreams were shattered. Lily's father had passed away five years earlier from some form of lung disease after suffering breathing problems for years. The family did not want to burden Lily with their problems, as they saw it, so she was never informed.

At the time of her father's death ten years after the end of hostilities, many people, particularly southerners, were still being rounded up and incarcerated in re-education centres, often for years at a time. As such, *Viet Kieu* family members were discouraged from returning to Vietnam. In addition, Vietnam's inexperienced and oft-times paranoid government suspected that Western nations were encouraging dissidents to undermine the relatively new socialist republic. Within any government, inexperience and paranoia can be an explosive mixture. This deep-seated paranoia meant that thousands of citizens were accused of subversive activities and, for many of them, long periods of incarceration followed.

Lily's family had long ago ceased corresponding with her on matters of ill-health among family members. They feared she would feel compelled to return, running the risk of being arrested and shipped off to a re-education centre.

The newly-established socialist republic attracted little international interest or support apart from a few Eastern Bloc countries at least until 1986 when *doi moi*, the open market economy, was introduced. The concept followed along the lines of an idea originally proposed by Deng Xiaoping, then Paramount Leader of the People's Republic of China.   Even though reunification of the north and south of Vietnam took place after the communists won control in 1975, many people believed the union had yet to be consummated. As it was, political and social activities continued very much on the basis of "one system, two countries". It was a dichotomy that both challenged and annoyed legions of diehard communist cadres in Hanoi.

The other alarming news confronting Lily was that her mother had been diagnosed with breast cancer. It was not a happy homecoming and worse was to come.

———

As agreed, Yu Ming waited outside Da Nang Rehabilitation and Re-education Centre with a taxi at the ready.

Remarkably, Lily's appointment lasted just minutes. Never in her wildest dreams could she have imagined a more distressing and aberrant outcome to the meeting she had with Mr Nguyen Tan Giap, deputy governor of the centre.

At first he refused to see her, relenting only after looking her over from a distance. He like what he saw but soon changed his mind when she badgered him with awkward questions. He was angry at first then became downright rude. And what he had to say about Kim left Lily totally devastated.

Stunned as though she'd been clubbed around the head, she staggered out of the centre weighed down by news so dreadful she willed the floor to open up and swallow her whole. What a shock! Her problems at home paled in comparison to what the deputy governor had told her. At that moment, she longed to be anywhere other than Da Nang...even California with her wretched husband Harold.

Just a few days ago, it would have been inconceivable for Lily to even entertain the notion of returning to the United States in the short term. For years she had planned a trip to Vietnam to see her family and sever the ties with her dysfunctional husband. Harold Crenshaw had treated her like a slave. To him she was wife, housekeeper, waiter and general factotum. To her, he was the greatest mistake of her life.

Between sobs, she explained to Yu Ming what had transpired. In view of her stressful condition he offered to call Yu Lee to convey the awful news. But Lily wanted Yu Lee to hear it directly from her. After all, she was the one who had gone face to face with the deputy governor.

———

Back in Ho Chi Minh City, eagerly awaiting a news update from Lily, Yu Lee impatiently plucked the phone from its cradle before the first ring had dissipated.

"I am with Yu Ming in a call box near my house. It's very noisy in the village. Can you hear me brother?"

"Yes Lily I can hear you." Odd, he thought, that she chose to address him as "brother" in such a respectful and polite manner. "What news do you have of Kim?"

There was no way to tone down the message or take the sting out of what she had to say. Taking a deep breath she came right out with it. "Kim is dead," she spluttered in a trembling voice. "She died the day after she arrived at the centre in Da Nang."

Lily bit into her lower lip to help endure the painful silence that ensued. She had to stay on the line to allow Yu Lee time to digest the awful news. And that seemed like an age. She gripped Yu Ming's arm for moral support. He placed an arm around her shoulders.

"Dead, you say...my Kim is dead? How...accident? There must be some mistake...this cannot be happening..."

In that single, emotionally-charged moment, Lily thought it would have been an act of kindness if someone had dynamited the telephone booth. Emotionally spent after delivering her distressing news, Lily broke down and wept uncontrollably into the telephone. With a heavy heart, Yu Ming could only look on. He knew how his brother would feel at that moment.

Stunned, Yu Lee was rooted to the spot, eyes transfixed on the wall ahead. His world had imploded. He went weak at the knees; sentiments alternating between extreme despair, from a sense of hopelessness, to virulent anger directed toward one Officer Nguyen whose actions had caused the pain.

More composed, but still shaking, Lily hurriedly related details of her incredible meeting in Da Nang.

"When I met with Mr Giap...he's the deputy director...he said Kim died the day after she arrived at the centre. The circumstances, he said, were still a mystery but subject to investigation. But I doubt anything is being done. I felt he wasn't being sincere with me."

Yu Lee listened patiently as Lily relayed the full extent of the meeting. He felt a deepening sadness and growing anger.

"But how could the man reach such a conclusion? Was anybody informed? Where is Kim's body? Oh, Lily, what terrible things are happening in Da Nang?"

"As we agreed before I left Saigon, I told Mr Giap I was Kim's cousin and showed him a copy of her ID. I asked about her belongings, clothes, money...things like that. I also asked what my cousin was doing there in the first place.

"Mr Giap became very aggressive when I questioned him. He told me that Kim was tried before a magistrate in Saigon and found guilty of subversive activities. An officer attached to Ho Chi Minh City's secret police supported the charge laid by Officer Nguyen. Kim was sentenced to six months of correctional training at the centre in Da Nang. He refused to answer questions and asked me to leave."

"I am heartbroken Lily...at a loss to understand how one human being could be treated so cruelly by another."

Recalling Lily's previous willingness to help, he suddenly felt sensitive about her own situation. How difficult this must all be for her. Unwittingly, Yu Lee had brought so much grief into Lily's life. He was also unaware of the disturbing family situation that confronted Lily upon her arrival in Hoi An.

"I must ask your forgiveness for asking you to do this on my behalf. It was not right to involve you in my private life and bring you so much distress.   Please go back to your family Lily; they need your support. We can talk again in a day or so."

Lily didn't respond; she did not want to add to Yu Lee's obvious grief.

And he needed time to think...to understand...to try to regroup and get back on track. The humiliation and pain he had suffered in Shanghai during the Cultural Revolution resurfaced as he recalled the cruel injustices perpetrated on him and his family. People cite man's inhumanity to man but do they really know what that means? To truly understand you need to feel physical pain driven by mental anguish over a lengthy period of time with no end in sight. And then get over it.

Although a devout pacifist, Yu Lee felt strongly that Officer Nguyen should be held accountable for Kim's death. But it would be Yu Ming, acutely aware of his brother's aversion towards any form of cruelty, who would make the necessary arrangements to deal with Nguyen.

———

Sleep was impossible for Yu Lee as thoughts of retribution entered his mind. The manner of Kim's disappearance and complete lack of accountability at the centre in Da Nang called for decisive action. But what should he do?

In the background, Yu Ming was already using his connections to make enquiries at the Da Nang Rehabilitation and Re-education Centre. Lily's account of Kim's demise was confirmed but no further details were available.

Yu Ming was ready to act and was prepared to do so without his brother's knowledge. The main burden of culpability, everyone seemed to agree, rested squarely on the shoulders of Officer Phan Van Nguyen. The part he played was a callous and calculated act of deception designed to exploit Kim's vulnerability. What happened in Da Nang was a direct consequence of his unbridled greed. The manner of his departure from this life to the next, and the timing, was all that had to be decided.

This would be handled the Chinese way: speedily, efficiently and without drawing undue attention.

———

Cholon's Golden Lotus triads, the pride of Saigon's Chinatown, were both feared and loved in equal measure. They were the perfect choice, Yu Ming concluded, to dispose of Officer Nguyen.

After being fully briefed by Yu Ming, the triad leader decided Wednesday, July 13, 1988 was the day the nefarious policeman would meet his demise. It was an auspicious date according to triad members. The day and date was of no consequence. What mattered most was that Golden Lotus gang members would oversee Officer Nguyen's final act in this life.

The triad members chosen for the important task went about their preparatory work efficiently and without attracting attention. They checked and double-checked

Nguyen's pattern of movements. Nothing was left to chance.

Early on Wednesday, July 13, Officer Nguyen dropped his lunchbox into the front basket of his bicycle, and set out for work just as he had done the day before and for years before that. It was just after six in the morning and the sun was still below the horizon.   The prospect of a fine morning lay ahead for Saigon residents but it would be a gruesome day for Officer Nguyen.

It took him a half hour to cycle to the police station. Slowly, as dawn broke, he edged his bicycle toward the River Saigon nursing a slight hangover from several days of unrestrained celebrations.

Near the river on Hai Ba Trung Road he was flagged down and pulled over by two fellow "police officers". Not another change in orders, he thought to himself. This is the third time in as many weeks.

It was not unusual to be flagged down in the city, and Officer Nguyen had no reason to suspect the uniformed officers were triad members in possession of instructions reassigning Nguyen's daily duties. His new orders, they told him, required him to report to another police station further along the river near Saigon Bridge. Special duties, they said. This meant cycling for another three kilometres. At least the weather was fine, although more humid than an hour earlier. The forecast said more rain but there was no need to hurry; he had plenty of time to get there.

Officer Nguyen steered his bicycle to the side of the road and set it against the rear wall of the police station. Few people were on the street. Picking up his lunchbox, he turned to walk to the front entrance. He had only taken two steps when he was grabbed from behind by two powerfully-built men.   They were also police officers so, at first, he thought it was some kind of a joke.

Unable to utter a word, he began to choke as one man stuffed a rolled-up wad of paper into his mouth. Any thoughts of the incident being a joke quickly dissipated. The paper gag was held in place with duct tape.   Nobody noticed as Officer Nguyen was frogmarched across a bridge to the east side of the River Saigon, a three-minute walk.

Choking now, his face beetroot red, Nguyen was in a catatonic state of sheer terror; eyes wide-open in horror; hangover forgotten. He could not defend himself and began to panic. It made his situation worse. Silently, one of the men lunged at his stomach with what looked like a ceremonial sword. It was all over in an instant.

Officer Nguyen was dead before he hit the water, taken out by a single thrust of a long bladed weapon expertly wielded by an experienced assassin. The ritual killing was watched by Yu Ming from his vantage point on the opposite river bank.

———

The police officer's disappearance went unnoticed until the following morning when his body bobbed up with the tide about two kilometres from where it entered the river. The corpse's mouth still contained a rolled-up wad of fake notes, like those burnt at temples to accompany deceased on their final journey.

The police superintendent, an ethnic Chinese assigned to investigate the case, quickly identified the unfortunate victim.

"Clearly this was a ritual killing," he said at the press conference, "I would say the work of triads." Money stuffed into the mouth signified greed on the part of the victim. Triads had carried out this form of killing before in some cases favouring disembowelment, the superintendent explained to the fascination of a dozen reporters.

"I have no doubt this is the work of local triads with a grudge against law enforcement officers. It's time to round up the usual suspects."

———

"Officer Nguyen's body was fished out of the River Saigon earlier this morning," Yu Ming informed Yu Lee.

Yu Lee accepted the news without comment; he suspected Yu Ming had been active behind the scenes and had decided not to intervene. He derived no particular pleasure from Nguyen's demise but, deep down, he felt justice had been served. Of course it would not bring back Kim. But, sending the errant police officer to the next life would serve as a warning to anyone who had a hand in Kim's disappearance. Word would soon spread, and that important thought kept him focused. He was getting back into his stride; thinking more clearly now ready to continue with the assignments.

But before that, he wanted to acknowledge Yu Ming's contribution in the wake of Kim's death: "Thank you for holding Officer Nguyen accountable for his unforgiveable crime. It will not bring back Kim but I want you to know I am grateful for what you did and proud that you are my brother."

Yu Ming was also fond of Kim and the manner of her passing had upset him greatly.

"She did not deserve such an end. I knew how you felt Yu Lee and I also knew you would never take personal revenge. That is why I acted for you brother.

"But there is something else you must concern yourself with," he cautioned. "The secret police will probably hear about the case of Officer Nguyen. And if someone links Nguyen to Kim it will not be long before they talk to you and me."

It was difficult to argue with Yu Ming's reasoning. It made good sense. Apart from Mrs Vanh only Jimmy Yuen knew of the link between Kim and Nguyen. It was Yuen who told Yu Lee how Nguyen had bragged about taking money from Kim.

A shout from John Mackenzie broke their train of thought. "Is anyone at home?" Mac dropped his small suitcase in the hall and headed to the kitchen where the two men were engaged in conversation.

"So, this is where you're hiding," Mac stated cheerily as he reached into the fridge for a beer. "I decided to take an earlier flight from Noi Bai," he said lighting up a cigarette.

Yu Lee gripped his friend's arm as he was about to open the fridge door. "We have bad news...very bad news."

"In that case I'll make it a scotch," Mac said grabbing his whisky bottle from the top of the fridge not sure what to expect. "What's going on?"

"Kim was killed the day after arriving in Da Nang. Lily gave me the news after her meeting with the deputy governor and..."

"For chrissakes...are you serious professor? What the hell's going on in this country?" Mac threw back his

160

drink: "I can't believe it. We were all fond of Kim...a lovely lady and..." Mac was caught in mid-sentence, steered away from the fridge by Yu Lee.

"Sit down my friend...please...I have more to say. You may not agree with this but my brother, knowing how I felt about Kim, decided her cousin Phan Van Nguyen should pay with his life for his part in this. He can give you more details but, for now, you need to know that Nguyen's body was pulled from the River Saigon this morning.

"And I hope the miserable wretch comes back as a cockroach in his next life because that is what he deserves for killing my Kim."

Immediately, Mac knew that local triads had been hired to deal with Officer Nguyen in the Chinese way. It was difficult to argue with Yu Lee's heart-breaking description of events. Perhaps now was not a good time to raise such matters, but something had to be discussed sooner rather than later in respect of their assignments.

Though his friend was going through his own private hell, Mackenzie was aware of Yu Lee's remarkable capacity to overcome adversity. "You know that I can't agree with the action Yu Ming took professor, but I can understand your feelings. And we all loved Kim and share your grief my friend."

Irrespective of their personal feelings both men knew they had to put Kim's death behind them if they were to meet their commitments.

"Let me pick this up tomorrow," Mac offered. "I will go to the Continental and confront Jimmy Yuen. Meet me later at the small, street-side cafe at the end of Dong Khoi

Street – make it around midday; you know the one...near the Floating Hotel. And try to keep a low profile will you?"

———

Next morning when Mackenzie sauntered into the lobby of the Hotel Continental he was surprised to find the place crawling with painters. Workmen were everywhere, busily painting the ornate ceiling and high walls. The bar was empty apart from paint pots, stepladders, tarpaulins and lots of paint-splashed workers.

Mac approached one of them. No-one, he was told, had heard of Jimmy Yuen. Their only concern, the foreman insisted when pressed again, was to finish a rush paintjob. They had one week to get it done to comply with the timetable passed down by Mr Dai the director of Saigontourism. All regular bar staff, apart from a few, were on forced leave of absence.

What a total waste of time that turned out to be, Mac muttered to himself as he left the hotel. Lighting up a Marlboro Lite he crossed to the opposite side of Dong Khoi Street. Outside the Caravelle Hotel he paused to gather his thoughts before walking a few blocks to link up with Yu Lee.

Above the noise of passing traffic, someone called out his name: "Over here, Mr John," a young man was shouting and waving an arm at him. Emerging from a doorway the caller introduced himself as Trinh Tan Son.

"Well, Mr Son, you gave me quite a fright. Do you always hang around in hotel doorways? Are you hiding from somebody? And how come you know my name?"

162

"Sorry Mr John. I was behind bar stocking bottles when you come into Continental. My English not good but I know you look for Jimmy Yuen. I tell you about him, yes?"

"Whoa, hold the phone young feller," Mac responded not entirely convinced of the young man's approach. "Let me think about that." He mulled it over for a minute or two. There was nothing to lose by listening to what the young man had to say. And right now, he didn't have any better ideas.

"Okay, Mister Son, I will listen to what you have to tell me, but not here. Walk with me to a cafe near the river. I will buy you a coffee." He wanted Yu Lee to be present.

———

By sheer good fortune, Yu Lee got to the cafe five minutes after Mackenzie and Mr Son, some fifteen minutes ahead of the appointed time. Glancing towards the River Saigon, Yu Lee was mindful that Officer Nguyen's body was found not far from where he was now standing.

Stepping inside the cafe he spotted Mac in conversation with someone he didn't recognise. Had there been some new development he wondered?

"Who is your friend Mr John?"

Yu Lee signalled to a waiter to bring another cup of coffee. He addressed Mr Son in Vietnamese. "Have I seen you before?"

"Yu Lee, say hello to Mr Son. He told me he works the bar at the Continental," Mac added by way of introduction "He has something to tell us about Jimmy Yuen. We haven't got started on that. You're just in time."

Yu Lee took a seat opposite Mr Son. "I see. So what do you have to say brother?" Again Yu Lee spoke in Vietnamese.

"I know who you are," Mr Son answered in English, "I have seen you before at Hotel Continental sometimes with lady."

Yu Lee acknowledged Mr Son's accurate observation with a smile and a nod.

Trinh Tan Son explained that apart from seeing Yu Lee and Kim at the Hotel Continental on one or two previous occasions, his mother, who had a stall at Ben Thanh Market, had known Kim for several years.

"My mother sells pork and Miss Kim shops at her stall sometimes," he declared with some pride.

"So what do you have for us Mr Son," Yu Lee asked again, not seeking to correct the remark about Kim into the past tense.

"Mr John, he ask about Jimmy Yuen this morning. I know something about him.

"I am twenty-five years old," he announced looking at each man in turn, "and I want to study English...improve myself. I have two pieces of information...and I want to be paid for helping you."

Yu Lee kept Mac updated with the exchange that swung between English and Vietnamese. "Listen to me Mr Son," Yu Lee said in English keeping his voice low, "if you have any information that is useful to us I will pay you fifty dollars for it. And if your information turns out to be very helpful then Mr John and I will pay for a one year course of English lessons for you. What do you say to that?"

"That is fair brother. I am grateful."

Yu Lee ordered another round of coffees as Mr Son got into his stride: "Earlier this year...I think January...Jimmy Yuen's mother come to my mother's stall. She tell how her son fix up her old house near market. She very happy.

"Jimmy buy for her electric washing machine, stereo, TV, furniture and new Honda Dream motorcycle," he explained rattling off a list of expensive items. In Vietnam in the late 1980's such items were luxuries and out of the reach of most people.

"Are you saying that someone earning around thirty thousand dong a month would not be able to afford such luxuries?" Mac asked even though he knew the answer.

"Yes sir. But there is more...I think I know how he gets money to buy expensive things. Jimmy Yuen's mother say Jimmy do jobs for foreign company. Company near Da Nang...make lot of money doing jobs for them."

"What sort of work?" Yu Lee asked.

"Not sure," Mr Son replied.

It sounded interesting, Mac wanted to learn more. "So what sort of work buys you a Honda Dream motorcycle, Mr Son?"

"Brother Jimmy...he talk on telephone with someone in Da Nang often. Use lobby phone...sometimes speak English. My English not good but I remember he say out loud '...you want me to find more girls...do you know how difficult it is?' Talk drugs also, once or twice."

"That is very interesting Mr Son. Do you remember anything else?" Mac asked.

"Just before lobby bar close, call come from Da Nang for Jimmy Yuen. He not in hotel so I take message."

"This man is foreigner...sound like you Mr John. He ask Jimmy Yuen call school as soon as he come back."

"Is that all?" asked Yu Lee, "did he mention the name of the school?"

"That was all. I wrote down message give to Jimmy Yuen next day. He looked at it quickly and put into pocket."

———

After meeting with Mr Son, Yu Lee and Mac spent a short time outside the cafe.

"I don't know about you prof, but I am inclined to think the young man's information is authentic. It is definitely timely. Everything we have seen and heard suggests Jimmy Yuen was the bastard who organised Linh's disappearance." He wanted to say "kidnap" but checked himself.

Unwisely, they had trusted someone they hardly knew and had to take responsibility for their bad judgment. But they had to look ahead, to move on.

"I guess we have to face the prospect my friend that Linh may have been abducted and taken out of Ho Chi Minh City to somewhere upcountry...some place that could be acting as a front for trafficking."

It could very well be the case and, as things stood at that moment, it was all they had to go on.

Though neither man was eager to give David Gervasoni an update both felt honour-bound to do so.

166

"How are we going to explain," Yu Lee asked, "that we found Linh and lost her again within days?"

Neither man wanted to appear incompetent before Gervasoni though that's how they felt. But, in simple terms there was nothing to be gained by making a call at this particular juncture. Mac nodded. "I agree prof. It will only increase concern on his and everyone else's part and Gervasoni can't help us anyway."

They were in need of help to make any progress. On the way back to Yu Ming's house, Yu Lee shared an idea with Mac. It was something he'd had on his mind for days.

"In my opinion Mr John we need to get the army involved. This may sound a bit strange to you and I will explain my reasons later," he promised Mac who was sporting a very worried look on his face.

———

After being confined indoors for more than a week it came as welcome relief when Linh and the other girls were told to get ready to leave. Just after six thirty in the morning all six were hustled into a white, windowless van.

"You are going on a five-and-a-half hour journey; an adventure trip," Mr Bill told them, "to a school near Da Nang. Right now that is all you need to know," he said slamming shut the van door.

It was an uneventful journey during which the girls spent time getting to know more about one another. The time passed quickly.

On arrival at the school, Linh and her five companions were taken to see the principal, Madame Ha, who hurriedly assigned living quarters in the dormitory building.

"Tomorrow all of you should report to Miss Thien. She will tell you what you have to do."

When Linh and the others arrived at L'Ecole des Filles, Mr Bill was not present. He was with Thien at the local market buying provisions and making payment protection rounds to the local police. The most important task, the school principal constantly stressed, was to protect the school's reputation as a centre of education.

———

The "school", located on the outskirts of Da Nang, was not as advertised. Madame Ha, its self-styled "principal", was the last in a long line of mamasan who, for decades, had fostered the myth of running a school for young ladies. Like those before her, Madame Ha coaxed and cajoled hundreds of unfortunate girls and young women into a life of prostitution. For her it was a lucrative business; for the girls it was a prison sentence.

In French colonial times, this particular L'Ecole des Filles was a highly respected school; an accredited educational institute for young ladies. French expatriates, and other foreign nationals living in the Hue-Da Nang conurbation, willingly sent their young girls to be educated, schooled in etiquette and groomed to become fine young ladies. Back then, it was a day school; young girls did not stay over but were taken to and fro by nannies six days a week.

For years it was run as a family business even after the French were driven out in the mid-fifties, thirty years earlier. That was when Madame Ha began to manipulate and cultivate local officials, including the police, to allow her to maintain the outward facade of running a school, which she did, while operating a walled-in, walk-in brothel. It became a rewarding enterprise from which everyone benefited apart from the unfortunate young women.

Spread over seven hectares of land, the facility stands back from the main road. The school's secluded location proved ideal for the gifted Madame Ha to build a dormitory facility deep within the grounds where girls and young women could be secretly detained and trained for a life of prostitution. When they reached the ripe old age of thirty, or began to look a little battle-weary or worse for wear, as Mr Bill indelicately put it, they were stood down from active service and retained as deputies to the mamasan to train new, young recruits. Some managed to escape after establishing outside contacts but they were few in number. Women deemed unsuitable as "trainers" were thrown out on to the streets to face an uncertain future.

During the latter part of the Eighties Madame Ha focused on building a clientele composed mainly of foreign businessmen as Vietnam opened up to the outside world. First, she targeted Koreans, then Taiwanese, men from Hong Kong and Singapore, and ultimately men from the USSR and other Eastern Bloc countries employed by petrochemical companies drilling offshore for oil and gas. Many workers were accommodated in the Da Nang-Hue neighbourhood. But her prized clientele by far were local dignitaries whom she deemed "persons of great importance". She was referring to them in the context of her business interests of course.

Bound by clandestine and closely-controlled "arrangements", many clients were entertained at the school.   Some girls were hired out under escort to approved hotels. That side of the business was handled by Mr Bill, Madame Ha's business partner. A tough, ex-serviceman, Mr Bill controlled the girls, and the clients, with an element of military discipline.

Madame Ha's girls were in great demand particularly the female *bui-doi* because of their singularly attractive features. Relatively tall and slender in build, with light or olive-coloured skin, long black hair and blue or green eyes some *bui-doi* were stunningly beautiful. They were greatly sought after and commanded a higher price than those of pure Vietnamese ethnicity.

For almost eight years, Madam Ha had enjoyed a steady flow of "students" from southern Vietnam thanks to the combined efforts of the perceptively cunning Jimmy Yuen in Ho Chi Minh City and master pimp Mr Bill who oversaw the Da Nang end of the operation.

When first introduced to Madame Ha, Mr Bill had proudly touted his vast experience gained peddling drugs to fellow servicemen during the Vietnam War. That was a good business, he told her, which continued after the war. She was impressed.   Later, after building up a network of contacts, including Jimmy Yuen, he turned to trafficking young women from the south of Vietnam to Da Nang. Although Madame Ha warmed to the idea of teaming up with him she remained cautious. She had to retain control of her own destiny though she had no experience dealing in drugs.

Later, around 1980, Mr Bill took up with a Vietnamese girl called Thien. She had made her way to Madame Ha's seeking work. Mister Bill saw her, took a liking to her, and decided to keep her for himself.

Confiding in Thien after their friendship blossomed, Mr Bill told her something of his own background, starting with his "new life" in Laos after America withdrew from Vietnam in 1973. She, in turn, told him how she had left her home near Ho Chi Minh City to find work to feed her family. At twenty-seven years of age, she was burned out and found it difficult working the bars and competing with the younger girls.

She learned about the existence of L'Ecole des Filles from other women working the bars in downtown Ho Chi Minh City. This prompted her to pack her bags and board a bus for Da Nang. Now, at thirty-five, she was too old to entertain Madame Ha's picky clientele. Instead, she was assigned to groom and train the new girls and she was good at it.

Apart from Madame Ha, nobody at the school knew of Mr Bill's service record, and even she was not aware of the scale of the lucrative trafficking business he had operated with another ex-serviceman, Robert Johnson. Together they had trafficked drugs – opium, heroin and marijuana – to American servicemen up until America's withdrawal from Vietnam. The two men went AWOL when the United States declared its intention to withdraw its fighting forces. They stayed behind and prudently developed their business interests.

Then they moved to Laos and, by some quirk of fate, married sisters in the same family. That was an opportunistic move that boosted their credibility. And the women proved useful when it came to bribing local law enforcement officers and other government officials to allow the two men to conduct business unhindered. Consequently, their trafficking operations in drugs and girls expanded at a rapid pace and became an extremely lucrative source of income.

Everything went along smoothly until one fateful day. Again by sheer chance, Robert Johnson returned home early from a trip upcountry to find his good buddy in bed with both women. For some time Johnson had suspected that something was amiss but couldn't pin it down. Behind his back, his pal had not only engineered the ménage à trois, he had insisted on secrecy and threatened both women with unspeakable harm if they mentioned it. Aware of Mr Bill's violent tendencies after watching him use his strength to settle disputes over drugs and girls – drawing his knife on more than one occasion – the sisters decided this was not a man to mess with.

Seeing all three together in a compromising state Johnson's reaction was predictable. He flew into a rage, throwing around furniture and screaming at his wife and her sister in turn. Terrified, both women hugged and tried to console each other in a corner of the bedroom, hardly daring to watch. Johnson, wielding the leg from a broken chair, made a desperate lunge at his former friend. The big man saw it coming. With lightning speed, Johnson's one-time good buddy unsheathed his Bowie knife from a bedside table and, with a single underarm stroke, plunged the nine-and-a-half-inch blade into Johnson's stomach. He died in a pool of blood amidst wild screams from two terrified women who were scrambling and stumbling away from the scene.

Johnson's death put an end marker on Mr Bill's love affair with Laos. He had to leave the country in a hurry. For sure, the women would turn against him and inform the authorities what had happened if only to protect their own interests. That could not be allowed to happen. For Mr Bill there was too much at stake.

Throwing together a few belongings, most of the cash, his passport and Johnson's, he got ready to leave for Vietnam secure in the knowledge the women could not follow him because they did not have passports.

Placing Johnson's dog tag around his own neck like a trophy, he buried the body in the jungle. Crossing over to Vietnam he hid out near Da Nang. Later, through contacts, he was introduced to Madame Ha and entered into an arrangement to traffic girls and young women striking deals with Jimmy Yuen to ensure a steady flow of girls from the South to Da Nang. For ex-US serviceman William Petroni, a.k.a. Mr Bill, it was business as usual.

Yu Lee and Mac regrouped at Yu Ming's house to mull over their options. Uncharacteristically, Ho Chi Minh City was bathed in sunshine and humidity was relatively low for July, so the duo withdrew to the small garden at the rear of the house.

Yu Lee laid out his plan: "Since our meeting with Trinh Tan Son, which I think was useful, I have thought of little else other than how to make the best of any positive leads we get to help our assignments. Mr John, it is my strong opinion that we need special assistance from inside this country to find Linh and the two Americans," he said with marked emphasis not normally his forte.

Mac had already voiced his support for any useful suggestions that would help push forward their commitments to find Linh and the Americans.

"I did consider asking Madame Ho for help," Yu Lee continued, "and I am sure she would agree. But she has been through enough, thanks to me. I do not wish to compromise her position and friendship with the cadres. I also thought of approaching the British ambassador in Hanoi because of his close working relationships with senior ministers."

"Yes, why not ask for Braithwaite's help?" Mac queried. "There is no doubt he is on side prof."

"I agree. But I think his special relationship with the American consulate in Hong Kong could act against us under certain circumstances. No, I think we have to work with Vietnamese people and I feel strongly about this."

"So, what do you have in mind?"

"This might sound strange to you but I believe we have to approach the army for help."

"I assumed your earlier reference to the army did relate to the Social Republic of Vietnam," Mac said. "Do you mind if I ask how the hell you arrived at what seems to me to be such a radical approach?"

"We need powerful friends behind us if we are to keep clear of the secret police...any police in fact. The army can give us the cover we need. Also, as we are searching for two American ex-servicemen it is logical to seek help from the army."

"But why would the Vietnam army want to help us?"

"Be easy my friend. We must look at this through the eyes of local people," Yu Lee cautioned. "The police force is not the only state entity in Vietnam that holds records of visitors entering and leaving the country. The army has its own records; I know because I have used them on previous occasions. More importantly, I have a very good friend in the army, a general, who I have known since I was a young boy. I have made an appointment to see him and I want you to come with me today to meet him.

"From now on we must work with reliable contacts; people we can confide in and who have the power to arrange safe passage for us within Vietnam. If our assignments are to succeed we must keep clear of state officials who might ask awkward questions – particularly local police and the secret police. Do you understand my point of view?"

"I can agree with you on that last point."

"What we need is an unrestricted pass that allows us to go wherever we wish. And I can get that from my friend General Nguyen Van Vo."

Yu Lee could see from the pained expression on Mac's face that he had reservations. Further explanation was required. "We can avoid interference from the police, Mr John, if we have protection from the army. In this country it is important to know the right people. That is how things work here as I believe you know from our many experiences together."

"And I can't argue with that either," Mac conceded lighting up another cigarette. "Okay…okay prof; let's do it your way. Why don't you just let me know what you want me to do and I'll do it?"

With a basic plan in mind and his good friend pretty much on board, Yu Lee was confident and felt he could go forward with renewed energy. His enthusiasm was returning; crucial if he was to keep his mind off Kim and concentrate on the challenges facing them.

"In my dealings with the army, I have never encountered any problems with the police. The police stay clear of army business. So please can we get going now Mr John? We have much to do and time is not on our side."

———

The Hong Kong-based hotel development group that helped finance and construct the army's VIP accommodation by the River Saigon also chose the hostelry's unusual name of Riverside GuestHotel.

It had proven to be another successful gambit on Yu Lee's part in matching foreign expertise with local landowners – in this case a branch of the Vietnam army. As in many countries in Asia, military units boast ownership of land and property; invest in factories; administer golf courses and, in General Vo's case, operate an upscale business hotel. It wasn't the first project Yu Lee had worked on for his good friend and mentor – though on those occasions without John Mackenzie's assistance.

Situated on the banks of the fast-flowing River Saigon, the stylish, three-storey boutique hotel opened for service in 1987. Though small and compact, the hotel's sixty, good-sized and well-appointed suites offered some of the most comfortable accommodation to be found anywhere in Ho Chi Minh City in the Eighties.

It was late in the afternoon when the duo arrived at the hotel. The weather had turned particularly humid. During the rainy season downpours in Saigon were commonplace from around four-o'clock onward.

The two guards manning the main entrance snapped to attention. How many hotels, Mac wondered, could boast armed guards to protect their clientele? Perhaps not quite in the mould of some of the five-star hotels in Hong Kong, Singapore or Bangkok, he thought, as the guard waved them through, but pretty darn good for war-torn Vietnam.

As they neared the hotel entrance General Vo stepped out and strode purposefully toward Yu Lee. Both men were smiling broadly at one another. Pulling Yu Lee towards him the general embraced him: "Professor...well, well, well...what a wonderful surprise, it is good to see you my boy."

The general's excellent command of the English language took Mac by surprise. Yu Lee had failed to mention that General Vo had spent some time in England.

"When you contacted me yesterday," the general said, smiling broadly, "I hoped you could find time to visit us and see the finished product. You did not come to the opening as I recall.

"And who is your friend?" he asked glancing over Yu Lee's shoulder.

Managing to extricate himself from the general's overzealous embrace, Yu Lee introduced John Mackenzie as his very close friend, explaining how together they had worked on numerous projects in Southeast Asia and in China.

"But all that can wait for now general: first let me tell you how good it is to see you and find you in good health."

It was clear from General Vo's bright eyes, smooth skin and upright stature that he had weathered well for his eighty-odd years. Yu Lee was well aware of some of the hardships suffered by the general over many years of conflict with the French, Chinese and Americans. The general was not tall, but his wiry physique was remarkable for a man in his eighties particularly considering what he had been through in the Indochina wars.

"A friend of Yu Lee is always welcome here," he said squeezing Mac's hand. "Allow me to show you around the hotel Mr John." He tapped Mac's shoulder. "Perhaps you can give me your opinion on how we compare with hotels in Hong Kong."

For an old soldier the general cut an imposing figure. Anyone meeting him for the first time could not fail to be impressed by the man's commanding presence and unbridled appetite for life despite his advancing age. Mac could see why Yu Lee insisted on having the Army as an ally, even though General Vo was no longer in active service. And it was obvious the general held Yu Lee in great esteem; an excellent example of the importance of who you know, not what you know. Yu Lee was almost always right about such things.

Ushering his guests into a ground floor suite, General Vo spoke with pride about the hotel facilities: "As you can see my friends, we have everything a man could ask for to make him comfortable. Every suite is similarly equipped," he said gesturing with his hands.

"I have to say I am impressed with what I've seen so far general," Mac told him. "Do you also have hot and cold running maids – in uniforms of course?" It was a test of the general's sense of humour.

"Quite so, Mr John; just dial 2 for room service and our battle-ready housemaids will come running...at the double of course."

Yu Lee smiled at the light-hearted banter taking place between the two men -- invaluable as a bridge-builder.

On the cyclo ride to the hotel, Yu Lee explained to Mackenzie how his father had introduced him to General Vo. Ever since then, as a close and valued friend of the family, Yu Lee said he felt duty-bound to assist the general in any way he could. His father would have expected it.

Although a career soldier, the general had learnt a lot about man-management over the years. But he was aware of his shortcomings and limitations in the world of commerce, and why he greatly appreciated advice from others particularly family friends.

It was Yu Lee who had sourced an architect from Hong Kong to draw up plans to transform the old, French colonial-style mansion into a high-quality boutique hotel. Now a full year since it opened, the Riverside GuestHotel was a firm favourite with overseas visitors and local army brass.

Small hotels in Ho Chi Minh City in the late Eighties were notorious for dishing out poor service or no service at all. The communists allowed everything to fall into disrepair. It was a rare event to find a room where the air-conditioner worked according to specification or come across a bathroom with a toilet that flushed. Mac's practice in Vietnam was to travel with a small toolkit to carry out running repairs when required. It had been pressed into service more times than he could remember.

"Again, general, I have to say I am greatly impressed; all the suites seem to be well-appointed and, unlike some hotels in the city, everything here appears to work. I might have difficulty getting used to that," he said with more than a hint of sarcasm, but expressed knowing the good general had a keen sense of humour.

"Let me tell you something: One good thing about the army running a hotel, Mr John, is that we have experts from all walks of life just waiting to be ordered to fix something."

Amidst loud laughter the general directed his visitors towards the riverside of the hotel. It was difficult not to like this old soldier whose rapier-like wit was a breath of fresh air in an increasingly conservative Vietnam.

The men peered out across the fast-flowing river their attention drawn by the endless clumps of water hyacinth heading towards the South China Sea.

"My dear professor, I would like to change the subject. Are you aware that the body of a police officer was found in the river not far from where we are standing?"

Mac stiffened, wondering what had prompted the general to raise that at this time. Yu Lee kept his composure. "Yes general…and I know why it happened," he added inviting the general to take a seat alongside Mackenzie.

"In fact, it has much to do with our visit today."

Attentive waiters handed out glasses of iced water. General Vo gratefully accepted a cigarette from Mac. Yu Lee had anticipated the general would be aware of Officer Nguyen's demise and also have some idea why it happened. If the two men were to get help from the army they had to come clean and place all their cards on the table. The general's distinguished military service marked him as a man not to be trifled with. Measuring each move carefully was the order of the day.

One of Vietnam's four national heroes and a protégé of Ho Chi Minh himself, the general was a highly-decorated and greatly respected army officer – a man not to upset or underestimate without good reason. Some would say he has enjoyed increased importance since his retirement from the army. He saw action against French colonialists and "American imperialists", and his considered views and opinions still carried a lot of weight among active servicemen, compatriots and party cadres.

Rain fell like pebbles on the River Saigon, greatly reducing visibility and almost obscuring the Floating Hotel upriver. Against a noise-filled background of driving wind and rain Yu Lee related all that had happened from the moment he and Mac arrived in Vietnam -- right up to Kim's disappearance, the consequences of that, and their assignments.

Out on the river, bountiful clumps of water hyacinth drifted towards the hotel's veranda. Some nestled alongside the boardwalk to be fended off by the general using a strategically placed broom handle.

Yu Lee took his time to deliver an unemotional account of everything that had transpired. Mac was impressed, but what would the general think?

"I was sure that the Saigon police force would never conduct a fair investigation into Kim's death," Yu Lee told General Vo. "And yes, general, my emotions did take over. I have no regrets that Kim's death has been avenged.

"Please believe me sir when I say that all we wish to do now is to continue our search for the Amerasian girl to honour the commitment I gave to her father. And it is imperative we find out what these two Americans are up to because it could have a significant effect on future relationships between Vietnam and the United States. We are here today because we need your help to successfully complete both assignments."

Everything was on the table; nothing had been held back. Now it was up to the general either to support them or have them dumped into the fast flowing river to drift downstream with the water hyacinths.

Anxious to show support, Mackenzie voiced his opinion: "General, when I was briefed by Colonel Nathan about our assignment I was given to understand that if these two Americans are dealing drugs or trafficking in women, or both, talks taking place between the two countries could be severely compromised – stalling chances of reconciliation for months if not years."

"Exactly who is going to be compromised; America or Vietnam?" General Vo asked probing the two men as he tried to gauge the level of commitment they had for their assignments.

"I guess both countries will be affected in equal measure sir," Mac responded. "America will be embarrassed if two ex-US servicemen are found to be trafficking in young women or drugs or both. And Vietnam will be embarrassed if some of its citizens are found to be implicated and providing some form of security for the Americans."

The general took a moment to think it over. He accepted a cigar from Mackenzie.

"This is how I see it," Mac said lighting the general's cigar. "First-stage bilateral talks are already underway. The British ambassador informed me the talks were being mediated by EU representatives in Hanoi. These meetings are vital, aimed at establishing a climate of trust with a promise to ease sanctions as soon as possible. The Americans are very serious about this general and that goes right up to the White House."

Neither man could have known that General Vo was already aware of low-key talks taking place in Vietnam. In fact they had started just before the Americans left Vietnam in 1973. He was careful not to mention it because, strategically, he wanted to occupy the high ground; to make the men ask for his help directly which they had. Additionally, he wanted them to make a clear case for assistance before he was prepared to offer any help or give advice. If nothing else, the general was a cautious octogenarian.

Adopting a more serious tone of voice the general expressed his views: "Gentlemen, these are my observations. First of all professor, I cannot disregard the action taken regarding the police officer. He may have deserved his fate but it was not for you to assume the role of judge and executioner.

"But I understand how you feel and I commiserate with you for your sad loss. For now, we will set that aside.

"Secondly, I believe you should complete your missions like good soldiers. If that is your intention, and the main reason for coming to see me here today, I will help for the sake of good relations between my country and the United States.

"I have a third point, and this is purely for your information: I will order an army unit to conduct an investigation into Americans trafficking in drugs and young women in Vietnam. This starts now. If there is a chance to shake free from America's punishing sanctions we have to take it. Mac, I am inclined to agree with your Colonel Nathan: whatever happens, we must avoid any potentially embarrassing situation from developing between Vietnam and the United States. As you both already know, Vietnam is twenty years behind the rest of the world. We have a lot of catching up to do and we must start by getting our own house in order and be prepared to embrace change."

The old soldier reclaimed his seat: "It is a great pity you do not have any names to pass to me. No matter, I will get to the bottom of this. As of tomorrow you will have use of a vehicle and an armed driver from my personal staff. This man will be at your disposal while you are in Vietnam. He will have with him a travel pass that will give you right-of-way including access to military bases so long as he accompanies you. When I have any interesting information about American ex-servicemen I will pass a message via the driver."

The general stood again to take a telephone call. The meeting was at an end. He made his excuses, bade farewell and disappeared into his office.

On the way back to Yu Ming's place, Yu Lee voiced his satisfaction at the way the meeting had gone. "That sort of discussion might not mean much in Canada or the United States, John, but as one of Vietnam's most decorated war heroes he commands respect from everyone. What I am trying to say is that military personnel, politicians and business people alike must all give the general their full respect – just as if he were still a serving officer. In Vietnam, a soldier's sacrifices in the service of his country are never forgotten, not even by future generations. And we have to remember that General Vo killed many American soldiers during the conflict. You would never guess he was a tunnel rat and lived most of the time underground with a team of army specialists."

"You mean he carried out hit-and-run missions against the Americans?"

"More than that; he transformed underground guerrilla raids into an art form, surviving on meagre rations and living in total isolation for months on end. There is another interesting thing about this old man," Yu Lee recalled. "His weapon of choice is a Ghurkha *kukri*.   He told me he got it in England. Next time you see him, ask him about that."

"I will, because that doesn't ring true," Mac replied, frowning in disbelief. "The only way to wrest a kukri from a Ghurkha is to kill him...unless of course he's already dead! But I will ask General Vo next time I see him."

The general's twenty-year old, slightly battered, gunmetal-grey Mercedes saloon arrived outside Yu Ming's house at first light. Now they could make an early start. General's Vo's pennants prominently displayed on the front mudguards constituted a welcome sign for their trip upcountry. It would be a brave man or woman who stopped the car without good reason.

The general's personal driver, a staff sergeant in his fifties, dutifully snapped to attention and, as ordered, handed two envelopes to Yu Lee. One envelope held an official letter of authorisation signed by General Vo for full use of the vehicle and driver. Attached to it was a handwritten note from the general requesting "whosoever it concerned" to render full assistance to the two men during their time in Vietnam. It was exactly what Yu Lee wanted.

The second envelope contained a hand-scribbled note in Vietnamese: *A man called William Petroni spends time at a school near Da Nang called L'Ecole des Filles. Good hunting.* The general had been very busy overnight.

It seems all roads lead to Da Nang.

Burning up kilometre after kilometre of the highway, the Mercedes wound its way along Vietnam's main south-north trunk route. Occasionally, the driver slowed down to skirt around deep holes in the road, inevitable hazards during the rainy season. Despite the pockmarked road surface, Mac managed to doze off. Yu Lee looked straight ahead with thoughts only of Kim. Try as he may, he could not get her out of his head. But he had promised himself that his personal pain would not be allowed to impair his judgement. General Vo's timely intervention had improved their chances of success. For the first time there was cause for cautious optimism.

A few kilometres abeam of the coastal town of Nha Trang, they rounded a tight bend to be confronted by a road obstruction. Exercising great skill, the driver brought the Mercedes to a halt inches from a heavy metal barrier that blocked the way. Mac was shaken awake in time to see two police officers emerge from behind the barrier. They were reeling from side to side.

"Good work sergeant," Yu Lee tapped the driver on his back just as he was about to open his door to leave the vehicle. "Please stay where you are. It will be better if I talk to the police officers."

The driver regained his seat and began to reach for the AK47 stowed above the windscreen. Mac saw the move and shook his finger from side to side.

"Stay calm please. These two are very drunk," Yu Lee said leaving the vehicle "This should not take long."

It was barely two-o-clock in the afternoon and both officers were totally inebriated. And in their near-paralytic state they had failed to notice the general's twin pennants hanging limply on the mudguards. Yu Lee walked towards them: "Good afternoon officers," he said politely, "how can I help you?" He had already checked to make sure the papers from the general were safely tucked into the side pocket of his safari suit.

Slurring his words, the officer to the left of Yu Lee spoke first. As he did he caught sight of the pennants and the uniformed driver. "You have...*hic*...general's pennants on your vehicle," he muttered, "but I only see a sergeant in the car. How do you...*burp*...explain that?"

"My authority is here," Yu Lee responded patting his pocket without lifting out the envelope. "Our business in Vietnam," he continued "has been authorised by General Nguyen Van Vo." The policemen, like everyone else in the country, would be aware of the general's status as a national hero.

Mouths agape, both officers stared first at Yu Lee then at the car and its occupants unsure of what to do next. Yu Lee was keen to end the confrontation peacefully and get on their way. It was one of those occasions, he decided, when a cash donation would serve a useful purpose.

"This is my permit," Yu Lee announced holding the envelope above his head. And here is fifty dollars for you gentlemen to enjoy yourselves. So what do you say?"

The offer of fifty dollars was tempting. One police officer held out his hand.

"I am sure we can be thankful to you both for keeping the roads safe," Yu Lee called back to them as he joined Mackenzie.

"Carry on driver, Yu Lee instructed." Nobody looked back.

"Well done professor; I guess we can call this a fifty dollar technical stop right?"

"When you travel by car around this country you must expect to be stopped by bandits. And in Vietnam, Mr John, most of them are in uniforms."

———

The coastal stretch of National Highway 1 narrows as it approaches the central provinces. The driver's skills were not in doubt but it was a challenge to keep the vehicle on the right side of the centreline because of the road's uneven surface. Fatigue could also be playing a part after five hours at the wheel not counting the time wasted with two drunken policemen.

What occurred next happened quickly and took everyone by surprise.

Approaching Tam Ky, seventy kilometres south of Da Nang, the driver swung the steering wheel hard right in a dramatic, split-second manoeuvre -- but not fast enough to avoid a collision. The Mercedes clashed side-on with a large army truck as it sidled across the centreline. The sound of grating metal, breaking glass and a shower of golden sparks confirmed the army driver had lost control of his ten-wheel, two-and-a-half tonne vehicle. Propelled sideways by its own weight, the truck sideswiped the Mercedes forcing it into a roadside ditch a couple of metres short of a sheer drop into the valley below.

The robust army truck, virtually unscathed, juddered to a halt, tyres smoking. A dozen excited soldiers disembarked at the double. "Stand by the vehicle," the squad's sergeant ordered as the officer in charge strode purposefully towards the Mercedes. Unlike the drunken police officers from their previous encounter, the lieutenant immediately noticed the general's pennants fluttering in the breeze.

By now, both men had scrambled out of the roadside rear window. The rear doors were jammed but the windows had only a few shards of glass in place. Before leaving, Mac tapped the driver's shoulder and felt for a

190

pulse in his neck. No response. No sign of life. The driver's side had taken the brunt of the impact and the driver's head was resting on his right shoulder at an unnatural angle. It didn't look good.

The tortured expression on the lieutenant's face foretold the pair was about to be hit by a barrage of questions. Once again, Yu Lee checked the permit was still in his pocket. Using his fan to brush imaginary dust from his safari suit he stepped forward suitably braced for an incoming blast of harsh words from the officer.

But the lieutenant had his own concerns to juggle with: How was he to frame a credible explanation to give to his superiors before they got back to Marble Mountain Air Base? Questions would be asked because his platoon was part of an army unit assigned to participate in war games organised by Soviet advisors. They were already running late when the accident occurred. Technically, he was aware his driver was at fault for straying across the centreline. Lack of due care and attention was the reason the Mercedes was pushed off the road but how could he be expected to admit that? Accepting responsibility would surely quash any hopes of promotion.

After a quick assessment of the situation he decided the safest course of action would be to blame the other party. No one would be the wiser and his men would do and say as they were told. But then there was the matter of the general's pennants hanging limply on the Mercedes mudguards. This small, but important detail troubled the young lieutenant who was not long in the rank.

Sensing the officer's obvious discomfort, Yu Lee got in first, speaking in Vietnamese: "Lieutenant, your driver caused this accident and I will say as much to your superiors. More than that you should be aware we are travelling under the protection of General Nguyen Van Vo. I have the signed permit..."

The lieutenant raised a hand above his head as an indication to stop. "First things first, if you do not mind. I would like to see some identity...also, has your driver been injured?"

"Yes, seriously I think. His neck may be broken."

He probably died instantly but as neither Yu Lee nor Mac were qualified physicians they decided to defer to the senior officer at the scene to form his own judgement

The officer remained polite throughout the entire exchange: "I would like to know why two foreigners are in a Vietnam army vehicle. Hand over your passports and permit please to show to my CO at Marble Mountain Air Base.

The body of the driver was removed from the Mercedes and placed in the back of the truck. The sergeant covered it with a blanket. It was a sad and defining moment that left Yu Lee and Mac feeling helpless. General Vo would not be happy either when he got the news.

"And you two," the lieutenant enquired in English, "are either of you injured?"

"A few bruises and scratches from broken glass," Mac said, holding up his bruised left arm. His shoulder had also taken a knock as he dragged himself out of the car. Yu Lee, probably because of his slighter build, was shaken but otherwise unscathed in his escape from the vehicle.

"Lieutenant, I believe you will find this is in order," Yu Lee said handing over the permit. The general's name and stamp were clear to see. "I will show you our passports later when we can get to our luggage if that meets with your approval."

"We will transport you to an army hospital near Da Nang. And, yes, I am aware of General Vo," he said, in a voice loud enough for all his men to hear.

"Get into the truck, please."

After being treated for minor cuts and bruises at a military hospital near Da Nang, Yu Lee and Mac were moved to a ward. It was a precaution, they were told, to make certain they were not suffering from concussion. Mac's left shoulder and arm ached, not from the accident so much as from being manhandled by an ugly, heavy-handed male nurse.

Considering their driver's plight – pronounced dead at the scene of the accident -- they were lucky to be alive. But they still had to face the matter of the lieutenant's report. Also their travel permit had been confiscated despite Yu Lee's protestations. Their passports had not been retained, though that could change given their run of bad luck since leaving Ho Chi Minh City.

The ward catered for a maximum of twelve patients. Each bed had a small locker for stowing clothes and personal belongings. Boxes of dressings and medical supplies were positioned at two, unmanned nursing stations. A solitary row of hooks along one wall accommodated freshly-laundered surgical gowns. Few nurses were to be seen – male or female -- and even fewer doctors, which suggested this was not a busy military hospital. So what was its main purpose? The ward's two windows had external bars like a prison hospital ward.

Assigned adjacent beds, the two men were left alone. Neither had any serious injuries but they were in need of a rest. It had been a long, frustrating and accident-prone day.

Mac noted that a single door led into the corridor to male and female toilets, a nurses' room and the exit. Yu Lee's bed was between Mac's and another patient to his right who was curtained-off and out of sight. An occasional cough betrayed his presence. So they were not the only patients.

On entering the ward, Mac made a mental note that the outer door had just one guard. But why have a guard on any door in a hospital ward? Was it for their benefit?

Suddenly, with a loud splintering sound, the ward door was thrown open. It banged against the wall before bouncing back into place. Accompanied by two heavily armed guards an army captain marched briskly into the ward and made a beeline for Yu Lee and Mackenzie. They both rose to their feet, ready to confront their visitors.

"I am Captain Nguyen Duc Dung," the officer announced proudly, head held high. "You two may consider yourselves under arrest. Later, you will be charged with stealing army property and causing the death of an army sergeant -- your driver."

Another incredible piece of Vietnamese logic, Yu Lee thought to himself. Leaping off his bed, Mac started to protest. The captain raised his hand and halted him in mid-leap. This was fast becoming an established negotiating stance among army officers, Yu Lee thought recalling the reaction they had received from the lieutenant at the scene of the accident. Rule number 1: Always deter others from speaking if you wish to win an argument.

A career soldier, who had chalked up thirty years of military service, Captain Dung did not relish his new assignment. He was even less pleased to be holding a right-of-way permit signed by one of the country's most decorated war heroes. He would have preferred not to have been given such a controversial assignment. Worse still, he had no idea how to handle the situation. It would have been easier if the foreigners had perished in the accident. He had said as much at the debriefing with the lieutenant who was much relieved at being stood down from a potentially tricky situation.

Predictably, the accident on National Highway 1 had galvanised all middle-rank officers -- air force and army -- at Marble Mountain Air Base to close ranks. They would stick to the same, fictitious, but official, account of what had happened on the road.

Brandishing a rolled-up sheaf of paper (possibly the travel permit) in a threatening manner Captain Dung stepped forward to address the new arrivals. It was plain from his body language that this openly arrogant captain was not having the best of days.

Puffing out his chest and struggling to find the right words -- in English -- he said his piece: "This report from the...hmm...lieutenant in charge of the convoy...accuses you of stealing government property. It also states," he went on, waving it in front of them, "that you caused the accident that resulted in loss of life. What do you have to say for yourselves?"

It was a baited trap. There was little point getting into a futile confrontation with the captain. It was necessary to find a solution they could all live with. The facts of the incident were indisputable. As usual, this would be about saving face. Being accused of causing an accident from the rear seats of a car was a preposterous notion and everyone involved knew that.

"Captain...if I may please," Yu Lee moved forward demonstratively waving his fan like the principal actor in a 12th century Chinese opera. "Listen with care to what I have to say. An army truck ran us off the road today. Our driver was killed, something we very much regret. And we were badly shaken. No other version of this incident presented by you or the lieutenant is acceptable by us. And I want you to understand captain that if you insist on making these ridiculous assertions General Vo will be informed." With a final swish of his fan, he returned it to the top pocket of his safari suit and went back to his bed, skilfully concluding the first act of the opera. But there was no applause.

Shaken slightly by Yu Lee's aggressive posturing Captain Dung, his face red with anger, had little option but to stand his ground.

But Yu Lee had not finished with him. He played what he thought to be his trump card: "On the other hand," he said getting up from his bed, "if you accept the true account of what happened, and return our permit, we will be on our way and nothing else will be said."

As a bluff it backfired. Captain Dung wasn't in a conciliatory mood: "This document is a forgery, and not a very good one," the captain fired back. He was confused and not thinking clearly. "I do not intend contacting General Vo because we do not trouble our war heroes with such trivial matters," he declared and hurriedly stuffed the permit back into the pocket of his tunic.

Outwardly Yu Lee maintained his composure. The captain's acerbic remarks and arm-waving indicated a lack of confidence. Dung had to know that the general would in all likelihood support Yu Lee and Mackenzie. These two men had to be important, at least to the general, otherwise he would not have afforded them carte blanche protection. It was something the captain had to balance against his present position. This confrontation was about finding a face-saving solution and, at that crucial moment, Yu Lee occupied the high ground.

Just as tension reached boiling point, an elderly doctor slipped into the ward and broke the impasse. Everyone looked in his direction as he approached Captain Dung. The doctor whispered something in the captain's ear. It brought an abrupt end to the proceedings and, possibly, further confrontation.

Still angry, Captain Dung spun around to salute Yu Lee and Mac then turned on his heels and headed for the door: "I am ordered to return to Marble Mountain Air Base. You will stay here with a guard outside the door. I will come back for you tomorrow at noon – with transport," he called over his shoulder as the doctor followed him out of the ward.

"Mr John, I am almost one hundred percent sure this matter will not reach the ears of senior military personnel. I believe the captain just received a message to let go of the matter," Yu Lee told him. "To avoid any further embarrassment I suspect we will be sent back to Ho Chi Minh City and handed over to the secret police along with Dung's version of what happened. That, of course would not fit in with our plans so cannot be allowed to happen."

"What about the general," Mac asked, "won't he have something to say about this?"

"Not if he doesn't find out. We should not get him involved at this stage. General Vo will be informed that the driver lost his life in an accident and he will assume the driver was looking after us when it happened. In other words, the sergeant was carrying out the general's orders.

"The permit will probably be destroyed. We have to accept that. The way this is developing means we must get out of this hospital prison. And we need to do so before the captain returns to collect us at noon tomorrow. There is much to do and we cannot do it in here. Do you agree?"

"I'm way ahead of you on that last point prof. We have to make a run for it."

They had only one lead, but it was a good one. Yu Lee referred to it: "We must find that school near Da Nang that General Vo mentioned in his note. As strange as it may sound, it could come as some relief to the military if we escaped from here. They could allow the issue to die because of the potential embarrassment to all concerned. As I said before, this is all about saving face."

On the other hand, Mac thought to himself, the whole Vietnam army and secret police could be stirred into action. But the professor was probably right; he usually was.

Apart from the guard outside the door they were alone again...except for the man in the bed. Curious about him, Yu Lee drew back the curtain to take a peak. His eyes were closed and heavy breathing suggested he was sleeping soundly.

"Are you sleeping brother," Yu Lee asked in Vietnamese.

"I have been awake ever since you arrived. I remained quiet because I did not want to interfere in your business," he declared, in English.

Mackenzie heard him and, at the same time, noticed the chief petty officer's naval uniform hanging on a curtain rail: "Jesus, Joseph and Mackenzie...not another member of Vietnam's armed forces who speaks good English. So what's your story Chief?"

Propped upright with the help of a couple of pillows, the CPO said he had been in hospital for three weeks: "My head feels better but both of my wrists are sprained and still causing some pain."

"Do you want to tell us what happened?" Yu Lee pulled up a chair. Mac sat on the end of the man's bed.

Though he was in bed it was easy to see their ward mate was taller than the average Vietnamese male. Physically, Chief Petty Officer Phan Quang Minh was ruggedly built. His sunburned face accentuated his brown, piercing eyes, square jaw and high cheekbones.

"I was brought here after a road accident. Unfortunately, my motorcycle was struck from behind by a school bus just outside Da Nang on the Hue road.

"I regained consciousness in a school, my head bandaged. I had a terrible headache. When I got to this hospital my wrists had been bandaged. I do not remember much because my head ached so much. But I do remember one man...American I think...telling me he would take me to a school and from there get help. I was in uniform so he must have contacted a military base in the area. Anyway, I ended up here."

The chief petty officer's chance encounter with an American in central Vietnam was surprising and could prove relevant in the context of their quest. It certainly served to heighten their interest in the tall navy NCO.

In the late 1980s there were very few foreigners in Vietnam; some Asians and a few Brits and French. Most foreigners were from Soviet Bloc countries with close trading links with the country. Yu Lee probed further: "Did you get a good look at this American?"

"Well, I am just guessing he was American. He was definitely a military man -- or had been," the CPO replied. "I noticed regimental tattoos on both forearms...a shield with crossed rifles I think."

"For a man who butted heads with a school bus your memory held up well," Mac smiled, impressed with the CPO's ability to stay focused throughout his ordeal. "Do you remember anything else?"

"I saw the tattoos when he carried me into the school. By then I was feeling a bit better. He was a tall, well-built man and had what looked like a hunting knife strapped to his belt," Minh added.

Chief Petty Officer Minh's powers of observation and obvious self-discipline were impressive. Here was an alert and bright young man; very much on the ball especially for someone who had been hit by a bus.

"We are interested in learning more about this big man if you can think back," Mac said, impatiently pacing back and forth at the end of the CPO's bed. But before that, let's talk more about this hospital. The guard on the door...is he for us or was he here before we arrived?"

"He is here because of me. When I am discharged from this place, I will be taken before a military tribunal and tried as a deserter. I will be found guilty of course. When I was turned over to the MP's I was...how do you say...absent without permission to leave."

Mackenzie moved a little closer. "You mean AWOL...absent without leave...on the run from your unit, right? So what did you do, shoot some poor bastard?"

"No Mr John," Minh said screwing up his eyes forcing a deep frown. "I am in trouble because I did not shoot some poor bastard as you put it. I refused to shoot."

"Brother Minh," Yu Lee interjected, "perhaps you could you start from the beginning and tell us everything that happened?"

Minh described his duties as a crew member of the Vietnam People's Navy Coast Guard operating fast patrol boats from Marble Mountain Marine Base. "Our base is ten kilometres south of Da Nang and Marble Mountain Air Base," he said, "and one of our routine duties includes intercepting refugees trying to leave Vietnam in small boats."

"You mean boatpeople right?" Mac asked.

Thinking back to his last UNHCR meeting in Hong Kong, Mac recalled a UN report that three-hundred migrants a day were coming ashore in Hong Kong in addition to those who made it to Thailand, Malaysia or the Philippines.

It was the task of the CPO's naval patrol, Mr Minh explained, to intercept small craft and then return runaways to Da Nang. "Most refugees are from the South, including middle class people from Saigon. They carry forged ID's and travel over a thousand kilometres by road to sheltered coves on the Da Nang coast. They spend one or two days in safe houses waiting for fishing junks or trawlers to take small groups into international waters. The boatpeople, as you call them Mr John, take a chance they will be picked

202

up in sea lanes and taken to foreign ports but it does not always work out like that."

Mac was aware of the size and scale of the "boat people" problem because his company was fully engaged in organising flights from Hong Kong to Hanoi returning "economic migrants" to Vietnam.

"But what's bugging me is what the hell has this to do with you going AWOL? Mac asked.

"During my last trip around a month ago we intercepted a fishing trawler south of China's Hainan Island. It was dangerously overloaded with men, women and children. They had embarked at Da Nang and their trawler had hugged the coast for a while before rounding Hainan to head for Hong Kong."

"So what happened?"

"Their leaders resisted our offer of a towline and ignored instructions to come about. The lieutenant commanding our patrol boat instructed me to order my men to open fire on everyone in the vessel. I refused."

"Jesus, that's unbelievable," Mac said studying the vexed expression on Minh's face.

"Again he instructed me to order my men to open fire. Again I refused. How could I carry out such an order? Those people were my brothers and sisters and there were many children aboard."

Yu Lee could picture the horrific scene: "You must have known that refusing to obey orders would place you in serious trouble."

"I was aware of that brother, but I did not join the navy to fire on my own people and I would never do that.

Yes, I was relieved of active duty, restrained in leg irons and placed under close arrest until our vessel docked at Da Nang."

"This is bloody incredible, almost unbelievable..." Mac repeated becoming increasingly angry. "And what the hell happened to the trawler?"

"The lieutenant gave my men a direct order to shoot at everyone on board. They did as ordered and then scuttled the trawler so no-one would know what happened."

The men fell silent for a moment. Minh would never get over the incident. Yu Lee and Mackenzie felt sick to their stomachs at the CPO's graphic and shocking description of life -- and death -- in the South China Sea.

"It's easy to see why Minh decided to go AWOL when he had the opportunity," Mac whispered.

"Yes. Any sane man would have done the same," Yu Lee readily agreed.

With help from a couple of subordinates, Minh told how he was able to remove the leg irons and make a break on his motorcycle. "Well, that is when the accident occurred and I ended up here. So, to answer your question, Mr John, the guard on the door is to make sure I do not break out of here."

So that's how it was. And who would argue that Minh's actions were not warranted, indeed admirable? It was not their place to pass judgment on the Chief's actions. But it was their responsibility, as well as good manners, to share with him the reason for their appearance at the hospital.

"Under such trying circumstances Chief, I would say your actions were commendable and we thank you for bringing us into your confidence," Mac said firing up a cigarette he had found in the side locker by his bed. The CPO declined the offer of a smoke.

"You probably heard the earlier exchange with Captain Dung. So, now I will tell you why we are sharing this ward with you. It's like this...we are searching for two Americans who served in Vietnam during the war. They stayed behind when the Americans pulled out in '73. One or both may be working at a school near Da Nang. There can't be many schools in that area with foreign workers and even fewer Americans the way we figure it. The reason for our search is something we are not at liberty to disclose – not yet anyway. But it has nothing to do with educating young people."

"It is like this brother Minh," Yu Lee said picking up the story. "It is very important to a lot of people to find these men quickly. Their actions could damage efforts to integrate Vietnam into the international community. I ask you to try to appreciate the importance of what we are doing even though we cannot give you all the details -- not at the moment anyway."

"We have a contract and must fulfil it to succeed in our assignments," Mac stressed, "and from what you have told us you could be of some help. And we would value your contribution."

"How do you think I could assist you?" The CPO was interested, at the same time thinking of getting help to escape.

"Well, to begin with, you could start by remembering anything you can about the school," Mac suggested, "such as its exact location. Your accident may turn out to be the lucky break we've been looking for, no pun intended." He laughed at his own joke. Chief Petty Officer Minh looked on confused; His English was good but Mac's little joke went right over his head.

Turning to plump up his pillow the CPO stared up at the ceiling trying to recall details of the accident. "The school is somewhere off the Da Nang-Hue road...nearer to Da Nang I think. There was a side road I remember...narrow but paved. There was something written in French on a big iron gate...it said 'L'Ecole'..."

Yu Lee interrupted him: "Do you remember if it was L'Ecole des Filles?"

"Not sure...I saw the name 'L'Ecole' with 'Da Nang' below it. I also remember seeing a few girls...young women really...wearing white *ao dai*. As all schoolgirls in Vietnam wear white *ao dai* so I assumed they were from the school."

Could this be the school they were searching for? And could it lead them to American William Petroni? CPO Minh's information appeared to be in line with that given by General Vo but the chief's account of events begged verification. After all he had received a serious blow to the head. And there were lots of girls' schools in Vietnam.

Mac rummaged through his bedside locker and, with a modicum of joy, retrieved two packs of Marlboro cigarettes! Joy! No cigars unfortunately.

Yu Lee was anxious to press on. "John, we must investigate this school," he said out of earshot of CPO Minh.

"And we must get the hell out of this place tonight. And let me tell you something...I really would like to have Mr Minh on board," Mac said in a low whisper as he stubbed out his cigarette. "Look at it this way: He is AWOL, in deep *kimchi* in my view. He will face a truck load of grief when they get him back to base. His best move is to throw his lot in with us."

Together they walked over to Minh's bed to spell it out. The CPO saw them coming; he had been doing some of his own thinking: "Brother, please answer something for me. Captain Dung mentioned a General Vo. Was he referring to General Nguyen Van Vo, one of our national heroes?"

"That's right and I am pleased you asked. General Vo is an old friend of mine and a former compatriot of my father," Yu Lee answered. "He gave us our letter of authorisation and is helping us because he believes it is the right thing to do for the country."

Beaming with satisfaction, the chief petty officer laid back on his bed. It was just what he wanted to hear: "I am a great admirer of General Vo. He is a true nationalist and an inspiration to many people – myself included. It was his brave show of patriotism during the French time that inspired me to fight hard during my time with the Vietnam Peoples' Navy.

"I also studied and followed Uncle Ho's teachings on nationalism which you will know were supported by General Vo. His dreams were my dreams for a new Vietnam. That's why I fought against the Americans."

"Correct me if I'm wrong chief," Mac interjected, "but isn't all that in the past?"

"To me, Mr John, everything about Vietnam is in the past. We have been occupied and colonised for over a thousand years and have nothing to show for it. I served and fought so this country would become strong with a united people ready to build a future for our children," he added grimly, every single word tinged with heartfelt emotion.

"Instead, what do we have? Totally unqualified people running the government and our armed forces; a corrupt police force and state officials; drug problems, a total lack of planning...I could go on..." Minh was right and it was his prerogative – even birth right -- to state as much.

"I am leaving this place tonight," Minh announced almost as though his soapbox speech had helped make up his mind. "I have an escape plan worked out. If I stay here I will be tried and found guilty as a deserter and for disobeying a direct order. In Vietnam that means a court martial and at least ten years hard labour. It could be worse; a firing squad or life imprisonment. I will not wait around to find out which."

When it came to formulating an escape plan, the duo had to accept that CPO Minh had stolen a march on them: "I guess you have been planning this for a few days Mr Minh," Mac said. "So let me ask you something. Do you have a family...a wife...children perhaps, to go home to?"

"Just my parents; they are still alive. You need to understand that I do not just want to get out of this hospital; I want to get right out of Vietnam. I have had enough," he added with total resignation.

"Can we join forces?" Mac asked.

"If you wish to join me I will help you escape. But I want something in return."

"What do you have in mind?"

"I need your help to get to America where I can start a new life. I am thirty-six years old and have my whole life ahead of me. I do not see a future for me in Vietnam. I want to live in a free society where I can get married and start a family."

"Anything else?" Mac enquired.

"I want one thousand American dollars...my fee for helping you get out of here and for taking you to the school to find the Americans. I need money to fund my escape and get started in America."

The requests were not unreasonable. There was no doubt the United States would be sympathetic to CPO Minh's situation given his recent, disturbing incident at sea. There was also a good chance the IOM would profile him as a political refugee supporting the prospect of asylum in the States. His was a compelling case to escape persecution. It would not be difficult to enlist Colonel Nathan's support. And Minh would make a fine addition to the team; his expertise and local knowledge would add great value to their assignment.

"I learnt a lot when I was patrolling for refugee boatpeople. And that is how I will escape," he added, feeling better knowing he had support from the others. "I will make my escape from Da Nang port which I know well. Wherever I end up I will seek permission to go to the United States and give officials your names. I will put my trust in both of you."

"I guess we have a deal Mr Minh," Mac announced leaning forward his hand outstretched.

Yu Lee was delighted at the way their brief relationship was developing.

"Brother, we will do everything we can to help you get to America. You have a good case and we know how to present it. Now, if I may ask, just how do we get out of this hospital?"

"That part of my plan is simple. The guard on this ward will be relieved at 2300. The new guard takes coffee before settling into his chair for a six-hour work-shift. At 2330 hours I will overpower the incoming guard, take his uniform and leave him tied up here in my bed."

"You make it sound very easy," Mac said, impressed by Minh's confidence though slightly sceptical of achieving a successful outcome.

"I did say it was simple Mr John. And that is why it will work. The guards are older men sent to guard military hospitals after being stood down from active service. What I mean is they do not do the sort of things I did when I was in active service," Minh added.

"Are you saying you've had special ops training?" Mac asked hoping for an affirmative response.

"Let me put it this way: I have attended many courses in combat training for special operations," Minh said matter-of-factly. "Apart from being a dive instructor in the navy I am also a Vovinam Viet Vo Dao black belt. I was Navy champion for two years running and I taught Vovinam to new recruits."

Mackenzie stared at him, eyebrows raised, totally confused. "What the hell is Vovinam-Viet Vo Dao if I might ask?"

Yu Lee came to Mac's rescue: "It is a martial art form that started in the late thirties when Vietnam was under French rule. In those days young men in Vietnam were given a choice: follow the way of the French colonialists or join the revolution against them. Am I right about this brother?"

The chief petty officer nodded.

"That is all well and good professor," Mac interjected, "but what the hell has that to do with Vovinam?"

"We adapted Vovinam as a martial art in competitions and in the armed forces," CPO Minh explained. "For example Vovinam can be practiced with or without weapons such as sticks or swords. In most martial arts there is either a hard approach or soft approach. With Vovinam we recognise the need for both."

Mackenzie was still not convinced: "I'm not sure I follow you."

"Let me see if I can explain: I follow the theory of yin-yang by practising my fighting skills in a hard and soft way? I can subdue an opponent using both my physical and mental abilities even against someone who is armed. I disarm without killing."

Yu Lee had a question: "I understand what you say...but am I also correct in thinking that one important principle of Vovinam is to accept discipline without question?"

Mackenzie tried hard to follow the exchange but found himself lost in a fog of confusion.

Yu Lee had to make his point: "If that is the case then you not only disobeyed a direct order from your superior, you also broke a Vovinam principle...am I right?"

"Yes, but I was taught -- and taught my students -- in challenging circumstances to try to make intelligent choices. That is also a Vovinam principle. In my view, my refusal to shoot unarmed people was correct; an intelligent judgement on my part. I have to acknowledge, however, that my superiors did not agree."

Mac had to admire Minh for sticking to his principles: "You broke the rules, I guess for a good reason. I can understand that. But to get back to the present, just how will you handle the guard on the door? What about your wrists?"

"I will overpower the incoming guard. He will be unconscious for several hours but will fully recover. Before we leave, I will place the guard in my bed and draw the curtains. Do not worry about my wrists," he added, "I am aware of my physical limitations.

"I will wear the guard's uniform and escort both of you out of the hospital grounds. You will wear doctors' gowns to look like physicians. If I am challenged at the gate I will say I am escorting you to another hospital to perform an urgent operation. The guards on the main gate change regularly and I am sure nobody will recognise me."

"What about the night nurses doing their rounds?" Mackenzie wanted Minh's plan to be watertight:

"There is only one night nurse. He comes on duty at 1800 and always checks the ward around 2230, hands out medication, and then goes to the nurses' room to sleep." It seemed Minh had covered every eventuality. He had done his homework thoroughly and come up with a credible escape plan.

"OK, I agree your plan is simple," Mac nodded approvingly, "and simple plans are usually the best. What do you think prof?"

"I agree," Yu Lee said, "so let us make sure nobody is killed or injured in the process. But where do we go when we get out of here? Have you given any thought to that?" His question was not aimed at anyone in particular.

Minh also had that covered: "I know of a safe house near Da Nang unless you have a better idea."

"What about transportation?" Mac asked anxious to avoid any last minute hitches.

"Once our absence is discovered, alarms will go off," Minh replied, "and there will be a countrywide search – at least for me. I do not know whether anyone will be chasing you. To answer your question Mr John, we will use cyclos. And we can find a change of clothing at the safe house. We will need to get rid of my uniform and your surgical gowns."

"Fair enough," Mac acknowledged, "and in the morning we can make our way to our friend's house in Hoi An."

"Why would we want to go to Hoi An?" Yu Lee asked. "The only person I know in Hoi An is Lily and she may consider us unwelcome in view of recent events."

"I am sure the lovely Mrs Crenshaw has a shoot-on-sight policy where we are concerned," Mac conceded, "but who else can we turn to for help in this part of the country? Do you have a better idea prof?"

"Let me think about that my friend. We would surely need a very good excuse for getting her involved in our problems again although I must admit she did me a great favour by visiting the rehabilitation centre in Da Nang."

"Another important thing to keep in mind professor: Lily told me she had some teaching experience in California. This could be useful if she can be persuaded to join us."

———

Mac distracted the guard by offering him a cigarette as CPO Minh delivered a short, sharp chop to the man's neck with the heel of his right hand. He was unconscious before he hit the floor. Yu Lee expressed concern but Minh assured him the man would not suffer any long-term effects. "He will recover in three or four hours, but he will have a sore neck for a few days."

That should give us enough time, Mac thought, as he helped carry the unconscious guard into the ward. "I guess your hands are okay now, right Chief?"

Minh offered a curt nod as he struggled to relieve the guard of his uniform: "I will hide my navy uniform in one of those pillowcases at the nurses' station." With some difficulty he squeezed into the guard's uniform. It was slightly short in the arms and legs but would do.

Strapping on the guard's M20 pistol (a Chinese variation, he noted, of the Takarev TT-22 handgun he was used to) Minh picked up the AK 47 propped against the ward door. He glanced over his shoulder to see Mac staring at him: "Jesus Christ. I hope you don't have to use those." Mackenzie was only half-serious; he knew full well that to pass as a guard Mr Minh had to look the part and that meant being armed.

Putting on a freshly-laundered doctor's gown, Mac followed Yu Lee to the exit.

Taking one more glance around the ward to make sure everything was shipshape CPO Minh drew the curtain around his bed, checked that the guard was sleeping soundly, and followed the others along the corridor. Outside all was quiet apart from a dog barking somewhere in the night.

It was just before midnight when the guard at the outer gate lowered his newspaper for a better view of the approaching men.

Trying to appear alert, as the trio drew closer, the guard figured one doctor to be Russian, the other Vietnamese. Observing nothing untoward he waved them through the gate without a word. Minh saluted and the three men left the hospital compound. Later, in the duty logbook, the guard recorded that two doctors exited the hospital grounds escorted by a guard.

The balmy night air was refreshing after the stale atmosphere of the hospital. It was good to be free. Boarding two cyclos they set off for the safe house. Later they would hire a car to take them to Hoi An. Yu Lee did not have a better idea though he remained apprehensive about the kind of reception they could expect from Mrs Crenshaw.

———

The "safe house" CPO Minh had sourced was perfect for a short stay. Owned by one of Minh's trusted friends, a former naval colleague, the boutique hotel offered thirty, good-sized rooms. Its secluded location in a quiet cul-de-sac afforded good security.

Following a brief meeting with the owner they were shown into a large, twin-bedded room. A third bed was added so all three could stay in one room for the night. They would take turns watching the street outside.

"I served with the owner, he is a good man," Minh said in the privacy of the room. He did not disclose his friend's name. "But we need to stay alert in case the local police check the registration records. We have not been registered for obvious reasons, so we must keep a low profile."

Mac and Yu Lee had disposed of their doctors' gowns before entering the hotel. Minh's AK47, the barrel covered with a towel, and sidearm were in his navy rucksack. The weapons would only be used, he assured the others, if there was no alternative. Well, so far so good, thought Yu Lee who had a distinct loathing of firearms – any kind of weapon come to that.

By anyone's standard, their clean getaway from the military hospital was a commendable achievement – "an example of great teamwork," as the professor put it: "We are grateful to you Brother," Yu Lee announced while enthusiastically patting CPO Minh on his back. "It was a simple but good plan but we could not have got out of there without your able assistance. For that we are very grateful."

The CPO held onto Yu Lee's hand: "I know you are concerned about that guard I put to sleep. I promise he will fully recover. I am less sure about Vietnam's armed forces however; many senior officers are going to be very upset when they find out how we made our escape."

216

"That's probably an understatement Chief and it's something to chew over tomorrow. Right now, it's time to call it a day," Mac said encouraging his colleagues to turn in. "Tomorrow, we can review the plan, with your welcome input Mr Minh. You did a great job today and it's good to have you on board. I will take first watch," he offered as he switched off the light.

———

It was midday before anyone stirred. Mac drew aside the curtains to check on activities outside. Overnight rain had left the streets wet otherwise all was quite. The sky was overcast; the hotel owner said more rain was forecast.

For the most part, sleep had eluded all three men who had taken turns keeping watch on the street for any signs of unwelcome activity. It looked peaceful enough. But, by now search units from the army, navy and secret police could be combing the area for three men who had brutally clubbed a guard. Or the whole incident could be forgotten, swept under the carpet. Whatever action the authorities took, they had to remain alert and on their toes.

The second phase of their plan required one more night at the hotel before travelling to Hoi An to reunite with Lily Crenshaw and attempt to enlist her support – yet again!

Friday, July 22, 1988: Hoi An, Central Vietnam

The ancient city of Hoi An, situated in Vietnam's picturesque south-central, east coast province of Quang Nam, looks out over the South China Sea. A small conurbation, it has an impressive history as a regional trading post dating back to the sixteenth century. And as far back as the first century, Hoi An, formerly known as Champa City, boasted the biggest harbour in Southeast Asia. The Champas were admired as proficient sailors who constructed excellent, oceangoing vessels whose proven hull design, local folk say, is still used by Hoi An's celebrated boat-builders.

The house occupied by Lily Crenshaw's parents, in the older part of Hoi An, was not difficult to find. For ten thousand dong, a cheerful roadside vendor eagerly directed their taxi driver to a small, detached residence bordered by a small, tidy garden.

Clearly caught wrong-footed, Lily frowned disapprovingly as she watched the men approach the front door. Balancing mixed emotions, she couldn't decide whether or how to greet them.

Whereas she would always be grateful to both of them for their invaluable assistance there was no escaping the fact that their presence brought back unpleasant memories of recent events. Stacked up against common-sense, however, she had to concede that what had happened to Kim was no fault of theirs, or hers.

In the end, hands on hips in a threatening pose along with an expression of feigned shock and defiance on

218

her face, she received them. To the men, her whole demeanour appeared less than welcoming. I guess we couldn't have expected anything else Mac seemed to indicate in a sideways glance towards Yu Lee.

But, hold on a minute...the dynamic duo had a third member with them; someone she didn't know. Lily's curiosity was roused, she wanted to learn more. A faint smile replaced her scowl. Finding her manners, she invited all three into the house. Further judgement as to the men's arrival on her doorstep would be held in abeyance until she'd listened to what they had to say. But it would have to be good.

"It is a pleasure to see you again Miss Lily." As always, Yu Lee was sincere in his greeting. "We have missed you, haven't we Mr John?"

Mac's forced smile barely answered Yu Lee's question. He was willing to bet the farm his own real-estate value was at an all-time low in Mrs Crenshaw's reckoning. How could it be otherwise after everything she'd been through?

"That's all well and good professor," she said sourly, "but I am not sure if I am ready for either of you again.

"But, I am forgetting my manners...I see you have brought a friend with you," she observed in a more engaging tone, her eyes surveying the tall, handsome man standing before her. CPO Minh's chiselled features, rugged arms and shoulders, close-cropped hair and dark brown eyes gave him the look of an Asian movie star. His appearance on the scene had, to some extent, tempered Lily's initial and uncomfortable feeling of being reunited with Yu Lee and John Mackenzie. But it was early days.

"Have we met somewhere before?" she asked almost teasingly and in heavily-accented Vietnamese. No one could misconstrue the ominous glint in her eyes. For Mac, it brought to mind their first encounter in the check-in line at Bangkok Airport recalling how had had turned to see who was tapping on his shoulder. He had been confronted by the same mischievous look -- irresistible but full of danger.

The chief petty officer smiled back shaking his head. "I don't think so. I am sure I would remember if we had. I am happy to make your acquaintance Miss Lily and thank you for inviting me into your home."

She wasn't to know that Minh was indifferent to her teasing; a personal discipline he honed to perfection before and during his time in the navy. Whenever he was engaged in an important task, he worked to shut out distractions. Right now he was focused on the task ahead. Yes, he did consider her attractive but he was not about to show his feelings; at least not until they had been properly introduced.

Wisely, Mac kept a low profile. Displaying similar indifference, he ignored the chemical reaction that was clearly developing between Minh and Lily – on her part anyway.

Acquiring Lily's support was all that mattered to him at this particular juncture. He had no doubt that her experience as a qualified teacher would be very useful for the next phase of their assignment. Whatever happened they must not upset her again. Mac had already conceded to Yu Lee that his aside comments and repeated witticisms sometimes backfired. But it was something he couldn't control particularly where women were concerned. It wasn't even in his nature to try.

Lily introduced the visitors to her mother. Although only fifty-something, mother looked at least ten years older, another example of how the ravages of war can accelerate the ageing process.

With a distinct lack of enthusiasm, mother gazed at each of the three men in turn, not clear why they were visiting her daughter and not particularly interested.

"This is Mr John," Lily explained. "I told you how he came to my rescue in Bangkok. Mother stared at Mackenzie, hardly impressed with what she saw.

"My mother does not understand English Mr John, sorry about that. I can see you're surprised at what you see before you. I felt the same when I got here. And I can't pretend I am having a great time either."

When Lily got to Hoi An she found the situation at home was not as she had expected. Her father passed away five years earlier. "I wasn't sure whether to be sad or angry at not being told before. I just cried for a few days after I got here.

"I was so stressed out after just a few weeks back in Vietnam I began to wonder if I'd done the right thing." At least her grandparents were alive, she added, and living with her mother. "They provide some comfort for her though both are in poor health," she sighed as if resigned to living in a world of bad news.

The men felt they were intruding on Lily's privacy. The atmosphere changed, becoming quite awkward and uncomfortable. It was beginning to look as though they'd picked a bad moment to ask for help.

"We are all very sorry to learn of your problems Lily," Mac told her. "When we met in Bangkok I know you never expected anything like this and I'm sorry it's turned out this way."

"It gets worse, Mr John," she said through tear-filled eyes, "my grandfather, who is resting in the bedroom, has stomach cancer. My grandmother is so worried she hardly leaves his side."

Lily Crenshaw had been in Hoi An for only a short while but had already decided it was too long. She missed everything she loved about America, particularly the freedom and ability to do almost anything she wanted. But how could she just get up and leave a house full of sick family members?

That wasn't all: Lily's mother was suffering from breast cancer. There was hope she could make a full recovery given the right treatment but Lily did not know if Vietnam's medical facilities were up to it. At the very least she figured she had to get her mother to the United States.

Pulling herself together she turned to Yu Lee and Mackenzie, two recently-found friends who had helped her in her hour of need and who had now driven over a thousand kilometres to see her. The reason for their visit must be important she figured. Might it have something to do with Kim? As the thought entered her head, she realised that Yu Lee must still be hurting from the loss of his cherished friend.

Thirty minutes ticked by before Mac felt it was appropriate to get to the point of their visit.

"Lily, since we last met quite a lot has happened to us in a short space of time. The shorthand version is we were involved in a road accident and ended up in a military hospital. With Mr Minh's help we escaped and now we're on the run from the military and the police."

Although her mother did not understand English, Lily felt it was better to take her to the bedroom. She could then give the men her undivided attention; she owed them that much. And they had brought Mr Minh into her life and that had brightened up an otherwise miserable day.

Yu Lee took his time bringing Lily up to speed with events, recounting everything that happened after learning of Kim's death; the disappearance of Linh; their meeting with General Vo in Saigon; the road accident; their time in the military hospital and their chance meeting with Mr Minh. He omitted the part about Officer Nguyen; that could wait for now.

"So you see Lily, we both believe that Mr Minh's decision to help us will improve our chances of finding Linh and tracking down the Americans," Mac added.

Lily listened with mounting interest, glancing approvingly towards CPO Minh each time his name was mentioned. What a man. Mac didn't miss the sparkle in her eyes; again it reminded him of their first meeting at Bangkok airport. That seemed like an age ago.

Yu Lee picked up the conversation. "As Mr John pointed out we have to find two American ex-servicemen who may be hiding out somewhere in this area. When we met up with Mr Minh at the military hospital near Da Nang he told us about his traffic accident and the help he received from someone who is of interest to us. This man has links with a nearby school. It is a promising lead and we must follow it."

Mackenzie outlined the accusations levelled against the Americans including trafficking in girls and drugs. "Apart from criminal activities their actions could seriously compromise future relationships between Vietnam and the United States. So, as you can see Lily, it is important we track them down so that our American friends can neutralise their activities asap."

"But these guys could be anywhere in Vietnam," Lily countered, placing her hands to each side of her head as she contemplated the size of the task.

"You are right of course," Yu Lee conceded, "but there are few Americans in Vietnam because of the embargo and lack of diplomatic relations. So this is a lead we need to follow."

"The prof is correct," Mac said. "And we have to bear in mind that the U.S. is discouraging its nationals from travelling here unless they are *Viet Kieu* and, like you, have good family reasons for doing so. So I would say that any American ex-servicemen found in this locality are probably throwbacks from the War."

"To get to the point of our visit Lily, we need your help," Yu Lee said looking directly at her.

To the men's surprise, she did not react angrily: "I am not sure how I can be of help but if what you ask is reasonable I will think about it but only if you help get my mother to the United States. She does not have a passport, even her house registration documents and other papers, such as her birth certificate, are missing."

The men had not expected such a positive response. Now it was a question of gauging Colonel Nathan's reaction to another request for a U.S. passport.

224

Would another request for one more passport be one too many? Probably not, was Mackenzie's view: "Don't' worry Lily, I will ask the U.S. consulate in Hong Kong to help your mother; and that's a promise."

"Prof, the way things are developing…I mean with General Vo involved, plus CPO Minh on board to some extent…and now Lily about to assist us and so forth…Well, I've been giving some thought to what happens after we find these two retards."

"Don't we just report that back to Colonel Nathan? You know, locate and report."

"Well that's the basis of our agreement. But look at it from the Americans' point of view. At the very least they will want to isolate these guys. And these days they can't just send in the marines or the C.I.A."

"What are you saying Mr John?" Yu Lee was puzzled. "You aren't suggesting we overpower them and take them with us to Hong Kong are you?"

"The longer these guys stay in their present roles, assuming we are correct in our assumptions, the more dangerous it will be for reconciliation talks to take hold. But to answer your question I am not up to blowing the heads off these guys and I don't suppose you are either professor, am I right?"

"I would not take too kindly to being asked to kill another human being if that is what you are asking Mr John. That I have to leave to someone else as you well know."

"Fortunately we don't have to face that prospect at this moment in time. I just want you to know I have been thinking ahead and I am concerned we may have to do a bit more than locate-and-report."

"I have been thinking ahead also. We still have to find Linh."

"Yep, that too prof.

The chief petty officer had watched the exchange from a distance but chose not to intervene. But Mac was keen for Minh to get more involved and went over to speak with him.

"I know you will agree that we have to help Lily. And we have to deal with the two Americans if we locate them as planned and..."

CPO Minh interrupted, "I guessed you and Yu Lee were discussing that point. I have been thinking, and worrying, about it also. I will help you find them, even help catch and restrain them but I will not kill anyone unless it is unavoidable. This much you already know Mr John."

"You are a good man to have on the team Mr Minh and I accept what you say. By the way, I am warming to your idea of using a boat to get out of Vietnam."

"Does that mean you have a plan Mr John?" he asked, smiling at Lily as she came back into the room. She was immediately impressed by Minh's show of good manners when he jumped to his feet and offered her his chair. It was something that had not featured greatly in her life in recent times.

"Chief...as I said, I have been thinking about what you said...escaping from Da Nang by boat. No, I don't have a firm plan yet but I think an escape into the shipping lanes to the east is worth further study. We will need outside assistance of course and this is where Yu Lee and I can get help."

Yu Lee turned to Lily: "If you agree to help us we will find a way to get your mother to the United States. I have been thinking about your situation. You were repatriated through the IOM programme so it should be possible for you to nominate family members to join you in America using your present residential status. We can check on that for you."

That was what she wanted to hear: "In that case gentlemen," she said, arms held high above her head in a submissive expression, "tell me what you want me to do?"

"Well, for a start Lily," Mackenzie replied, "you can borrow somebody's graduation gown and get ready to go back to school."

Monday July 25, 1988: L'Ecole des Filles near Da Nang

"You must believe me that today is an auspicious day," Yu Lee announced to the others, "therefore it is a good day to visit Mr Minh's school near Da Nang."

The professor's long-held belief concerning Chinese traditional wisdom was not challenged because no one really knew how to. On previous occasions, Mackenzie had made it clear he couldn't care less one way or the other. He always disassociated himself from such assertions. In his view it was another example of superstitious nonsense on the part of his good friend who could be unbearably Chinese at times.

"Whatever you say prof; I'm sure you know what you're talking about," Mac answered with total indifference.

As it turned out, it was a dry and sunny Monday with relatively low humidity so, as far as the weather was concerned the day had got off to an auspicious start. Everyone could agree with that.

Lily confirmed her agreement with the team plan but reserved the right to remain sceptical. At Yu Lee's request, she handed over some of Kim's belongings recovered from Da Nang. For both of them, it briefly rekindled bitter thoughts of that fateful day at the rehabilitation centre.

Living in rural Vietnam was fast becoming a lost cause for Lily considering her family's circumstances. She would prefer to move on, possibly returning to the States. But leaving Vietnam before finding a way to take care of her sick family was not an option. For now, her best option was to stay in touch with Yu Lee and John Mackenzie.

And there was the question of the handsome chief petty officer to whom she was attracted? Was there a place for him in her life?

"At least we'll be able to scratch one neighbourhood school from your list professor if this turns out to be a wild goose chase," Lily said sardonically as she stuffed a small bag with personal things including the photograph of Linh as a baby which she'd removed from Kim's belongings.

"I am sure you're right about that Lily," Yu Lee conceded not really appreciating the sarcasm laced in her remark.

"Listen everyone: I am becoming increasing concerned about Linh," Yu Lee announced to the others. He felt they should be making better progress. He had in mind a mental picture of Gervasoni nervously pacing back and forth at the Landmark Hotel in Bangkok waiting for news of his daughter.

His redirected his attention as a heavily-dented private car, hired by Yu Lee from the village, pulled up outside Lily's house its noisy engine spluttering indignantly. It was time to get started. Chief Petty Officer Minh slipped into the front seat to help with directions. The others piled into the back seat, Lily sandwiched between Yu Lee and Mackenzie. She would have preferred to be sitting next to Mr Minh. Mac caught the glint in her eyes.

Nobody said much during the journey, because there was a lot to think about. After an hour's drive they pulled up in a quiet lane a short distance from the main Da Nang-Hue road.

"This place looks familiar...I am sure I have been here before," the chief petty officer claimed after looking up and down the lane.

Mac got out of the cab first. Peering down the narrow lane he pointed to what could be a school. A closer look was called for.

The car was hidden underneath the vast canopy of a rain tree; the driver directed to stay with his vehicle. The others moved towards the main gate taking advantage of the natural cover offered by the undergrowth lining the lane. Lily walked the last few steps to the main gate leaving the men concealed behind a dense mulberry bush. From their vantage point they could read the circular sign on the wrought iron gate: "L'Ecole des Filles", on the top half; "Da Nang 1935" on the bottom.

"Jesus, this could be the place we are looking for," Mac whispered to Yu Lee.

"In that case," Yu Lee whispered back, "now is a good time to worry about Mrs Crenshaw. She has reached the gate."

What happened next would have a great influence on the success or failure of the assignment.

Lily rang the bell for a second time, unappreciative of the long distance between the gate and the reception area of the main building. Nor did she notice Yu Lee and Mac slip across the road to the left side of the perimeter fence. They crouched behind dense bushes out of sight from the school. Mr Minh positioned himself to the right of the gate. From the corner of her eye, Lily noticed him slip into the bushes pleased he was part of the team. Everyone was in place.

It would be fair to conclude that the little lady was confident but apprehensive. She had been well briefed by John Mackenzie who had stressed over and over again that flushing out the Americans – if they were there – could be very dangerous for her.

"If you feel someone is getting too suspicious," he insisted, "use your amateur acting skills. Convince them that you are a schoolteacher." Mac had great faith in her acting abilities. And he knew from personal experience she could be very persuasive.

Lily had a mental picture of the tattoos described in detail by CPO Minh. But she had no idea how she was going to persuade total strangers to roll up their sleeves for their bare arms to be examined. She could get lucky. Maybe the guys would be wearing short-sleeved shirts. "Nice tattoos you have there," she thought, smiling to herself as she pondered her likely reaction. Of course it may just turn out to be a girls' school tucked away in the countryside. She would soon find out.

Approaching from his patrol box, a uniformed guard saluted thirty metres from the gate without breaking step. At that same moment Lily spotted a young woman walking towards the gate from what looked like the school's main building. It was a very long walk.

"What do you want?" the woman called out in Vietnamese at the same time dismissing the guard.

"Oh hello, I am looking for work," Lily said as calmly as she could. Her insides were churning but her voice held steady.

"What sort of work?" the young woman had reached the gate and was looking up and down the lane probably for signs of a vehicle or motorcycle.

"Teaching...I am a qualified teacher. My name is Lily Crenshaw...Mrs Crenshaw. Recently I got back from the United States. I taught children at a school in California."

"So why did you come to this school and how did you get here?"

"Someone in Hoi An, near my family's house, suggested I try here. I came by cab. My driver is parked further down the lane." Lily stuck to the script and kept on smiling.

"What sort of teaching did you do in America?"

"Languages...I taught Vietnamese to American kids...ten-, eleven-year-olds. I was hoping there could be teaching vacancies at this school," she said staring through the bars.

"That depends," the young woman said, "I mean I can check for you. I am not in charge here. Please come inside."

The first phase of the plan was on track. Lily made a quick calculation that the school was about two hundred metres from the main gate. She counted the buildings and outhouses along the way. It was a very big place.

"My name is Thien," the young woman said showing Lily into a large room to the left of the main entrance door. "Wait here please. I will fetch the school principal."

The waiting room looked like a classroom. It had desks, chairs, blackboards and books. But where were the pupils?   Peering out of the window she counted several parked cars. As she watched, two men climbed into a silver Mercedes and drove away.   One of the men looked European or American. Maybe the others would get a closer look as the car passed by them.

Miss Thien returned with a man at her side...a tall man. Lily was caught off guard; she had assumed the principal would be female and Vietnamese.   Clearly, the man before her was neither.

"This is Mrs Lily Crenshaw," Thien said. "She return from the United States...is looking for a teaching job."

As directed, Lily sat at one of the small desks, the big man sat on the top table near the blackboard, arms folded across his chest.

"This gentleman is Mr Bill. The principal is busy with visitors."

"Petroni," the big man said without moving from the table, "my name is William Petroni."

Petroni...the name mentioned in General Vo's brief passed to Yu Lee. Is he one of the men they were searching for? Lily swallowed hard.

William Petroni looked long and hard at the school's new visitor. "So Miss Lily, you are looking for a teaching position is that right?" He spoke in English with an American accent. The big man remained seated on the desk, arms still folded across his chest. He was wearing blue jeans, a short-sleeved safari shirt and flip-flops. His arms were tattooed but he was too far away for her to see clearly.

"Yes sir," Lily responded cheerfully. "I came back from California a short while back only to find my mother and grandfather quite ill. I have to take care of them and to get the medical attention they need I have to earn some money." She spoke with conviction but was unsure if he would believe her?

Petroni released a long sigh. It sounded like one more improbable story from another *Viet Kieu*. Sliding off the table he walked towards her. "Well that's just fine and dandy," he said patronisingly. He placed his arm around her shoulders. She flinched briefly. He stared down at her ample chest. "So let's get a few questions out of the way before we go any further."

Lily was nervous. She bit her lip and tried to remain calm. The tone of his voice troubled her and she hated having his arm on her shoulder. But she resolved to stay cool. He was too big to fight off anyway if it came to that. Everything would be alright, she told herself, so long as Thien remained in the room.

"Bring us a couple of coffees," he instructed Thien. "I have a few questions for you," he informed Lily looking her over very carefully.

Lily's good looks and obvious charms had registered with Petroni. "I may be able to find some other use for you as well as teaching," he offered, smiling now.

He was good at that, Thien thought as she prepared the coffees. She had seen it all before.

Yes, Thien knew him all too well. The big American had teamed up with her a few days after she arrived at Madame Ha's school in 1980. He had taken a shine to her and even confided in her on several matters including his arrival in Vietnam after living for a while in Laos at the end of the war. She found it quite strange at the time as he confessed to selling drugs to American servicemen. He must have thought he was on safe ground.

Petroni believed Thien when she told him she left her home near Saigon to find work to feed her family. At twenty-seven years of age she found it difficult competing with younger girls in the bars. Many more women faced the same predicament.

Journeying by bus to Da Nang she sought out Madame Ha. Thien had learnt of this particular girls' school from other women working the bars in downtown Ho Chi Minh City. Now thirty-five, Madame Ha had reassigned her to groom and prepare new arrivals to serve the "school's" clients. Thien's relationship with Petroni was in its eighth year.

Petroni handed Lily a cup of coffee. What her eyes chanced upon, as he did so, made her heart leap. Struggling to cope with a sudden rush of adrenalin she took a few deep breaths. Petroni's forearms were tattooed with a shield with crossed rifles. She looked again to make sure. There was no mistake; Lily was sharing space, and coffee, with the man who assisted CPO Minh when he had his motorcycle accident.

So what about the other American? Had he left the school earlier in the Mercedes? She thought of Mac's advice to act her teaching role and stay cool.

"Drink your coffee Miss Lily. Tell me what you've been up to in the States." Cup in hand, Petroni returned to his former position at the desk. "Thien, I don't need you for now. You can go."

This was a dangerous moment for Lily; how she handled the next few minutes could be crucial. Settling into her acting role, Lily fielded each of Petroni's probing questions: Where did you live in Vietnam during the war? When did you leave the country? Where did you live in the United States...full address? What sort of a place is Venice, Californian? Why did you return to Vietnam and where do you live now?

Apart from her parents' home address, she answered every question truthfully and confidently.

"Okay, Miss Lily that will do for now I guess," Petroni said getting up from the table. As he did so, Lily noticed the top three buttons of Petroni's safari shirt were undone and two dog tags were hanging loose. Why two dog tags? It struck her as odd; she would tell the others.

Pleased with her performance answering all of Petroni's questions, she took a chance and asked permission to take a look around the school. "Perhaps I could meet with some of the students?"

"Not until you meet Madame Ha, the school principal. She might have some questions for you. Follow me Mrs Crenshaw."

Arriving at the principal's office on the first floor Lily stood aside as Petroni knocked on the door. There was no acknowledgement. He knocked again, opened it, and walked in.

It was a little after eleven o'clock, the sun was high in the sky. Looking through the large window Lily noticed two young girls on the school lawns – probably teenagers.

At that moment a short, stout woman entered the office looking dazzling in peacock-blue *ao dai*. She walked over to Lily: "You must be Mrs Crenshaw," she smiled, "please take a seat...you too Mr Bill if you don't mind." Her English was good.

It was difficult to pin down Madame Ha's age. Her smooth, clear skin and jet-black hair, fashioned into a bun on the top of her head, made her look much younger than her sixty-one years.

"Thank you, it's a pleasure to meet you," Lily remained composed as she took a seat across from the school principal. Petroni was to her right. It was important, Lily figured, to maintain the pretence and air of optimism that had got her this far. She had to convince Madame Ha that she was looking for a job and for that she had to be convincing throughout the "interview" if that's what it turned out to be.

"Our school has students aged between five and eleven mostly from expatriate families," Madame Ha announced with more than an ounce of pride. "This school has been run by my family for generations. It has a long history of providing education right back to the French time," she added looking directly at Lily.

If something was going on at the school, other than teaching, every staff member Lily had met so far was doing a good job of covering up. The school appeared to be a genuine place of learning but no five to eleven-year-old students had so far been seen at close quarters. But that was about to change.

Thien knocked on the door and entered the principal's office accompanied by two young girls. They looked to be around ten and six years of age. Madame Ha directed them to stand either side of her: "These children are daughters of the consul general of the Laotian Consulate in Da Nang. We also have children from prominent families based in this area whose fathers work in the petrochemical industry...mostly Russian nationals and some from other Eastern Bloc countries."

Why was Madame Ha trying so hard to impress her when her status was nothing more than a prospective employee?

"Madame Ha, is it alright if I ask the children a question?"

"Please do. Ask Mai." The ten-year-old was gently pushed towards Lily.

"Do you like coming to this school Mai?" Lily asked in English.

"Yes miss, we like it here. Madame Ha and the teachers are very kind to us."

The school principal beamed with delight. Lily smiled politely. If she was going to learn more, she had to take care not to overreact or rush matters. "The children are well-mannered," Lily observed. "I can see why you are so proud of them Madame Ha." Thien guided the children back to their classrooms.

The school took its educational responsibilities seriously, Madame Ha informed Lily. "That aside, I do not mind telling you I have difficulty finding good teaching staff."

If this particular girls' school was a front for something else, keeping up the pretence of running a genuine school would be paramount. Madame Ha seemed to have that under control from what she'd seen so far. To support prostitution or engage in trafficking scams could prove quite difficult if a lot of people were involved. But it wouldn't be impossible for someone who was determined to succeed. In that respect, Madame Ha had impressed Lily.

And it looked as though Lily had impressed Madame Ha: "Why don't you collect your things and return...let's see...next Monday...August 1 I believe that will be. I will give you a class to run and see how you get on. Then we can talk about a permanent post for you." At that she got up from her chair and walked to the window.

"You are welcome to make use of the staff accommodation over there," she said pointing to a long, dormitory-like building at the side of the school's main building. "Come at nine o'clock and please bring with you your teaching credentials."

Petroni was not entirely convinced about Lily but had to accept the principal's decision. He had his doubts and the pained expression on this face spoke volumes. Lily pretended not to notice.

But Madame Ha had noticed. She waited until Lily left the room: "Please do not be concerned, Mr Bill," she told him. "I will keep Mrs Crenshaw confined to school classrooms and the dormitory building, away from other activities."

Later, she would brief her inner coterie to stay clear of the new teacher other than for matters concerning the children's education.

There was no need for her to know what went on behind the scenes, she told Petroni: "Expanding the business is essential Mr Bill, and I want to press on with our plans to set up a similar school in Vung Tao.

"We must keep L'Ecole des Filles functioning in Da Nang as a place of learning. In this respect Lily Crenshaw could be a great help to our plans."

Madame Ha always considered her chance encounter with William Petroni some time back to be fortuitous. The war had provided fertile ground for Petroni to build up a steady supply of opium, heroin and marijuana to sell to American servicemen. Trafficking in young women became a natural extension of the business as she saw it.

From Petroni's point of view it was essential to have a good partner; someone with good connections with the communist cadres running the country. Madame Ha fitted that role perfectly. As partners they were good for each other. But William Petroni was not in agreement with his partner's latest decision to offer Lily Crenshaw a job at the school.

"Madame Ha, I agree with what you say about expanding our business interests. But I have my suspicions about Miss Lily and you should know that I intend to keep a close watch on her."

———

Back in the car Lily debriefed the others. Their initial reaction, similar to Lily, was one of cautious optimism. Perhaps it had all been too easy. That aside, everyone agreed the primary objective had been achieved -- Lily was on the cusp of landing a teaching job at the school. Then she would be able to report from within.

It was a positive start. From now on, any information Lily could pick up as an insider would help frame a plan to deal with the Americans assuming they were the guys they were looking for.

"Why would Petroni be sporting two dog tags?" Mac asked the others.

"I can think of one reason," offered CPO Minh. "Maybe it belonged to a comrade and he's holding on to it as a sort of...how you say...keepsake?"

"Could be. Perhaps he killed someone and is wearing it as a trophy," Mac threw back.

As it turned out, Monday, July 25, 1988 had been an auspicious day after all. Yu Lee had been right about that; he usually was.

———

One week later, promptly at nine o'clock, Lily Crenshaw went back to school to begin her first day teaching English to a class of eleven-year-old girls. Madame Ha scrutinised her teaching diplomas and appeared satisfied. It was made official; Lily was on-board and she was raring to go.

The next two weeks flew by as the little lady worked tirelessly to earn Madame Ha's confidence.

"*Écoute beaucoup e parle peu,*" Yu Lee had told her. *"Listen a lot and speak little."* She followed his advice and kept her mouth shut and her ears open. It paid off because she learnt of plans to open up another, similar school in Vung Tao in southern Vietnam. Each time it came up, the principal said it was to keep up with the expansion of joint ventures in the petrochemical industry.

It was true that more Eastern Bloc nations were establishing cooperative ventures in Vietnam and the

241

media was full of such plans. It meant foreign workers with children had to find suitable schools. For reasons not clear to Lily, Madame Ha said she was thinking of accepting boys as well as girls into the school although this would break with a longstanding tradition. So it was just a girls' school after all.

"You know Miss Lily, this is a very good time to offer teaching services in Vietnam," Madame Ha had told her enthusiastically.

It could also be a great opportunity, Lily thought, for Madame Ha and Petroni to expand any illicit business practices they may be pursuing. And where was the other American? She had not seen another Westerner in the two weeks she'd been at the school.

———

"If Madame Ha and her partners are working to set up another school for drugs and human trafficking," Mac pointed out during a discussion at Lily's place, "it could set back America's plans for reconciliation for months or even years."

"In my humble view as a Vietnamese," CPO Minh interjected, "if the government of Vietnam find out about it and take the view that America is not doing enough to control its own citizens it could bring about a halt to any form of discussions. Unless of course it turns out that some government officials are also involved."

"If you are all correct," Lily chipped in, "and let's assume for one minute that you are, then don't we need to try to get the Americans out as soon as possible?"

"Yes Lily, but at the moment it all amounts to a whole lot of 'ifs'. And our brief, don't forget, is to locate-and-report. We need hard proof before the U.S. can act," Mac responded. "These guys will have to be removed but that can't be done until we have proof the school is definitely dealing drugs and trafficking in girls."

"In that case, and if I am to find out more of what's going on," Lily responded, "then I need to befriend Petroni's girlfriend Thien. She has already reached out to me. By the way, she is not happy in her life. I think I can learn more from her. I accept that's a few more 'ifs' to add to the mix though."

Just the same everyone agreed that in just over two weeks Lily had done an outstanding job compiling a dossier on life inside the "school" – at least the educational part. There were around one hundred girls (no boys) aged between five and eleven, mostly children of expatriates. The children attended school five days a week arriving and departing by school buses or in private vehicles. No one stayed overnight.

"As we have already discussed we need proof Lily," Yu Lee reminded her, "then we'll have something to present to Colonel Nathan in Hong Kong."

———

On Friday, August 19th all classrooms emptied at L'Ecole des Filles as the nation celebrated the August Revolution of 1945. On that day, under the leadership of the Communist Party of Vietnam, citizens from all parts of the country rose to seize power and establish the first worker-farmer state in Southeast Asia signalling an era of independence and freedom for the entire country.

To celebrate this important, gazetted holiday, the school closed for three days. All but a few staff enjoyed leave of absence; students were normally on holiday at weekends anyway. A few staff members remained at school including Lily and Thien.

Lily seized the opportunity to get closer to Thien.

"Did I tell you that oolong tea is my favourite," she called to her across the dormitory, "would you like to join me sister?"

Thien admired Lily because she was a good listener and she loved learning about life in the United States. It reminded her of an American pilot she knew during the war.

Madame Ha and Petroni had already left the school. On their departure they informed Lily about their plans to spend the national holiday in the South checking on construction progress at the school in Vung Tao. Madame Ha said it as if there could be a teaching role for Lily at the new school.

"Why are you staying at the school this weekend Miss Lily and not going home for the national holiday?" Thien asked sitting on the edge of Lily's bed nursing her oolong tea.

During occasional chats at school, mostly in English because that's how Thien wanted it, Thien had made it clear to Lily that she was not entirely happy with her present status. She never had a good word for Petroni, and even let it slip that he treated her badly, knocking her around on occasions. At the beginning, Thien claimed she was happy to be at the school. "But when Mr Bill get involved in other things," she said sadly, "my opinion of him change."

"To answer your question," Lily replied, "my family have friends joining them for the holiday. I decided not to join. May I ask you why you did not you go to the South with Mr Bill?" she asked leaning across to recharge Lily's cup.

"Mr Bill not ask me. I sometimes go to market or meet with local dignitaries. He never takes me anywhere nice."

"What do you mean by dignitaries Thien; do you mean the governors and students' parents?" Embarrassed at the question, Thien stared at the floor. At that moment Lily was concerned she was being too pushy?

It was easy to see that Thien was struggling with her inner feelings. She desperately needed a friend. She strived to find the right words: "Not exactly Sister Lily. I mean important people in this area...you know like the Chairman of the People's Committee of Da Nang, provincial governors and their business friends; these are all dignitaries."

"Thien, I would like to be your friend. And as your friend you will have someone to turn to for help and advice. Would you like that?"

Looking out over the compound behind the school Lily could sense that Thien was wrestling with her conscience. Thien had already said too much but, if she was honest with herself, she felt better whenever she met with Lily -- just talking to her took a great weight off her shoulders.

Deteting Thien's discomfort Lily changed tack. Placing an arm around her shoulders she asked about the building behind the school. "What is it used for? I haven't been there before."

It was another probing question that brought a frown to Thien's face. It was obvious that Thien had kept problems to herself for months possibly years. Consequently, unexpected offers of kindness, such as on Lily's part, threatened her fragile defences.

At first, she just sobbed quietly to herself...then came out with it. "I cannot tell you how unhappy I am, Sister Lily" she spluttered. "I do not like what happens here, but I do not know what I can do about it." She sat back, head in hands, shaking uncontrollably.

"Talk to me Thien. Tell me what's troubling you. We can work something out together. I promise you."

Dabbing her eyes, Thien looked around to make doubly sure they were alone – then she let it all out: "Sister Lily, this place is a school for girls but that is not all. Things happen here that have nothing to do with education." she added sheepishly.

"Before I say any more, I want to tell you something about me...my life...how I came to be here...how I met Mr Bill."

Expecting an outpouring related to sex and drugs Lily was taken by surprise when Thien went back to the war years.

"I had a love affair with American pilot...officer called David Gervasoni. We had a child, a girl."

It was a startling revelation. Lily wanted to interrupt but held back. "Did not last very long. Mr David not accept

246

his responsibility as the father. He go back to America. It was 1973 when Americans leave Vietnam."

Lily jumped up from her bed. "Are you telling me that the father of your child is a man called David Gervasoni," she questioned eyes wide in shocked disbelief. "So, is your daughter called Linh?"

They looked hard at one another. Lily felt like she had just won the lottery. Not only was she going to learn chapter and verse about the L'Ecole des Filles' extracurricular activities, she had hit the jackpot by finding Linh's mother.

Thien, on the other hand, felt she was nearing the end of a long, dark tunnel. Ahead were bright lights. Yet so many questions ran through her mind: What did Lily know about her daughter? Was Linh looking for her?

Thien had been out of direct contact with her parents for so long anything could have happened to Linh.

Frantically rummaging through her suitcase by the bed, Lily came up with the photograph of Linh and handed it to Thien: "Linh's father is sponsoring a search for this girl." Thien just stared at the photograph her right hand over her heart as if encouraging it to keep beating. "After sixteen years he obviously realised his mistake in deserting his daughter – your daughter I think -- and now wants to give her an opportunity to start a new life in America."

"Yes that is my baby," Thien said through tear-filled eyes. "I give Linh copy. But why search for her in Da Nang? My daughter in South. And if she like to go to America nobody stop her; not me and nobody in our family I mean."

"Listen carefully to what I have to tell you. My friends found your daughter at your parents' house. They talked to them – your mother and father – and it was agreed that Linh would go to America. Then it all went wrong when someone cheated my friends and took Linh away. We have been looking for her ever since."

It was good news and bad news. The relief Thien had experienced for one precious moment was shattered by Lily's further revelations. She was confused and felt more helpless than before. All along she had trusted her daughter would be safe with her parents; that the money she sent back from time to time would pay for Linh's education and be enough to buy a little food. Thien's own life might be in a mess but she had hoped for better things for her daughter. Now she craved to see her; to touch her face, to stroke her hair.

"I want to help you and I want you to trust me. I am sure my friends will feel the same way," Lily added reassuringly.

"Do not know what to say Sister Lily...my life turn upside down. I am frightened. I do trust you, but I am very afraid for Linh and for myself. I must find my daughter. Please help me."

Despite the highly-charged emotion of the moment, Lily had a job to do. She had to pump Thien to learn more about Madame Ha and William Petroni; to get the hard evidence Mac and Yu Lee spoke of: "Thien, it is very important for me, and my friends, to understand what is going on here. Please tell me more about the dignitaries you spoke of. What is their connection with this place?"

"The building you ask about," Thien said pointing out of the window, "is where Madame Ha keep young women...and girls, some only sixteen."

"So where does the chairman of the People's Committee of Da Nang fit into this?"

"He one of Madame's clients. She call him 'Mr Mayor'. Girls go to hotels in Da Nang and Hue...spend afternoon with the mayor and his friends."

"You mean sex, I assume. Do these afternoon sessions also involve drugs?"

"Yes. Mr Bill tell girls sell drug to clients...marijuana, but he also sell cocaine. You must understand Sister Lily the mayor can pick first of new girls...also take some money from Madame Ha."

"Is this to buy his silence? Does he allow the school to act as a front for sex and drugs so long as he is taken care of, is that how it works?"

"I hear when Madame Ha and Mr Bill talk on the telephone. Chairman of the Peoples' Committee in Ho Chi Minh City also involved...that why young women can be brought to school from South without problem.

"You must understand, everyone afraid of Mr Dai...him chairman, or mayor...want people to know that he important man."

"How do you mean?"

"People call him Bao Dai...you know, after last emperor of Vietnam. You are Vietnamese, and teacher, so you must remember him. He was a man not liked by people in South. Anyway, I hate Mr Dai."

What Thien couldn't know is that after leaving Vietnam Lily turned her back on Vietnam's history – Bao Dai and all. "So have you met Mr Dai?"

"During visit to school he force himself on me. I tell Mr Bill. He shrug shoulders," Thien explained, tears streaming down her cheeks again. "He say business more important and I should do anything Mr Dai ask or Mr Bill throw me out. That is something I do not want, Sister. I have been on streets and do not want to go back again."

"You will never go back on the streets and that's a promise."

So, it was confirmed...the school was an elaborate cover for trafficking in women and narcotics. This was hard evidence and Lily had Thien's detailed account to take to the others. Would it be enough?

"Thien, I am going to change my plans and meet with my friends as soon as I can. By Monday, when school reopens, we will have a plan. Don't worry. And don't discuss anything of this with anybody. It would be dangerous for both of us and will not help to find Linh.

"Take a rest during the school break. I will talk to you on Monday. Get together a few of your belongings in case we have to move out of here quickly.

"And don't worry. I am certain you will soon be reunited with your daughter," she assured Thien. All she wanted was to give Thien some hope. Little did she realise her promise was about to be fulfilled.

———

At the conclusion of the August Revolution holiday celebrations, activities at L'Ecole des Filles returned to normal. Arriving at school early, Lily had not expected to find Madame Ha and William Petroni already on the premises.

As she prepared for class, Lily spotted Thien on the school lawn. She was talking to Petroni. It looked like a heated exchange. He had his hands on her shoulders and was shaking her so much both dog tags jumped out of his shirt.

Lily had to wait until the lunch break to learn more about the apparent confrontation. Thien had refused to brief six new girls, recent arrivals at the school, on how to behave. Petroni was assigned to help change her mind. Madame Ha scolded her reminding her it was standard practice to brief all new girls on how to "service" clients and it was Thien's job to do the briefing. No dissent, no discussion. But Thien had resisted, stood her ground, and had paid the price. Her right eye was blackened and swollen after Petroni had swung at her wildly with both fists.

Moments after the confrontation on the lawn, Petroni left the school with Madame Ha to attend a meeting in nearby Hue. The new girls from the South were instructed to wait in the dormitory – the same one pointed out earlier by Thien.

Taking advantage of the principal's absence, Lily grabbed Thien by the arm and steered her into the dormitory. "It is time to check on the new arrivals." Together they entered the dorm. The new girls, frightened at first, stood silently by their beds. Thien approached the two Amerasian girls. They recoiled in fright; Linh reached for Mai's hand and held it tightly.

"Linh, is it you...my dear daughter?" Although Thien hadn't seen her daughter for eight years she knew immediately the girl before her was Linh. It was solely a mother's instinct and Linh's peerless complexion and cornflower blue eyes were dead giveaways. Mother and daughter became locked in embrace, Linh weeping openly as the other girls looked on not knowing what to make of it all.

For Thien the chance meeting brought on an acute sense of guilt. She hadn't made any effort to visit her daughter in eight years and that played on her mind, particularly after learning how David Gervasoni had surfaced after a sixteen-year absence. She said to Linh, "I am so sorry I stayed away from you for such a long time. I try to earn money to give you a better life. But I am very upset to see you in this place...this is the last place I would want to find you my dear daughter."

But she could not hide her joy at being reunited with her daughter: "We must get you out of here, and the other girls. Miss Lily will help us."   Whatever happened next, she made a promise that neither William Petroni nor any of Madame Ha's cronies – particularly the disgusting and vile "dignitaries" – would get their hands on Linh. "I will not fail you again," she said drawing her daughter close.

Breaking away from her mother's embrace, and dabbing tears from her eyes, Linh went to her bunk and retrieved the photograph given to her so many years ago. If there were any lingering doubts they were dispelled instantly at the sight of the photograph.

"My darling Linh," Thien sobbed openly as she stared at the old photograph. "I am so sorry and ashamed for everything that has happened to you. I will take care of

252

you...make sure you are safe...we have much to say to each other."

"But not now and not here," Lily interjected firmly. "I have to get back to inform my friends of these developments. Stay with the girls, Thien, and keep out of Petroni's line of fire. Can you do that for me?"

Lily was pumped up and beginning to relish her dual role as teacher and guardian – all five-foot two of her.

———

On his return from Hue, Petroni sent word for Thien to meet him in the principal's office. Afraid of being beaten again she turned to Lily for help who again willed her to stay the course: "You must cooperate with him. Think of Linh. So long as she's here she is in danger so you must go along with whatever you're asked to do until we find a way out of this mess."

Both Madame Ha and Petroni were waiting for Thien when she arrived.

"Sit down Thien," Madame Ha said brusquely. "Mr Bill asked you to brief the girls and you refused. You have one last chance. We are leaving for Ho Chi Minh City in a short while and will not be back until Saturday. We will return with some senior officials from the People's Committee including the chairman Mr Dai."

Thien was crestfallen; she knew what that entailed and didn't like the sound of it one bit. She became even more concerned for Linh and the others.

"I want you to arrange a boat trip for next Sunday for the new girls and some of our dignitaries to get acquainted.

No more nonsense please...you must prepare the new girls...get it done."

Leaving the principal's office Thien went straight to Lily: "Good news sister," she said in stunted English, "Madame Ha and Mr Bill away from school for five-six days, come back for harbour boat trip Sunday."

"That is good news. It will give us time to put together a plan before the boat trip. And this means the girls should be safe for a few days."

"One thing more sister: Other dog tag on Mr Bill neck has name Robert Johnson."

Another piece of the jigsaw had fallen into place.

————

Lily walked out of the school gate and turned right. Courtesy of Yu Lee, a car was parked a short way down the lane. Lily had called the night before to explain the latest revelations deemed by all to be a significant step forward. They had to get a move on if they were to benefit from Madame Ha's absence from the school. Johnson was no longer a player so full attention would be directed towards Petroni.

"Johnson's disappearance," Mac suggested to the others, "is a matter for Colonel Nathan to decide about. But let's face it prof, things are beginning to move quickly. Linh is now part of our locate-and-report assignment whether we like it or not. It seems to me the only option we have is to remove Petroni from the scene," he added.

"But we would be changing our assignment without the colonel's approval Mr John. And for...how do you say…an extraction to take place the colonel will certainly need state department approval. Is that correct?"

"Correct professor. And any successful extraction or attempt to escape from Vietnam will have to be by sea as I see it. I certainly can't imagine any other options given our present circumstances.

"As I see it my friend we must grasp this opportunity before Petroni or Madame Ha get wind of what's happening. We have the advantage of surprise and we also have CPO Minh's seamanship and fighting skills on our side. And unless I am mistaken Mr Minh will go wherever Miss Lily goes and that makes me feel a whole lot better than when I dragged myself out of bed this morning."

But will the colonel and the state department go along with a seaborne extraction in the South China Sea? There was only one way to find out: Mac would put a call through to the U.S. Consulate in Hong Kong without delay.

3

Thursday, August 25, 1988: Call to U.S. Consulate, Hong Kong

"Go ahead Mac, this is a secure line. So where are we with the assignment or should that read assignments?" Colonel Nathan closed his office door, put the call on the speaker and reached for his notepad.

"For sure William Petroni is dealing drugs and trafficking in young women," Mac explained setting the scene. "He partners a certain Madame Ha, a control freak with a PhD in pimping. Both of them are in thick with some very influential Vietnamese contacts. Petroni is probably certifiable Dick...he's gotta be removed from active duty as I see it."

"Understood Mac...and Robert Johnson?"

"No sign of him so far. Petroni sports two dog-tags around his neck and one is Johnson's. We can't explain this at this time."

"And Gervasoni's daughter...what about her?"

"Just coming to her Dick and this is where it really gets complicated and probably dangerous."

"Why am I not surprised?" Nathan asked, deep in thought as he turned his chair to stare out of the office window along Hong Kong Island's windswept Garden Road.

Mackenzie checked himself before responding. Colonel Nathan was aware of both missions but unaware they had converged after the discovery of Linh and her mother at L'Ecole des Filles. And nobody had updated the colonel or Gervasoni on events following the disappearance of Linh outside the Hotel Continental.

"As I said, it's complicated so let's back up a bit. We have pieced together a lot of this puzzle but a few important pieces are still out there. By the way you might check if the Pentagon has anything on Petroni or Johnson dealing drugs during the war and still peddling dope after the U.S. pulled out in '73. It looks as though they went AWOL and hid in Laos. At some point Petroni crossed into Vietnam. Not sure about the other guy.

"Okay, now fast forward to the present: We can confirm that Petroni and Madam Ha operate a thriving drugs and human trafficking business at a school in central Vietnam. They have plans to spread drugs throughout the country. That's in addition to making young ladies available to dignitaries as Madame Ha calls them. The school, L'Ecole des Filles, near Da Nang teaches children – all girls. But it's a cover, a front they use to gain support from local and regional authorities in the centre and south of the country."

"Darned clever wouldn't you say Mac? And what about the Gervasoni case," Colonel Nathan prompted, "what's the link if there is one?"

"I was just getting to that colonel. The link is Linh's mother Thien and William Petroni. This is what we know: Eight years ago, Petroni took up with Thien. At that time, and even now, Petroni doesn't know Thien had a child with Gervasoni. Thien has identified Linh as her daughter and Linh was one of the girls recently abducted from Saigon. Anytime at all Petroni will catch on."

257

"Then the fat will be in the fire, I guess," Colonel Nathan supposed.

"For sure he will be well and truly pissed colonel. And things could get much worse. He could hold Linh for ransom. Petroni is one ruthless son of a bitch. He sports a blue-handled, long-bladed Bowie knife -- and not just because it matches his denims.

"We need to move fast. Petroni and Madame Ha are due back from Vung Tao to join a boat trip arranged for this Sunday to introduce the new girls, including Linh, to Madame Ha's dignitaries."

Colonel Nathan pushed back from his desk and stared at the ceiling his brain processing Mac's comprehensive report. "Okay pal, I think I get the picture: Politically, it's potentially highly explosive and dangerous. And there's plenty of danger for you guys too. No need to tell you that your locate-and-report assignment appears to have turned into something else – something potentially dangerous.

"So, I need your recommendations Mac. How do we defuse the situation and protect Uncle Sam's reputation?"

"We have given this a whole load of thought Dick and this is the plan we came up with..."

Referring to his notes, Mac walked Colonel Nathan step-by-step through the extraction and escape plan prepared by the team without any attempt to minimise or overstate the risks involved.

"Based on what you say, I agree with you it's risky. But from where I'm sitting Mac, we have no alternative. We can't send in the marines, yet Petroni must be taken

258

out...and I mean right out of Vietnam. So, this is what we'll do. I'll call the state department this evening when Washington wakes up and discuss your plan and extraction options. You call me again around nine pal. This will give me time to get my ducks in a row.

"Let me ask you something else: Just how much of Linh's situation have you communicated to David Gervasoni? I guess you know that he went back to California a while back to take care of his law business. I said we'd keep him posted of any developments. We'll handle that from the consulate, no need for you or Yu Lee to get involved.

"No, sir I didn't know about Gervasoni's change of plan, but thanks for the heads-up. I'll make sure Yu Lee is briefed accordingly."

"I also have some concern about this CPO Minh guy," the colonel continued. "I hear what you say but can you trust the man; someone you hardly know? It I understand your plan he will be pivotal to its success. Don't bother giving me an answer now...just make sure he comes through Mac...on your head if he doesn't.

"From now on everyone must exercise extreme care. This assignment must succeed. And I have no doubt that relationships between the United States and Vietnam could be seriously affected if the plan backfired. Now go and earn your keep. Good night Mac and give my best regards to the professor."

———

"The Americans want Petroni taken out of Vietnam," Mackenzie told the team as he set out a coastal map of Da Nang on Lily's kitchen table. "We are instructed to coordinate with the U.S. Navy so we have to refine our strategy a bit."

"And we have to double-check everything," Yu Lee told the others. "Once the plan is set in motion we must all follow it to the letter."

Lily and CPO Minh looked askance at Yu Lee, as if questioning why he had felt it necessary to interject. But it wasn't some mercurial twist of temperament on Yu Lee's part. He, and Mac to a greater extent, had noticed how Lily and Chief Petty Officer Minh were becoming more intimate in their relationship. Both were anxious to gauge the intensity of the couple's blossoming courtship preferably without spooking either of them. Their only concern was to protect the integrity of the escape plan. As Colonel Nathan had commented the role the chief petty officer would play in the extraction and exit strategy could prove crucial to its success – particularly because of his nautical abilities and martial art skills.

Lily sensed Yu Lee had had something on his mind for the past few days about her and CPO Minh. Maybe he thought they were becoming too friendly. Was he afraid it might affect Mr Minh's ability to perform when the time came to face-down Petroni?

Whatever the reason, she wanted to clear the air.

"I have something to say," she announced looking up from the map and addressing Yu Lee directly. "Mister Minh has agreed to help me support my parents if he can get charges against him dropped. I intended to ask for your help professor after we completed the mission. But I think it is only fair to everyone that I mention it now because I don't want it to affect our work ahead.

"Concerning my mother's cancer; my original thoughts were to get treatment for her in the United States. But now I'm not so sure."

Minh remained silent as Lily explained their growing friendship which she did in English for John Mackenzie's benefit.

"Recent events have influenced my whole outlook on life," she said, "even provided me with a good reason for not leaving Vietnam. Let's just say I have renewed hope about staying here."

No one doubted that Lily had grown in stature by helping Yu Lee and Mackenzie -- and working at L'Ecole des Filles: "I don't mind telling you I feel good about Thien being reunited with her daughter and I'd like to be around to witness a happy ending."

The loss of Kim was still fresh in everyone's mind and like other members in the team Lily nurtured thoughts of bringing Petroni to book even though he was not directly responsible for Kim's death.

"What I'm trying to say is I feel I belong here...in Vietnam...with Mr Minh."

There was no going back on the plan approved by Colonel Nathan and whether Lily and Minh agreed to go or stay they had to press ahead. But for the plan to have any real chance of success CPO Minh had to stay the course. The part he would play would be crucial to its success.

"We understand and appreciate what you have told us Lily," Yu Lee reassured her. "And it is important that we find a way to make both of you feel comfortable going forward. If you and Mr Minh want to stay together in

261

Vietnam, I will find some way of getting your mother to Hong Kong for treatment."

Minh looked at Lily before responding to Yu Lee: "Both of us will see this through, you have my word. When it is all over brother I will ask you to help me regain my post in the navy. Until then you can count on our full support."

"That's great to hear Chief. I guess we are all moving in the same direction," Mackenzie said, visibly relieved. "I was sure Yu Lee would be able to tease out the problem and find a solution without a falling-out among friends. Let's go over details for tomorrow's action points just one more time and then we can call it a day and get some shut-eye."

Sealed orders from the Secretary of the U.S. Navy detailed USS Blue Ridge, the control and command ship of the Seventh Fleet, to put to sea from Subic Bay in the Philippines and rendezvous with a Vietnam Navy patrol boat off the Paracel Islands in the South China Sea. Its mission: to intercept and pick up a small group including a high-value prisoner, then set course for Hong Kong. The navy was responding to an urgent request from the Department of State on a matter classified as "Most Urgent: of National Importance".

Captain Theodore S. Brewster USN, a twenty-year veteran had skippered the U.S. Seventh Fleet's highly sophisticated flagship since its forward deployment to Yokosuka navy base in Tokyo Bay ten years earlier.

Following an on-board review of his sailing orders Brewster, and his senior officers, formulated an intercept plan. Skilfully they coaxed the "large cabin cruiser" (as the crew like to call it) out of Subic Bay and into the South China Sea. At 0100 hours Vietnam time on Saturday, August 28, Blue Ridge came onto a west-north-west heading for Triton Island some 800 nautical miles west of Subic Bay. At a top speed of 23 knots the vessel faced a thirty-four hour cruise to the rendezvous point. With good weather, she would be hove-to off Triton Island by 1100 on Sunday morning a few hours ahead of the planned rendezvous time.

———

China and the Republic of Vietnam fought one another for possession of the Paracel Islands in 1974 believing them to be at the centre of an oil-rich region. Although it has no indigenous inhabitants, Woody Island, the largest in the island cluster, is administered by the People's Republic of China which maintains a contingent of soldiers from the People's Liberation Army.

It was reasonable to suppose that Chinese patrol vessels could be in the area. Captain Brewster's standing orders were to avoid any untoward incidents with China which was the reason for choosing the uninhabited and more southern island of Triton as the intercept point in the western Pacific.

Details of the captain's orders were on a need-to-know basis, yet everyone on board ship was aware the mission included a stopover in Hong Kong. Crew members were already making plans for shore leave and a date with the convivial fleshpots that flourish under the neon lights of Wanchai and Tsimshatsui.

Though lacking on-board hangar facilities, USS Blue Ridge had two Sikorsky SH-3G Sea King helicopters housed on deck. Airworthiness checks for both were conducted prior to the vessel setting sail. The U.S. Navy was ready for any test put before them.

———

Just before 0700 on Sunday, the day of the school cruise, Chief Petty Officer Minh, clad in navy fatigues, marched briskly and confidently through the dock gates of Marble Mountain Naval Base. Mac and Yu Lee, on plan, remained out of sight a short distance from the main gate.

264

Whether it was a bold bluff or a calculated risk on Minh's part, neither of the two guards on duty looked closely at the ID pinned to the top left pocket of the CPO's fatigues. So far so good Minh mouthed to himself.

Coolly stepping through the door of the NCO's mess he walked towards two petty officers who were standing apart from a dozen or so fellow mariners. No one paid any special attention to the three men but, to be on the safe side, CPO Minh remained near the door his woollen hat pulled down masking most of his face.

One petty officer opened his hand and revealed three sets of ignition keys for three navy patrol boats. His mate presented a set of navigation charts, a compass and a leather brief case containing the side-arms that CPO Minh had specified. Placing the charts under his arm he walked out of the door briefcase in hand.

Both petty officers were now in danger of jeopardising their careers, perhaps even their lives, by helping their CPO who was also their friend. But neither man was unduly concerned because their motivation and inspiration stemmed from their admiration of a brave man who had refused to comply with an unjust and unwarranted order. Because he had taken a firm stand, they would support him in whatever way they could. And, as they saw it, the action they were about to embark upon was justified, even warranted. Time would tell.

———

All told, the Vietnam Navy had some fourteen navy patrol boats berthed in a number of coastal bases around the country. Three were at Marble Mountain Naval Base employed mainly for coastal patrol work including

265

interception and repatriation of boatpeople trying to leave the country as CPO Minh had experienced first-hand and to his cost.

The entrance gate to the navy patrol boat anchorage had a two-man guard at weekends. Surprisingly, the guards turned, stood to attention and saluted Minh as he approached. Without breaking step he returned the salute and walked briskly towards two more guards on duty at the quayside, close to the vessels.

Using the heel of his hand, he expertly delivered two sharp chops to the neck of each man. As their knees buckled, Minh put his arms around their shoulders and gently lowered them to the ground. It was all over in seconds.

Moving quickly, and as quietly as possible, he dragged the inert figures landside of the quay, covered them with an old tarpaulin and left them to sleep it off. It would be four hours before they regained consciousness by which time Minh expected to be clear of Vietnam waters.

Minutes later, Yu Lee and Mackenzie broke cover to join the CPO at the quayside positioning themselves alongside the patrol boats.

———

The mass-produced, Russian-built Grif ("Zhul") class patrol boats have a maximum speed of thirty knots, around 56 kilometres an hour. They were designed for harbour patrol and general mission duties. Machine gun turrets, mounted fore and aft, are not linked to any firing control system and must be operated manually. Electronics include a 12-channel HF radio and one, single, simple radar. But CPO Minh already had all the navigation equipment that would be required for the task ahead.

Minh stepped aboard and assumed command of the nearest patrol boat: "Deploy below decks and await my signal," he ordered the two petty officers. "We are undermanned," he told Yu Lee and Mac, "so please attend to the bow and stern lines."

Dropping two sets of ignition keys into the harbour, Minh gunned the vessel's diesels. Start-up problems with the other vessels would be easily overcome but it would take time for the navy to organise and man one or two pursuit vessels. Scuttling the other two patrol boats was not an option in Minh's view. He was already in deep trouble with the strong possibility of more on the way.

Fully committed to making a fresh start with the charming Mrs Crenshaw, Minh's confidence was buoyed and at an all-time high. He had never been so sure about anyone in his life even though he had only known her for just over a month. Like Lily, Minh had found a new lease of life and he intended to make the best of it.

"Let go fore and aft," Minh ordered.

Slowly and skilfully the CPO manoeuvred the vessel away from the quayside and into open water. He plotted a course to intercept the school cruise boat not sure how the next few hours would affect his and Lily's plans for the future and the lives of others. But there was no turning back.

————

The school's forty-foot boat was a converted pleasure craft with rows of seats lining either side of the boat deck. Its shallow draught and single diesel engine made it suitable for inshore waters only. Below decks, two cabins separated by a small galley were configured as dining areas. Cushioned seats and polished wooden tables converted into bunks as required.

Madame Ha's important dignitaries included the nefarious Mr Bao Dai, Chairman of the People's Committee of Ho Chi Minh City and his assistant. Also, Mr Nguyen Tan Giap, the deputy governor of the Da Nang Rehabilitation and Re-education Centre – a.k.a. Kim's tormentor and Lily's antagonist; Mr Nguyen Van Nguyen, Chairman of the People's Committee of Da Nang; the ambitious General Ngo Banh, Chairman of the People's Committee of Ba Ria-Vung Tao Province and his deputy Mr Phan Tanh Hung – all carefully groomed by Madame Ha to protect the "school's'" current business interests and with an eye on future expansion.

There was a cheery air of expectation among the group characterised by their spontaneous jokes and laughter. No one seemed to have a care in the world. But that was about to change.

The six "new girls", Thien and William Petroni were already on board when Madame Ha's convoy arrived at the quayside. All girls were dressed in white *ao dai* -- the "school" uniform -- which pleased her very much. Thien had been paying attention at the pre-briefing after all.

Madame Ha's ambitious plans to expand operations to Vung Tao had already been outlined and given a nod of approval by General Banh.

"I am very pleased you approve of our future plans general. Today, my dear brother, you have first pick of the new arrivals."

The general was already eyeing Linh up and down. His lascivious gaze had not escaped Thien's notice but she kept herself in check.

Just after 0900 the pleasure craft made its way to the outer reaches of Da Nang harbour. The dignitaries had retreated below deck to avoid attracting any undue attention from onlookers on the quayside. Apart from a slight, south-westerly breeze sailing conditions were perfect. The air was warm and sultry but the forecast was for fair weather all day.

Looking towards the far side of the harbour Petroni caught sight of a Navy patrol boat heading in their direction at great speed. He figured there was nothing to be concerned about as there were enough dignitaries aboard the pleasure craft to divert any unwanted attention from the school's Sunday cruise. But the navy vessel continued to bear down on the pleasure craft and Petroni was becoming more and more agitated. "Madame Ha," he shouted, "we have company. Looks like a Vietnam naval vessel is coming our way."

By the time the school principal responded to Petroni's request to join him topside, Minh had manoeuvred the patrol boat to within one hundred metres of the pleasure craft. Everyone went on deck to see what the navy wanted.

"What the hell's all this?" Mr Dai asked indignantly. "Why are we being followed?" The other dignitaries announced similar annoyance everyone talking at once.

Using a loud hailer, Minh outlined his instructions: "Heave to and prepare to be boarded."

Observing two crewmen positioned by the patrol boat's forward AA gun, Petroni felt obliged to comply with Minh's instructions. He turned to Thien: "Push the fenders over the left side...now!" he shouted over the noise of the engines, as the patrol boat came smoothly alongside. Petroni mumbled something about someone having a lot of explaining to do.   By now Madame Ha had stepped out of the wheelhouse. She was fuming but not sure where to direct her complaints or vent her anger. All she could do was watch anxiously and await the opportunity to set matters right.

On cue, the petty officers threw stern and bow lines onto the pleasure craft to be made fast by Thien who ran fore and aft as fast as her legs could carry her.

"For your sake sailor, you better have a watertight excuse for boarding us. This is a damned intrusion," Petroni yelled in Vietnamese through a loud hailer. "You are screwing up a pleasure cruise for schoolchildren and governors. We have some very important people on board my friend."

Below decks Petroni's "pleasure cruise" remark brought a chuckle from Yu Lee who watched as one of the petty officers threw a rope ladder over the starboard rail of the patrol boat. The hull was two metres higher than the pleasure craft and the deck guardrail added another one and a half metres. As soon as the rope ladder hit the deck of the pleasure craft Minh picked up his loud hailer: "Girls...listen to me. Get to the rope ladder immediately and board my boat now! Move yourselves."

The plan was not to board the pleasure boat -- quite the opposite.

Responding to Mr Minh's instructions, Linh and Mai, the other Amerasian girl, and two of the Vietnamese girls grabbed at the rope ladder as it swung back and forth as the boats' hulls scraped together. Everything happened quickly and Petroni was caught flatfooted. Creating that element of surprise had been a vital part of the plan.

A moment after gathering his thoughts and getting his act together, the big American sprang into action. Vacating the small wheelhouse and confronting Madame Ha and the governors, he turned angry at first then became totally unhinged when he realised no one was aware of what was happening around them. The dignitaries would be of no help in the present circumstances -- that much was clear. They were perturbed but disinclined to help in any way.

Moving as quickly as possible, Mac and Yu Lee scrambled topside to find all hell had broken loose. "Whatever goes down in the next few minutes," Mac said to Yu Lee, "we must make sure all the girls get safely aboard the patrol boat."

"What the fuck's going on?" Petroni screamed at CPO Minh who, by now, had jumped from the patrol boat's raised bridge to stand alongside the 12mm AA stern gun. "And who the hell are you?" he yelled. For the first time in years, Petroni was floundering outside his comfort zone. Ignoring the man's pleas Minh stayed on plan.

Mac took up position behind the forward 12mm gun both hands on the weapon. "Stay exactly where you are," he commanded pointing the weapon towards Petroni. Mac's nerves were taught and his stomach churned with apprehension, but there was neither time for reflection nor a change of mind.

Yu Lee instructed Thien to help the last two girls mount the rope ladder. Four girls were now safely on board.

Mac's threat to open fire on the pleasure craft was an obvious bluff and Petroni called it. Instinctively, the big man made a grab for Thien. His lunge caused the rope ladder to twist and spill two of the Vietnamese girls back on deck. Uninjured, they got up immediately and tried again, this time without assistance from Thien.

Unsheathing his Bowie knife, a now frantic Petroni bounded towards the girls. He slashed wildly at the rope ladder. Screaming hysterically, the girls lost their grip and dropped out of sight just as both vessels were driven apart by the quickening swell. Distraught and unable to help, Thien could only watch. From on board the patrol boat Linh and Mai, rooted in horror, watched as their compatriots disappeared below the waves, crushed as the two hulls scraped together. It was all over in seconds. Screams rang out and Thien became distracted. Petroni saw it and charged at her, the long, shiny blade missing her face by inches.

Petroni's cowardly attack on an unarmed and defenceless woman was all the motivation CPO Minh needed to enter the fray. Screaming like a man possessed, he leapt high over the patrol boat guardrail his rattan fighting sticks poised to strike. "Prepare to defend yourself American," he yelled. Petroni was about to receive his first lesson in Vovinam-Vet Vo Dao; a lesson that would bring intense pain.

Turning away from Thien, Petroni braced to confront the incoming, pumped-up, chief petty officer who was expertly twirling his fighting sticks in mid-flight. Falling deadweight on Petroni, Minh delivered a stinging blow to the left side of the man's neck also catching his jaw with a sickening crunch. Severe pain forced Petroni to let go of his knife. Crouching on deck, Minh brought one stick to Petroni's left leg scything him to the ground. At that juncture, it would have been easy to terminate the man's life with a blow to the head. But that was not part of the plan. The American had to be immobilised and transferred to the patrol boat. That was the plan and Minh would follow it implicitly.

"Come here, you bastard, I'm not finished with you yet," Petroni screamed in pain as he fell backwards as the next blow from Minh's rattan stick bit into his shins.

"Don't worry my friend," Minh said enjoying the moment, "there is plenty of time. I am just getting started."

Neck, jaw and legs burning with pain Petroni managed to scramble to his feet, retrieve his knife and stagger towards Thien. Astonishingly, this wild and dangerous man, crazy with pain, fought back with grim determination to regain the upper hand. The American had guts, but he hadn't reckoned for the pumped-up CPO from Marble Mountain Naval Base.

"I will take it out on you," Petroni snarled. In a blind rage he cursed and struck out wildly at Thien. She ducked and weaved to stay out of reach.

"Got you bitch," he screamed, holding her by the hair, a sickening grin spreading across his tortured face. The unthinkable happened. In one swift movement he brought his Bowie knife to her neck and slit her throat from ear to ear. Distraught, Linh watched it all from the relative security of the patrol boat's wheelhouse.

The sight of blood spurting across the deck caused everybody on both boats to gasp in horror. Even the indomitable Madame Ha showed concern.

Seconds later, the stick-wielding chief petty officer repeatedly delivered sharp, crippling blows to each side of Petroni's head. The big man's knees buckled for a second time and he went down like a stricken buffalo. Minh neatly cross-gripped his sticks around Petroni's neck ready to strangle the life out of the broken man.

"No, not yet Chief...hold hard," Mac yelled at him. "We need this bastard alive, so back off now. Restrain him quickly." Mac picked up Petroni's Bowie knife from the deck.

"I have some rope Mr John," Yu Lee shouted. Responding to Mac's plea, Yu Lee bounded forward with a length of rope and helped Minh tie Petroni's hands behind his back. Pulling the rope tight around Petroni's waist, Mac and Yu Lee struggled to haul the inert body on to the deck of the patrol boat. Unable to carry their 230 pound bundle, they dragged and shoved Petroni towards the bow. Setting the unconscious man upright, they lashed him to the forward gun emplacement.

"Stay there, be quiet and don't do anything stupid or I'll let the navy loose on you again," Mac cautioned the unconscious American with a pat on the head. Then he stooped down to yank Johnson's dog tag from around his neck. Later, he thought, someone would have to determine what had happened to him.

Madame Ha and her guests watched in shocked disbelief. Everyone was stunned, unable to believe what was happening before their eyes. Dreams of an afternoon of extracurricular activities had turned into a nightmare for all concerned.

Everything happened so fast after Petroni was overpowered, trussed up and taken out of play. Her right hand man rendered unconscious, Madame Ha's immediate concern was to get back to the safety of the quayside and her school. Petroni, she figured, would have to fend for himself.

Madame Ha had a lot on her mind, much to consider: Should she approach the Vietnam Navy to report the unprovoked attack and lodge an official complaint? Or would that draw unwanted attention? Could she expect her dignitaries to come to her aid back on dry land? She had doubts about that.

The pitiful sight of Thien's body lying in a pool of blood for all to see was something none of them could have envisaged. One thing was certain: explaining what had just happened in Da Nang harbour would not be easy. And Madame Ha could not assume support from any of her special guests.

Would the day's events affect future business? That was her main concern. Could Jimmy Yuen maintain a constant supply of girls, even take Petroni's place? Would it be business as usual?

Before any of these questions could be addressed someone had to pilot the pleasure craft to shore. All of the "dignitaries", apart from Mr Dai, had gone below to work on their alibis.

———

With care, Mac wrapped Thien's body in a blanket pulled from the pleasure boat's cabin. Yu Lee helped him to transfer the body to the patrol boat. It was an incredibly sad moment. Reuniting Thien with her daughter had been a very brief affair. There was no knowing what sort of traumatic effect it would have on Linh who had clammed up since the tragedy occurred. Losing the other girls was also a major blow to the mission which nobody was inclined to characterise as successful. That was for others to decide. But they did have Petroni all trussed up and that was of vital importance.

"I expect Colonel Nathan will classify these unfortunate deaths as collateral damage," Mac whispered to Yu Lee.

By now the petty officers had retrieved the rope ladder, retracted the fenders and instructed Mr Dai, to let go of bow and stern lines to allow the two craft to drift apart.

With Mr Dai at the helm, the pleasure craft separated from the patrol boat and headed back to Da Nang. One seaborne drama was drawing to a close.

Moving into the wheelhouse to assist CPO Minh, Mac said: "I expect a major row will break out between Madame Ha and her guests. But that's not our concern."

"Madame Ha will talk her way out of this Mr John," Yu Lee offered, "blaming us for everything that happened. This is why you have to go to Saigon and approach General Vo for help."

———

"Chief, I need help to set a new course," Mac announced.

276

"What heading Mr John?"

"Plot a course to the Paracel group of islands, specifically Triton Island, which I ascertain to be 180 nautical miles east of Da Nang."

It was time to put into effect the remainder of the plan agreed with Colonel Nathan. They had sufficient stocks of food and water on board and enough diesel fuel to reach the rendezvous point.

Minh brought the vessel on to the new heading: "New course set as requested Mr John."

———

An hour later, Mac spotted two vessels on the horizon astern of their position. Through high-powered binoculars, Minh identified both vessels as Vietnam Navy patrol boats: "They are out of Marble Mountain Naval Base...following us about ninety minutes behind. They do not have any advantage in terms of speed; we should be able to stay ahead of them."

Sighting the two vessels giving chase meant they were not yet in the clear, but they were closing fast on their rendezvous reference point.

Mackenzie addressed everyone on deck, including Minh who surrendered the helm to one of the petty officers. "Listen up please. I want you to know that I intend to take this patrol boat on to Saigon. First, though, we will rendezvous with a U.S. navy vessel and transfer you to safety."   "Then I will press on with help from CPO Minh and our two petty officers."

Mac, Yu Lee and CPO Minh had already discussed and agreed a revised course of action.

The assignment was not yet finished but the contribution made by CPO Minh and Lily to date was of inestimable value. Both had gone the extra mile. Yet, both had their problems: Minh faced the prospect of a court martial, probably worse; Lily was worried sick about her mother and the rest of her family. It was important to set the record straight, particular in Minh's case.

Turning to the CPO, Mac said: "I will make it my solemn duty to introduce you to General Vo in Saigon. You will have an opportunity to explain all that had happened before and after we were thrown together in the military hospital.

"And when Minh is rightfully reinstated in the navy," Mac said, turning to the others, "he will be free to help Lily and her family."

Switching his attention back to Minh, still smiling at such welcome remarks, Mac told him that he and Lily could set about rebuilding their lives: "And I would like to be among the first to wish you both the best of luck."

One of the petty officers interrupted with an incoming message: "It is for you Mr John," he called out. Mac had gone over to check the condition of the unconscious Petroni.

He clicked the receive button on the radio telephone: "John Mackenzie here...over?"

"This is U.S.S. Blue Ridge. Patching you through to Captain Brewster sir; stand by."

"This is Captain Theodore S. Brewster commander of the Blue Ridge. Are you aware Mr Mackenzie that you have two Vietnam Navy vessels astern of you, over?"

"Affirmative sir...we estimate them to be ninety minutes away and not closing, over."

"Very well...I would be obliged if you could inform me of your current status...souls on board...their condition and the state of your vessel. My orders are to transport thirteen to Hong Kong including two prisoners. Do you concur, over?"

"Negative, sir, our complement has changed. The total for transportation to Hong Kong is six, including prisoner William Petroni, two Vietnamese girls, two Amerasian girls and Professor Yu Lee.

"Would you kindly explain the change in circumstances previously notified to me by Colonel Nathan, over?"

Mackenzie quickly apprised Captain Brewster of the string of events that had caused the group's reduction in number.

"In that case, Mr Mackenzie, let us concentrate on securing one William Petroni on board the Blue Ridge. What happens to the Vietnam Navy patrol boat afterwards is of no concern to the United States Navy. Is that understood?

"Understood sir. Captain, after the transfer I intend to journey on to Saigon. I respectfully request assistance with diesel supplies, food, water and a temporary casket. We have one fatality on board the patrol vessel and I intend to take the body to Ho Chi Minh City to hand over to the next of kin. Are you able to assist, over?"

Minh checked on the trailing Vietnam Navy patrol boats. He judged them to be slowing down or even hove to. The sight of the Blue Ridge probably caused them to take stock of their situation. Surely their pursuit orders did not include picking a fight with the control and command ship of the U.S. Navy's Seventh Fleet. But, one way or another, the navy's presence so close to Vietnam would certainly be reported to Hanoi.

Within thirty minutes, Lt. Cmdr. Wilson Smith had positioned a tender alongside the patrol boat: "I am ordered to collect a party of six." Commander Smith shouted through his loud hailer as the tender came alongside the patrol boat. John Mackenzie stepped forward and identified himself

The two boats bobbed up and down in unison: "I have the provisions you requested Mr Mackenzie including some ready-to-eat meals. Compliments of Captain Brewster, sir, and the best we could do I'm afraid at short notice."

The dynamics of the mission changed after Thien's untimely death. CPO Minh wanted to be with Lily to help her with her problems and he was desperately concerned to clear his name. At first, Minh wanted Lily to go on to Hong Kong leaving him to take the patrol boat back to Marble Mountain Naval Base to try to clear his name. But Yu Lee and John Mackenzie's idea was better. The CPO would never receive a fair hearing in Da Nang, but Mac had convinced him he would get a fair hearing from General Vo in Ho Chi Minh City.

"After all you have done for us Brother Minh," Yu Lee told him as he prepared to board the tender, "I could not sleep soundly knowing you had to defend yourself at your naval base. You, and your brave petty officers, deserve to be recognised for the parts you have played. Take my advice and put your trust in Mr John.

"Remember what I told you before: General Vo is aware of our assignments in Vietnam," Yu Lee reminded Minh. "He helped us get started and I am sure he would not approve of the way you have been treated by the navy. If I know him, and I think I do, he will do all he can to destroy Madame Ha's trafficking network. And nobody can better explain everything that has happened in the past month than Mr John. So go now and be safe."

The petty officers finished loading the stores onto the patrol boat and turned their attention to Petroni lashed to the forward gun emplacement. He had regained consciousness. Mac prescribed shackles for the prisoner and cautioned Commander Smith to have them applied before releasing any of the ropes: "This sorry example of human waste is a mean and dangerous bastard commander. He murdered one of our party, caused the death of two Vietnamese girls who were crushed when they fell overboard, and I believe he murdered at least one other person – probably with this weapon," he said handing over the Bowie knife. I urge great care handling his transfer."

Petroni was sore from the beating he received from CPO Minh. His head hurt and his legs felt numb partly from the fight and partly due to restricted circulation caused by the restraining ropes.

It was of crucial importance to get Petroni to Hong Kong in one piece: "I guess it's up to you prof to explain to the colonel all that happened. I will also leave it to you to square things with David Gervasoni who's probably pretty pissed with us. But the sight of Linh after sixteen years should help a bit, what do you think?"

"Be easy my friend. I will take care of everything in Hong Kong including Mr David. Be sure to give my regards to General Vo," he smiled, triumphantly swishing his fan back and forth.

"Will do prof, you take good care now," Mac called back.

"Mr Minh let's get under way if you please, let's get this tub to the River Saigon and get you reinstated in the Vietnam Navy where you damn well belong."

A short distance away the U.S.S. Blue Ridge was preparing to get under way.

"Set course for Subic Bay," Captain Brewster ordered.

"Aye sir," Lt. Cmdr. Wilson Smith acknowledged though puzzled to some extent why they were not setting a course heading for Hong Kong.

"Don't worry commander, we will go to Hong Kong in due course," Captain Brewster reassured him at the same time bringing smiles back to the faces of some of the confused naval officers and ratings around him, "but first we have an important package to drop off at Subic Bay."

For security reasons the state department modified the extraction plan so William Petroni could be debriefed at Clark Air Base before being flown stateside. It was done on a need to know basis.

Epilogue

The clandestine undertaking in 1988 by John Mackenzie and Yu Lee to locate and determine the fate of two, wayward Americans took four months. The colonel's initial locate-and-report request placed before them was only the start of a process. During the engagement the men found it crucial to remove Petroni from the scene, without waiting for approval. They had to act if the U.S. was to have any chance of establishing bilateral relations with Vietnam. Neither man had signed up for active duty in the field but that's how it turned out. There were no financial bonuses for the extra effort, but neither Yu Lee nor John Mackenzie felt inclined to raise that as an issue.

The White House considered the proactive action taken by Yu Lee and John Mackenzie with Colonel Nathan's blessing to be justified and acceptable. The emotive phrase "collateral damage" was not used but, if pushed for an answer, any White House spokesman would surely use it to justify the untimely deaths of Thien and two, young Vietnamese girls in the prime of life.

As for Kim and Officer Nguyen, their deaths would be deemed by the Administration to be unrelated to its strategic goal of achieving normalisation talks with Vietnam. In politics -- anybody's politics -- the end always justifies the means. And John Mackenzie was well aware of how things worked in D.C.

———

Relieved to see the back of the whole escapade, John Mackenzie returned to running China Orient Airways in his beloved Hong Kong. Thoughts of having to creep back to Ottawa, tail between legs due to financial concerns, became a thing of the past. There was plenty of work to go around. And his "real estate value" in the eyes of the U.S. government had soared tenfold. He went back to handling U.S. military aircraft and crews arriving at Kai Tak from Clark Air Base with the occasional business soiree to China and Indochina with the redoubtable Yu Lee. Life was especially good for John Mackenzie.

Life was also good for Yu Lee but in a different way. He was a man skilled at managing his own expectations so when it came to business he never aimed so high he would break any bones in the event of a fall.

———

Just before Christmas 1988, four months after completing the assignments, Colonel Nathan called Yu Lee and asked him to drop by the consulate.

"Professor, I have good news and some not-so-good news," he pronounced cheerfully as Yu Lee jauntily entered his office.

"First the good news: Here are U.S. passports for Gabrielle and the children. Keep them safe."

"I suppose the not-so-good news is no passport for me," Yu Lee said with more than a hint of sarcasm.

"It seems the excellent work you did all those years ago as a translator for Zhou Enlai and Uncle Ho on the side-lines of the Geneva Accords raised a red flag in D.C.

284

"That's not all. The facilitation work you did working for the PRC's foreign affairs ministry, where Zhou Enlai was minister at the time, rankled with some people in the U.S. Department of State."

Yu Lee just smiled. He had anticipated problems obtaining U.S. passports for everyone. But deep down, he was greatly relieved. His family would not have to worry when the sovereignty of Hong Kong reverted to China in 1997.

"Colonel, I would like you to know, officially, that I am very grateful to you for giving my family hope for the future. I could not ask for more."

"You are very welcome prof. But I have to tell you that I deeply regret not being about to get a passport for you. I guess some situations are difficult to explain years after they happen – especially to someone who wasn't there and probably hadn't even been born."

"There are almost ten years to go before the handover, Colonel, so I hope we can continue working as before – I mean my Mandarin classes at the consulate." After shaking hands on it, he walked briskly out of the consulate and onto Garden Road bringing to close another auspicious day in Yu Lee's complicated life.

———

Months later, in August 1989, prior to Vietnam's occupation force withdrawing from Democratic Kampuchea which it had overtly occupied to put an end to genocide perpetrated by the Khmer Rouge, General Nguyen Van Vo called Yu Lee at his office in Wanchai on Hong Kong Island.

"This is a social call my dear boy," he announced to a surprised Yu Lee. "I would like to invite you to come to Saigon next month to talk about something important. Can you do that?"

"It would by my pleasure general, but only if you permit me to stay in a suite at your very fine GuestHotel on the river."

"That can be arranged. And bring Mackenzie with you if he's available. Tell him he can stay in a suite also. And, if he asks, tell him the plumbing is working just fine."

All three men contrived to meet on a warm, sunny September day in Ho Chi Minh City. It was really too warm for a military parade, but this parade was different. On a sheltered dais hastily erected in Dien Bien Phu Road, General Vo stood proudly to attention taking the salute as hundreds of ten-wheeler army trucks filed by one after the other bumper to bumper. Each truck held thirty to forty soldiers – men and women – standing erect, completely exposed to the elements because the trucks' canvas canopies had been deliberately rolled back. Not one soldier dared to mop the beads of sweat from his or her face.

It took over two hours for Vietnam's victorious occupation force to drive by and General Vo remained at attention throughout, not wavering once.

Comfortable in VIP seats on the platform, Yu Lee and Mac watched with unconstrained admiration as this old man – a national hero – saluted the country's brave men and women in uniform on their return from Kampuchea. It was an honour, both men told the general, to be present at such a remarkable event; something they would never forget.

————

Early that evening, they got back at the GuestHotel to find that General Vo's staff had prepared a celebratory dinner for his guests: "Mr John, may I have your undivided attention please," he asked motioning Mackenzie and Yu Lee to be seated.

"On behalf of Vietnam I would like to officially thank you for the part you played in the reconciliation process. We are not there yet but, thanks to you Mr John, we have made excellent progress.

"Also, you did the right thing asking for my help with CPO Minh who went AWOL with justifiable reasons. I thought you would like to know his case was reviewed at my request and he was reinstated, promoted to lieutenant and given command of a patrol boat out of Da Nang.

"So, Mr John, I would like to present you with this kukri as a keepsake to remind you of your work here and as a token of our gratitude for a job well done."

It was one of the few times in his life that Mac began to feel uncomfortable. He was embarrassed and fidgeted with his napkin. And what about Yu Lee; his contribution was enormous. Why wasn't the general honouring him Mac wondered?

"General Vo, I was just happy to be of help to you and Colonel Nathan. But thanks for the wonderful gift. It is way more than I deserve and I will cherish it forever.

"But I have to ask you something: Did you kill a Ghurkha soldier to get his kukri?"

Shaking his head from side to side the general suppressed the urge to laugh: "No, my friend, I bought it at a pawn shop in Saint George's Place in Liverpool." There was a brief pause then all three men collapsed in fits of laughter.

It was Yu Lee's turn. "As for you, professor, I thought you could use this," he said, passing over a brand new passport.

"Mr John told me what happened at the consulate in Hong Kong when you met with Colonel Nathan. So now you can apply for a visa if you want to take your family to the United States."

"Or Canada, or the UK," Mackenzie added.

"Precisely so Mr John. And to answer your next question professor, Cambodia's ambassador to Vietnam is an old friend of mine. He was only too happy to provide a passport issued by the Kingdom of Cambodia."

"Thank you general," Yu Lee stepped forward to embrace the old soldier. "This is a generous gift, and a great weight off my mind. Whenever I use this passport it will remind me of you, my very good friend.

"As we have discussed many times Mr John," Yu Lee said turning to Mac. "In this part of the world is all about whom you know n'est-ce pas?"

"I seem to recall you mentioning something like that before...on several occasions. I guess I can't argue with you about that prof."

———

In a brief ceremony in the East Room of the White House President William J. Clinton announced the normalisation of relations with Vietnam. Military representatives, families of those still missing in action, members of Congress who were veterans of the war, and former prisoners-of-war were in attendance. Neither Yu Lee nor John Mackenzie received invitations. As far as the Administration was concerned they had played no part in the normalisation process. And that was fine by both men.

Tan Thoi Hiep Village, Vietnam

If Vietnam held its own official service to announce normalisation with the United States it went unnoticed. But there was a little-known, informal service that did take place at a graveside in Thien Thoi Hiep Village where a few people had gathered to commemorate the seventh anniversary of Thien's untimely passing.

Yu Lee contacted David Gervasoni. They spoke on the telephone for more than an hour. Gervasoni spoke proudly of Linh's achievements at school and at the University of California, Los Angeles where she was studying at the UCLA School of Law.

Accompanied by wife Mary, Gervasoni jumped at the invitation to attend the memorial service along with Linh whom, he said, had taken all of seven years to put the tragic events of the past behind her. Now in her early twenties she was able to appreciate the harsh life suffered by her mother. It was time for understanding, forgiveness and reconciliation.

Only a few other members of Thien's family were present including Aunt Vanh who had played such an important part in finding Linh. Yu Lee and John Mackenzie, who organised the gathering along with Lily Crenshaw, helped make up the numbers. It was a solemn affair but brighter for the presence of Lieutenant Phan Quang Minh, his partner Nguyen Thi Minh Lili and their seven year old daughter. Lily carried a vase of fresh flowers.

Watching as the three of them set the vase down by the grave, Yu Lee, curious about the note, walked over to read it:

Dear Thien, We will never forget your sacrifice. You will always be in our thoughts

RIP

Much love from Minh, Lily and our beautiful daughter Kim

With a heavy heart and tear-filled eyes, Yu Lee pressed his fan into action and swiftly left the graveside.

8280270R00162

Printed in Great Britain
by Amazon.co.uk, Ltd.,
Marston Gate.